BITTERSWEET GOODBYE

Stacy Boatman

Stacy Boatman
Proverbs 3: 5,6

Bittersweet Goodbye

© 2018 Stacy Boatman

Print ISBN: 978-1-54392-321-6
eBook ISBN: 978-1-54392-322-3

A heartfelt thank you to my friends and family who read this, my first-ever novel, in manuscript form. The bravery you showed in daring to read an aspiring author's work was not lost on me. Your honesty in pointing out mistakes allowed me to make the story better. (I accept full responsibility for any lingering errors!) I can't thank you enough! So here's a shout out to Jason, Chloe, Mom, Dad, Kristen, Laura, Ingrid, Grandma O., Cathy, Jan, Mary, Sylvia, Margaret, Erica, Barb, Jaime the Great, and Nancy. Love to you all!

Chapter One

AUDREY CHAPMAN'S LEGS BURNED WITH LACTIC ACID, but that didn't stop her from picking up the pace as her house came into view. She sprinted the last fifty yards, pumping her arms harder. Sucking in the humid August air with controlled breaths. Reminding herself to finish strong.

At the mailbox, she stopped her watch, satisfied with her workout, and eased into a walking pace. A shocking spray of cold water pelted her back. She screamed loud enough to set off the neighborhood dogs.

"You looked like you needed to cool off." Trevor Hayes, Audrey's next-door neighbor and closest friend, stood next to his sudsy car, aiming a garden hose in her direction. He wore a tank top with basketball shorts, flip flops, and his signature University of Minnesota cap turned backwards.

Audrey couldn't stop a smile from spreading across her face. Even pretending she was mad at Trevor was impossible. "I sure did. Thank you so much." She squeezed water from her curly blonde ponytail and waddled up Trevor's driveway in her sopping shorts. "It felt great. I mean, there's nothing better than wet socks and underwear."

"Glad I could help." Trevor began rinsing the bubbles off his car. "You look fast. Are you ready for cross-country?"

Audrey sprawled out in the Hayes' lawn, looking up into the cloudless sky. It was the last Friday of the summer. On Monday she'd be starting her freshman year at Bethel University in Saint Paul, Minnesota. It was only a half-hour drive from her hometown of Hastings. But still, the excitement of moving away from home, living on campus and running for a collegiate team sent butterflies twirling in her stomach. "I'm so ready!"

She sat up to remove her shoes and peel off her wet socks. "And you? Are you ready to go down in history as the Gophers' best wide receiver?" Trevor, a year older than Audrey, was a sophomore at the University of Minnesota.

He cracked his typical modest grin. "I'll do my best."

"I'm going to the Michigan game with Becca." She knew Trevor's football schedule wouldn't allow him the opportunity to cheer her on at any of her races. As much as she looked forward to college life, she dreaded the separation from Trevor. She'd missed him last year when he went to the U. But they had lots of time to catch up over the summer, and she felt closer to him now than ever before.

Trevor picked up a rag, wiping away the water spots on the hood of the car. Time for payback. She pulled herself up off the ground, still tired from her run, and grabbed the hose. She took a long drink of the cold water, and then doused Trevor from head to toe. "You asked for it, buddy."

He lunged at her, wrestling the hose from her grasp. She grabbed a soapy sponge off the ground and hurled it at his chest, sending a burst of bubbles into the air.

"Wait." Trevor held up his hands.

Audrey laughed. "I'm not letting you off that easy." She picked up a bucket of soapy water for ammunition.

"No, wait. My phone is in my pocket." He pulled his phone from his pocket and held it in front of himself like a shield. "You break it, you buy it."

Audrey set down the bucket, and put her hands on her hips. "That is so not fair. You got off easy this time, but watch your back. This isn't over." It was never over between them. Truth be told, Trevor was the one always keeping her on her toes. She loved Trevor's goofiness, even when it was at her expense.

Trevor flicked water from his fingers, and then swiped the screen of his phone. "Jake texted me. Wants to know if I'll team up with him for two-on-two basketball at his place tonight." Jake Preston, like Becca Olson, was a friend Trevor and Audrey had grown up with at Hope Church. The circle of friends became especially tight over the last few years in the youth group, despite their differing ages. Jake and Becca were slated to start their senior year at Hastings High School.

"Is Becca gonna be there?" She was usually only a stone's throw from Jake's side.

"I'll ask." Trevor typed on his phone. "Yep. She's already there." He held up the phone, displaying a selfie of Jake and Becca. "Wanna go?"

"Sure. Pick me up in an hour. That should give you enough time to wipe away those water spots." She pointed to his clean car that had suffered in the crossfire of their water fight.

"Yes, your highness." Trevor bowed down.

Audrey hurried home, eager to jump into the shower and get ready for the night. This weekend was dedicated to hanging out with her hometown friends. Because on Monday, she would tell them goodbye and start a new chapter of her life.

* * *

Forty-five minutes later, Audrey slipped her feet into sandals and glanced out the front window just as Trevor pulled up in front of her house.

"Bye, Mom and Dad," she called over her shoulder. "I'm hanging out at the Prestons' house tonight." The screen door clapped shut behind her as she stepped into the evening sunlight. The humidity had lightened enough that she felt comfortable in an ensemble of jeans and an emerald tank top. She'd dressed up her simple outfit just a bit with the modest teardrop diamond necklace and earrings her parents had given to her as a high school graduation gift.

Sliding into the passenger seat of Trevor's car, she noticed he'd spritzed on a little cologne even though tonight's get-together was just a casual meet-up...playing basketball, no less. She considered giving him a hard time about it, but decided instead to just enjoy the delicious musky scent. It suited him well.

Audrey buckled her seat belt. "Ready when you are."

Trevor pointed toward the house, a smirk on his face. "Did you forget to give your mom a goodbye hug?" Audrey's mom ran out to the car, barefoot, and in her typical attire of capris and a button-down shirt, waving a book. Audrey rolled down her window.

Trevor leaned over, peering out Audrey's window. "Hi, Mrs. Chapman."

"Hey, Trev. I'm so glad I caught you guys." She handed the book to Audrey. "Can you please give this to Mrs. Preston? It's my study Bible. I told her I'd lend it to her, but we haven't crossed paths lately."

"Sure thing, Mom."

"Thank you so much." She blew a kiss to Audrey, and then flitted onto the porch where she stood waving.

Audrey waved back, rolling her eyes. "My mom is all sad about me moving away from home. She's been babying me all week."

"She's going to miss you. Making sure you're up for school every morning. Waiting for your return each evening." Trevor waved sweetly to her mom. "Those are the things my mom said she missed last year when I moved out."

Audrey's heart melted a bit. She looked over at Trevor, admiring the sincere look emanating from his light blue eyes. She might get homesick and miss her parents, but she knew for sure that she'd miss Trevor. Still, after building a childhood of memories together, she had confidence that nothing could ever make them grow apart.

At the first glimpse of Jake's house, Audrey's stomach dropped. The place looked like it had been attacked by a fraternity club. Beer cans littered the lawn, and a group of kids mingled in the yard. "What has Jake gotten himself into now?" Not only was Jake under the legal drinking age, but getting busted for consuming alcohol could get him kicked off the high school football team.

Trevor squeezed his car into a parking space along the normally quiet suburban street of Hastings, Minnesota. "This looks like trouble. I know Jake parties once in a while, but this is crazy."

"I thought it was just gonna be a few of us hanging out." This wasn't turning out to be the carefree night she'd hoped for. As much as she wanted to see her friends, she didn't want to engage in the party scene she'd managed to avoid her entire high school career.

Trevor turned off the ignition. "Me too. I can text him and say we decided not to come. He knows you and I don't drink."

"What about this?" Audrey held up the Bible. "Let's just go in for a few minutes. I'll deliver the Bible and say hi to Becca."

"I did promise Jake we'd team up for basketball. We can leave right after that."

Audrey knocked on the door of the sprawling craftsman home, clutching the Bible in her other hand. She twisted the band of her running watch, waiting for an answer. Tucking a strand of her blonde curly hair behind her ear, she tilted her head toward the door. From inside the house, a muffled cacophony of hip-hop music and laughter seeped into the still night air.

Some guys toting a case of beer pushed past Audrey and Trevor, opening the door without knocking. Trevor followed suit, taking hold of Audrey's hand and stepping into the entryway. The house was packed with teens, many of whom Audrey didn't recognize. Trevor put his arm around her shoulders. He leaned down so that his face was close to hers; the scent of his cologne wafted over her. "Are you thirsty?" Even with him shouting in her ear, Audrey could barely hear him over the loud drumming music. She nodded, placing her arm around his back so they wouldn't get separated in the crowd.

Trevor led her through the throng of partiers to the kitchen island that served as a makeshift bar. A bucket of ice was centered amidst half-empty bottles of hard liquor, plastic two-liter pop bottles, and stacks of red Solo cups. The display reminded her of movies she'd seen of college frat parties. She preferred watching it on a screen over experiencing it for herself. Glancing over her shoulder at the entryway, she debated making a run for it. But she needed to set the Bible down somewhere and talk to Becca.

"Here you go." Trevor handed her a cup of pop. She took a sip, enjoying the familiar fizz of sweetness on her tongue. She smiled at the notion that he hadn't had to ask what she'd like to drink. He knew Coke was her favorite beverage. The security of being with Trevor, her best friend, put her at ease. She stood on her toes, shouting into his ear so that he could hear her voice over the music, "Let's hurry up and mingle and then get outta here."

"Hey, Trevor." Jake yanked Trevor into a bro hug, causing Trevor's drink to slosh out of the cup. "It's about time you showed up. You up for a game of hoops? We'll make a killer team."

Trevor, wiping Mountain Dew from his shirt, looked to Audrey.

She shrugged, attempting to appear nonchalant. "Go ahead. Show them who's boss." It would be infantile to tell him she didn't want him to leave her side.

He slung his arm over her shoulder again. "Come out and watch." Again, he knew her too well.

Becca Olson sidled up next to Jake. "I'm going to be your personal cheerleader." Her eyes were sleepy, her movements exaggerated and unsteady. She leaned against Jake as much to flirt as to steady herself, it seemed. Her half-masted eyes swept over Audrey. "Hey, girl! I didn't expect to see you here."

Jake, brushing Becca off, pushed Trevor toward the back door. "Let's school these boys!"

Becca swayed without the support of Jake. Audrey linked arms with her friend, holding her steady. It was no secret that Becca partied from time to time, but Audrey had never witnessed Becca's drinking before. Becca was normally super concerned with her appearance. Her brown hair was usually coiffed in silky waves that cascaded down her back, and her makeup was pure artistry. She posted tutorials on YouTube that got thousands of views. So seeing Becca disheveled and tripping over her own feet was unsettling. "Becca, how about if we watch them together? You can teach me some football cheers." Becca clearly needed some looking-after.

They made their way outside and followed a stone pathway lit by garden lights to the sport court. The fresh air was a relief after being in that congested house. They sat on the outskirts of the court, leaning their backs against the fence. The other duo was already shooting around as Jake and Trevor discussed game tactics. They'd be playing against their friend Gavin and some guy who played Hastings football. Trevor dribbled the ball to the three-point line and sunk a shot. Audrey clapped. "Nice shot, Hayes!"

Becca laughed. "Settle down. They're just warming up."

Audrey gave her inebriated friend a playful shove. "We need to get them psyched up. We're their cheerleaders, right?"

Becca cupped her hands around her mouth. "Shirts against skins. Jake and Trevor are skins!"

Jake pulled his shirt over his head and tossed it to Becca. "Is this your idea or Audrey's?" He flexed his pectorals.

Becca slipped his shirt on over her own T-shirt. "It was a mutual decision." She winked at Audrey.

"Whatever!" Audrey shoved Becca again. This time Becca tipped over and sprawled out on the ground laughing. Trevor took off his shirt and tossed it out of bounds on the other side of the court. Their friends had always teased Audrey and Trevor about harboring a surreptitious romance. Truthfully, their relationship was unequivocally platonic.

So why did she blush and force herself to look away when Trevor took off his shirt? She took a gulp of cold, refreshing Coke.

Becca sat up and nudged Audrey with her elbow. "You're welcome." She winked again. "That's what friends are for."

The guys played a couple of games under the lights. Trevor was an amazing athlete. It was fun to watch him play any sport, even just a pickup game of basketball. It wasn't surprising that he'd been recruited to play Division I football. Audrey watched Trevor deftly steal the ball from Gavin. He dribbled effortlessly down the court and made a slam dunk. She held her hand up to Becca prompting a high five.

Becca just sat there and groaned. "I don't feel so good."

"What do you mean?" Audrey examined her friend's face. She was white as a sheet. "You're not going to throw up, are you?"

Becca shielded her eyes from the bright lights illuminating the sport court. "I'm a little woozy."

Audrey jumped up, out of the line of fire. She looked around for help. The guys were focused on their game, and no one else was outside. "Stand up. Let's get to the bathroom." She pulled Becca onto her feet. Audrey eased open the gate to the sport court and ushered Becca across the yard. "Remind me why you think drinking is so much fun."

Becca stopped dead in her tracks just as they were about to step onto the back patio. She hunched over, planting her hands on her knees. "I'm not sure it's such a good idea either." Audrey lifted Becca's hair away from her face. Becca looked up at her. "Why can't I be like you?" Becca coughed a couple of times. "Wholesome. That's what you are."

Audrey rolled her eyes. She wasn't sure she wanted to be described as wholesome. In a way it was a good thing, but at the same time, it sounded lame. "I'll take that as a compliment. Now let's keep going." She tugged on Becca's arm, but met resistance.

Becca grunted. Then she vomited on the manicured lawn.

Holding Becca's hair with one hand, Audrey dug a ponytail holder out of her pocket with the other hand. She fastened Becca's hair at the base of her neck, trying not to get queasy from her friend's retching. "Becca, I'll take you home. Did you drive here?"

Becca nodded.

"How were you planning to get home?"

Becca didn't answer. She remained hunched over.

Audrey texted Trevor to let him know she'd be driving Becca home. She looked over at him out on the basketball court. He was focused on the game, guarding an opponent. His long arms stretched out to the sides, his muscles flexed. Undeniably attractive.

She reminded herself to blink.

He blocked a pass, and took possession of the ball. He passed it to Jake who ran it down the court for a layup. Trevor backpedaled, getting into position. A light sheen of sweat on his chest and arms glistened—

"Hello?" Becca waved a hand inches from Audrey's eyes. "As soon as you're done drooling over Hayes we can go inside."

"I'm not drooling." Audrey peeled her eyes off Trevor. "I'm just watching the game and…admiring his athleticism."

"You keep telling yourself that." Becca placed a hand on her stomach. She still looked ill. "When are you two gonna hook up?"

Audrey scoffed. "First of all, we're just friends. For another thing, I don't plan to *hook up* with anybody until I'm married."

Becca held up her hands in surrender. "Okay, Miss Wholesome. Whatever you say."

Audrey rolled her eyes. She led the way to the bathroom, parting the crowd for her over-indulgent friend. Becca knocked into people as they went. Audrey set her Coke down on a kitchen counter behind the coffeepot and linked arms with Becca.

In the bathroom, Audrey fixed Becca's hair while Becca splashed water on her face. Her color improved with the help of lip gloss. The two friends stood side by side, gazing at their reflections. Becca was tall and slightly curvy. She was strikingly pretty with coffee-colored eyes and light brown skin. In contrast, Audrey was petite with shoulder-length curly blonde hair, blue-green eyes, and a smattering of freckles. She wasn't strikingly beautiful like Becca, but people often told her she was cute. Cute and wholesome. Made her sound like a puppy.

"You know," Becca said, looking at Audrey in the mirror, "you don't need to take me home."

Audrey faced her friend. She planted her hands on her hips. "You're not driving. I won't let you. Not after you've been drinking."

Becca tipped her head toward the floor and traced the grout between tiles with the toe of her shoe. "I'm not driving home." She stared into Audrey's eyes. "I'm staying with Jake."

"Oh." Audrey blushed. She felt foolish for not understanding at first. "Are you sure you're ready? I mean, you're only seventeen, and you guys aren't really even dating."

Becca smiled coyly. "It won't be the first time. I mean, it will be the first time I stay the night. His parents are at some family reunion in Wisconsin for the weekend. But it won't be the first time that Jake and I…" Her voice trailed off.

Audrey leaned a hip against the vanity. She felt naïve. Yet at the same time horrified that her closest girlfriend had sex, and Audrey had no idea. Growing up in the same church, she thought they shared morals on waiting until marriage. "Do your parents know?"

"No!" Becca's eyes grew wide. "And they better not find out." Her words came out like a threat.

Audrey rolled her eyes. "I'm not going to tell anyone. That's your deal."

Becca's demeanor softened. "But my mom did put me on the pill and gave me a speech about condoms just to be safe. So embarrassing." Becca turned to the mirror and fluffed her hair. "She told me she hoped I wouldn't need the protection but that it was better to be safe than sorry."

Audrey sighed. She was more naive than she'd realized. Way more naive than Becca.

"You don't have to worry about me." Becca twirled a strand of her dark hair. "I'm sorry I didn't tell you sooner. I just didn't think you'd understand. I thought you might judge me."

Probably true.

Becca flashed her gorgeous smile. "Let's go have some fun while Trevor and Jake are playing basketball. Then you can take off."

"I can't talk you into going home?"

Becca shook her head. "Not a chance. Besides, I need to help Jake clean up this house in the morning."

Audrey shrugged. "Fine. But you're not drinking anymore as long as I'm here. I am not suffering through another of your puking episodes."

"Fair enough." Becca yawned. "Don't worry. I'm done for the night."

Audrey opened the bathroom door, bracing herself as she reentered the party scene. The crowd had lightened some. She found her drink where she'd stashed it on the counter and finished it off. It didn't taste as good, having lost its fizz and the ice cubes had dissolved. Becca grabbed her hand. "Let's mingle." They talked to graduates and the in-coming seniors. Most kids weren't completely smashed like Becca had been. Audrey loosened up and chided herself for being such a goody-goody. She was warming up to the party scene. It really wasn't such a big deal. Just a bunch of kids hanging out—having a good time.

They meandered into the dimly lit living room, lured by the source of the music. Jake's mom's exquisite area rug had been rolled up and propped in a corner, revealing the polished hardwood flooring that currently served as a dance floor. Audrey and Becca joined a crowd that encircled a couple of guys competing in a dance-off. A hip-hop beat rattled the windows and shook the walls. Audrey kept time by clapping a hand on her thigh as a weak attempt at appearing interested. In truth, she felt like an intruder in Mr. and Mrs. Preston's home. They would be horrified by these kids trashing their house. Plus, the loud music screaming in her ears was giving her a headache. She rubbed her temples with her thumbs while shielding her eyes from the flashing strobe lights. How did strobe lights get in here anyway?

Becca looked over at her. "You really need to loosen up."

Audrey laughed despite herself. "Am I really that bad?"

"How do I put this nicely?" Becca pursed her lips and placed her pointer finger on her chin, pretending to be searching for the perfect words. "You look like my grandma at my cousin's wedding dance." Becca ran to a cooler and grabbed a beer, cracking it open. "Just take a couple sips. It'll relax you."

Audrey considered it. It would be nice to loosen up a bit. It's not like she would get drunk from a couple sips. Trevor was having fun with his friends. Sure, he wasn't drinking, but he was out having a good time. He would want her to have fun too.

Audrey put the can to her lips and took a swig. The bitter taste filled her mouth and burned as it ran down her throat. She coughed. "Gross!"

"Feel better?" Becca moved her curvy hips to the music.

Audrey nodded. Although she didn't feel the effects of just one sip of alcohol, in a way she did feel better because now she fit in. She still hated drinking and partying. She would much rather be hanging out with Trevor.

Her phone vibrated in her pocket. The caller ID read, *Trevor*. She was ecstatic to see his name. Maybe the guys were done with their game, and he was looking to meet up with her again. At the same time she felt a pang of guilt. What if he could tell by the sound of her voice that she had a drink? Would he be mad? He would definitely be shocked, knowing how she felt about underage drinking. She decided not to tell him. The call went to voicemail, and she put the phone in her back pocket. She would text him in a couple of minutes.

The cold beer can suddenly felt toxic in her hand. What did she think she was doing? She was such a hypocrite. Using hand signals, she motioned to Becca that she was going outside. She'd stay by Trevor's side for the night as planned. Becca made a pouty face, turning out her bottom lip. She pulled Audrey into a quick hug and then returned her attention to the dancers. Becca wouldn't miss her.

Audrey turned to head for the back door. She temporarily lost her balance. The combination of pounding music, flashing lights, and alcohol wreaked havoc in her wholesome brain. She rubbed her temples and regained her bearings. She didn't feel well. Could one swallow of beer make a girl drunk? Impossible. Nobody appeared to be smoking pot so she couldn't be suffering from secondhand inhalation. She took cautious steps.

Her head spun. A wingback chair sat vacant in a corner across the room. Audrey headed straight toward it, squeezing her way past the mass of dancers. The room continued to spin, and she couldn't keep her focus on the chair. Her head felt heavy, and a warm sensation crept through her veins, making her limbs feel weak and liquid. Her body swayed, or was it the room that was swaying? Just as her legs were giving out, strong arms circled around her waist. A deep, coaxing voice sounded in her ear. "Easy there. Looks like you could use a hand."

Audrey collapsed into the strong arms and blinked her eyes, trying to focus. She strained to turn around to see who was holding her. She wanted to tell him to get his hands off her, tell him she didn't need his help. But the dizziness was too intense; she was powerless to fight him. So instead, she accepted his help.

The warm sensation traveled up her spine to her head, soothing her headache and making her eyelids heavy. Unable to fight the strange sensation any longer, she allowed her body to relax and her eyelids to close. Her feet were dragging on the hardwood floor. He must be taking her to the wingback chair. But the music became muffled, more distant. He brought her to a different room, hopefully someplace where she could lie down for a while.

She tried to ask the stranger where they were going, but her tongue felt thick. Nothing more than a faint whisper passed her lips, left unheard. If only she could open her eyes. But it was impossible.

A door slammed shut. Plush carpet now brushed against her toes instead of hardwood. It was quiet. Finally. The stranger's hands tightened around her waist, and his fingers dug into her sides. A pang of panic shot through the fogginess in her brain.

She was in trouble. This guy was not helping her but was taking advantage of her. She wanted to scream but knew it was futile. Not only was she incapable of speaking, but no one would hear her over the noise of the party. She was utterly helpless.

The stranger released his grip on her waist where bruises were surely forming. She felt herself falling. She squeezed her eyes tight in anticipation of slamming against the floor, but instead she landed softly on what she could only guess to be a bed. Her body, wanting to drift into sleep, welcomed the softness, but her mind was frantic. The strong hands returned to her waist and then painfully traveled the length of her body, tearing at her clothing. Unable to fight him, she did the one thing she was capable of. She prayed.

Then everything went black.

Chapter Two

SATURDAY MORNING, TREVOR HAYES CRACKED THREE eggs into a bowl, beating them with a fork. He tossed a pat of butter into a hot frying pan and waited impatiently for it to melt. The news he would deliver to Audrey later that afternoon weighed heavily on his mind. All summer he'd been planning to make his confession when the perfect, romantic opportunity presented itself. Time was running out. Monday he'd be moving back to campus with his buddies. He had to design that idyllic moment today.

"Mmm, smells good." Trevor's older brother, Lucas, ambled into the kitchen shirtless, sporting only black athletic shorts, and suffering a major case of bed head. People always said Lucas and Trevor looked alike with their tall, athletic builds, dark wavy hair, and light blue eyes. This morning, Trevor was admittedly equally disheveled as his brother—if not more.

Trevor poured the eggs into the pan "Make your own, buddy." He grabbed a spatula and stirred the eggs.

Lucas grunted and then poured himself a bowl of Cheerios at the kitchen island. "Why are you so edgy this morning?"

He couldn't deny it. "I decided to talk to Audrey today." Trevor's crush on the next-door neighbor girl, Audrey Chapman, was no secret in the Hayes household. Lucas noticed the way Trevor got goo-goo eyed around Audrey back when they were little kids running around the backyard together. He hadn't stopped teasing him since.

"Are you planning to break it to her slowly or just sweep her off her feet with a big ole kiss?"

Trevor grabbed a potholder and chucked it at his brother. The hot pad bounced off his forehead and landed in his cereal bowl.

"Dude!" Lucas jumped off the stool. Milk was splattered on his chest and all over the countertop.

Trevor laughed. "Serves you right."

"I was just giving you helpful suggestions." Lucas wiped milk off his chest with a fistful of napkins.

To be honest, a little advice couldn't hurt. He scraped the steaming eggs onto a plate and sprinkled them with salt and pepper. "I'm just going to come right out and say it." He speared a lump of eggs with a fork and popped it into his mouth. "It can't come as surprise to her. I mean, she knows me so well—better than anyone else—so how can she not know this?" He opened the fridge and grabbed a carton of orange juice, unscrewed the cap, and took a swig.

Lucas grabbed the orange juice out of Trevor's hand, helping himself to a drink. "She probably has a hunch. But can I be honest with you?"

"Can I stop you?"

"Your timing stinks. Explain to me why you think it's a good idea to start dating right before you two move to separate colleges. You've waited this long. Maybe you should just wait until Christmas vacation or next summer. Maybe even let it happen naturally."

Trevor cringed. "Don't talk me out of this." He scooped the last of his eggs into his mouth. Lately it had seemed more than ever that Audrey might reciprocate his feelings. This summer had been one of the best they'd spent together—sharing fried food at the state fair, paddle boarding on Lake Minnetonka, and hanging out on Audrey's front porch stargazing and talking about God. To him, it almost felt like they were already dating. Why not make it official?

Dating across college campuses wasn't unheard of, especially since they each owned a car, and Bethel was only a thirty-minute drive from the U of M. He'd dated a few girls the last couple of years, but on each date, Audrey would pop into his mind. Deep down, Trevor felt that Audrey was the girl he was ultimately supposed to spend his life with. But he didn't feel an obligation to explain his rationale to Lucas.

He swiped the orange juice back from his brother and finished it off—seconds before their mom entered the kitchen. He stashed the empty carton in the garbage.

"Good morning, boys. I saw that, Trevor." She stood on her tiptoes and tousled his hair. "Didn't I teach you boys anything?" She poured herself a drink of water. "Next time, try using one of these." She tapped the glass with her index finger.

Trevor dutifully rinsed off his dirty dishes and stacked them in the dishwasher. "Sorry, Mom. You only have to put up with us for two more days."

Victoria Hayes frowned, exposing her true feelings. Trevor knew his mom missed him and his brother when they were living on campus. "What are you two up to today?"

"Yeah, Trevor." Lucas wore a mischievous grin. "What are your plans for this fine Saturday afternoon?"

His mom eyed him curiously. "Do tell." She filled the coffeepot with water.

Trevor gritted his teeth. "Hanging out with Audrey this afternoon and then we're going to the youth group thing at the Chapman's house. Pastor Mitchel is doing the annual youth group grad party tonight."

His mom sighed. "It's hard to believe little Audrey Chapman will be a college freshman." She took a bag of coffee from the cupboard, scooping grounds into the coffeepot.

Lucas snickered. "She's growing into quite a fine young lady. Isn't she Trevor? Or haven't you noticed?"

Trevor picked up the milk-saturated pot holder off the island and whipped it at his brother's head again.

His mom, no doubt fully comprehending the insinuation, laughed. "She sure is."

Trevor groaned. "You guys think you're so funny." He went upstairs to shower. That whole scenario demonstrated the absurdity of keeping his feelings a secret from Audrey. At twenty years old, he shouldn't be nervous to ask a girl on a date.

The problem was: Audrey wasn't just *any* girl. And he wasn't just going to invite her for movie and a pizza. By confessing his feelings, he was asking her—his best friend—to be his girlfriend. Once his feelings were out in the open, he could never take them back. Their friendship would be changed forever.

He checked his phone to see if she'd returned his call or texted him. No such luck. He tossed the phone onto his dresser and fished out a pair of basketball shorts and a T-shirt. He wasn't upset that she'd spent the night hanging out with Becca instead of watching him play basketball. He was concerned that he hadn't heard from her since his message he left last night. It was unlike Audrey to not have responded right away. Especially since he had told her there was something he wanted to talk to her about. On second thought, those words could be unnerving. Was she avoiding him?

He stood under the spray of warm water thinking how foolish he was to overthink the Audrey thing. She and Becca were probably sleeping in. Or they went out for breakfast. *Stop fixating on it, Hayes.* He turned the faucet handle to the little blue circle. Time to cool down.

Finally, he heard the *ding* signaling an incoming text. He turned off the freezing water, wrapped a towel around his waist, and grabbed his phone. Sure enough, the text was from Audrey.

Sorry I Didn't Hear Your Voicemail Until Now. Busy Packing. We Can Talk Tonight After Grad Party.

"No." Trevor leaned his hands on the counter and hung his head. Tonight wasn't soon enough. He couldn't wait to let her know how much he cared for her. When they were kids, he had a crush on her. But now, he'd fallen in love with her. Her ambition, her compassionate heart, the way she loved the Lord more than anything else.

He had envisioned taking her on a walk this afternoon through their childhood neighborhood, holding her hand while they recalled adventures of mischief during their childhood days. When the sun would get too hot, they would stop at the gas station to buy cans of pop just like they did when they were kids. Then they'd stroll back to her house and sit on the porch swing, sipping their drinks. He would put his arm around her and tell her that she was the love of his life. That he couldn't live without her knowing how special she was to him. She would lean into him and tell him she'd been waiting to hear him utter those words. If things ended really well, maybe they would even kiss. But he didn't want to plan that. He wanted their first kiss to happen spontaneously.

Trevor wiped the foggy mirror with his hand and filled the sink with warm water for shaving. He chuckled at his reflection. He may be a big football player with a five o'clock shadow, but he was also a hopeless romantic suffering a ridiculous case of puppy love. The only people who needed to know that were his brother and mom...and Audrey.

The sooner Audrey knew the truth, the better. Tonight would have to be soon enough.

* * *

Audrey spritzed the unruly blonde curls framing her face and struggled to pin them back. The silky tendrils slipped from her shaking fingers. A headband would have to do. She studied her reflection in the bathroom mirror, satisfied. The coral top she'd selected for the evening brought out the pink color in her cheeks. She held up her hand, waggling her fingers. The pale pink nail color was a perfect match with her lip gloss. She looked good enough. Nobody would suspect a thing.

The evidence was there if someone looked closely enough. She'd been practicing her smile for the last half hour but failed to make it reach her eyes. Her normally shiny blue green eyes now appeared matted and hollow. Spooky.

Seeing Trevor would make her smile come to life. She hoped. Since waking in Jake's guest room in the middle of the night—terrified and confused—the first person she thought about contacting was Trevor. She'd almost texted him to come get her and bring her home. But she couldn't make herself do it. He would've questioned her why she'd stayed at the party. She didn't have a good answer for that. Or he would've hugged her and comforted her. But the idea of being touched, even by Trevor, made her skin crawl.

It took a few minutes to figure out what had happened to her. The last thing she remembered was watching a hip-hop dance off. Next thing she knew she was lying in the dark with her ribs aching so much that it hurt to breathe. She was nauseated, and sore all over. Kind of like after she ran her first 400-meter dash, after eating a chili cheese dog for lunch. But worse. Maybe she was hung over. She did recall tasting beer. She remembered the feel of the icy cold can in her hand. Yep, she must've gotten drunk, passed out, and now she was suffering a hangover.

But her body told her more had happened than that.

The ugly truth had emerged when she flicked on the table lamp. Her clothes were mangled and torn. Upon straightening her jeans, she noticed tender purplish marks on her sides. Then bits and pieces of the night came back to her in short clips. Sudden dizziness. Being hauled across the living room. Falling—she squeezed her eyes shut as she'd done at the time, reliving it. She gasped in horror, putting the pieces together. She scrambled off the bed and ran to the nearest bathroom, stumbling around in the dark house. The party was long over. She washed herself, scrubbing until her skin was nearly raw. Then she'd run home, showered, crawled into bed, and cried herself to sleep.

Audrey drew a shaky breath, releasing it slowly to calm her nerves. She needed to shove last night into the recesses of her mind so she could get through this youth group gathering. This was a secret she needed to take to the grave. How could she explain to her parents that she was at a party? At Jake's house? Jake would get into trouble—so would Becca.

Audrey wondered if she could look Pastor Mitchel in the eye and tell him she'd been raped. If Trevor found out, what would he think of her?

Her sister pounded on the bathroom door. "Audrey! Get out of there. People are outside waiting for you." Darcy was two years younger than Audrey. She was the carefree, creative sister whereas Audrey was the responsible, studious one. At the moment, Audrey found herself envious of her younger sister, whose biggest worry was which shirt she would wear on the first day of eleventh grade.

"I'll be there in a minute." She accessorized her outfit with the diamond studded earrings from her parents. She ran her fingers over her bare collarbone. The necklace was missing. Somehow she'd lost it overnight. She blinked back tears, but one slipped down her cheek. She blotted it away with a tissue. Then she pasted on her best smile and hobbled downstairs to greet her guests.

Her mom was in the kitchen, preparing a tray of marshmallows, graham crackers, and Hershey chocolate bars. Their tabby cat, Simba, lay at her feet. "Hi, honey. You look nice." Her mom put down the box of crackers she was holding and gave Audrey a tight mama-bear hug. "I'm so proud of my graduate."

Audrey released a little whimper; her ribs were so sore they felt bruised.

Her mom stepped back, furrowing her brow in concern. "Are you all right?"

Audrey forced a giggle. "Just a little sore. I've been running a lot. You know, preparing for the cross-country season." She'd never lied to her mom before. Guilt instantly ensued.

"You better take it easy. I don't want to see you getting hurt." Her mom returned to the food preparations.

"Too late." Audrey muttered.

Her mom grinned, shaking her head. "You've always been one to push yourself too hard. Go easy on yourself your first year of college. Your GPA and running is important, but don't forget to have fun too. Okay, honey?"

"I'll try." Audrey could see through the window above the kitchen sink that some of the youth group kids had already arrived and were in the backyard. Her dad was stacking logs and twigs in the fire pit. She didn't feel ready to face everyone. "Do you need any help in here?"

Her mom wiped her hands on her apron. "Like I just said—go have fun."

The doorbell rang; Audrey's heart leapt into her throat. "I'll get it." She went to the door, hoping to see Trevor through the sidelight window. It was Pastor Andrew Mitchel and his wife Maggie. A guitar was slung over Pastor Mitchel's shoulder and Mrs. Mitchel was hiding something behind her back—probably a gift for Audrey. Each year, Pastor Mitchel gave each of the graduates a meaningful gift. This year, Audrey was the only graduate of the small youth group. She opened the door. "Come in. Can I help you with your stuff?"

"Don't you dare." Mrs. Mitchel backed away from Audrey. This is a surprise for later.

Audrey felt her spirit lighten in the presence of the Mitchels. They had to be the coolest couple on earth. "Nobody will let me help with anything tonight. Not even my mom." Audrey ushered them through the kitchen.

"Hi, Lydia." Mrs. Mitchel smiled at Audrey's mom. She shrugged her purse onto a kitchen chair while keeping the gift hidden behind her back. Even in her mid-thirties, Maggie Mitchel dressed in trendy clothes and always had her light brown hair styled. She was a first grade teacher. The kind who gave hugs to her students and actually remembered their names years later when kids stopped back in her classroom to visit.

Pastor Mitchel helped himself to a piece of chocolate from the tray. "Thank you for your hospitality tonight."

Audrey's mom moved the tray out of Pastor Mitchel's reach, giving him a dirty look. "You're welcome. And what time will this shin dig be ending?"

Pastor Mitchel laughed. "Not soon enough for you, I'm sure. But we'll stay outside for the most part."

"In that case, you're welcome to stay as long as you'd like."

The friendly banter between Pastor Mitchel and Audrey's mom cracked Audrey up every time. This graduation party couldn't have come at a better time. She put on a brave face and led the Mitchels outside to the fire pit.

"Hey, Audrey." Becca came barreling toward her practically knocking her over with a big hug. "It's about time you show up. I almost went up to your room and dragged you out here."

"I've been packing all day. There's so much to do before Monday."

"Hey, you and Trevor took off without saying goodbye last night. I turned around and you were gone."

"Sorry about that. Trevor called me when their game was done…I should've told you we were taking off." Another lie. Truthfully, she couldn't remember leaving Becca's side. Trevor had called, but she'd let it go to voicemail.

"Don't worry about it. You didn't miss much. The party ended soon after you left. A few people were getting out of hand so a bunch of people took off. Jake started kicking people out around midnight. He didn't mean for it to become such a big beer bash. The house was trashed. We were cleaning all day. I'm exhausted."

The back yard gate creaked open. Audrey watched Trevor walk through, holding a bouquet of wildflowers and wearing a goofy grin. He was so adorable. Audrey had to hold herself back from running to him like Becca had done to her.

Becca elbowed Audrey. "Aw, he brought you flowers. I'm so jelly. Jake has never brought me flowers."

Audrey skipped over to him, ignoring her aches and pains. She wrapped her arms around his waist and rested her cheek against his chest. She was so happy to see him. She didn't care that everybody was probably watching and whispering about them. Tears threatened to spill from her eyes, but she wouldn't let them. Not now. For now, she just wanted to bask in the safety of Trevor's embrace.

Trevor hugged her back. "I'm happy to see you too." He held out the flowers; the stems were tied to together with a yellow ribbon. "It's a little send-off gift. I realize you'll be leaving in two days and probably won't take them with you. They don't even smell good, but—"

"I love them! You know I love wildflowers! Did you pick them?" Audrey took them, admiring the arrangement and running the silky ribbon between her fingers. When she and Trevor were little kids, they went on adventures, trekking around the pond behind their houses. Audrey would fall behind, picking wildflowers from the hillside. The yellow ones that looked like daisies were her favorite. Trevor was always yelling at her to hurry up and stop picking the weeds. She smiled at the memory.

"Sure did. I got about twenty mosquito bites in the process." He held out his arms, showing multiple red bumps.

"That was sweet of you." It was the kind of gesture that made Audrey's heart beat a little faster. The kind of gesture that sparked a giddy feeling that Trevor could one day be more than just a friend. This time, the gesture also brought tears to her eyes that she couldn't repress. With the events of last night haunting her thoughts, her emotions were wildly unstable. She buried her face into Trevor's shirt, weeping.

Trevor rubbed her back. "Hey, what's up?" His voice contained a hint of amusement. "Are you homesick already?"

Becca and Darcy and Mrs. Mitchel surrounded Audrey as she clung to Trevor, making heartfelt reassurances that they would keep in touch over the school year. Mrs. Mitchel extended an open invitation for her to attend any youth events as an alumna.

Let them think that's why she was crying. She could never admit the truth.

Chapter Three

❧

THE SETTING WAS IDEAL. A CLEAR SKY SPARKLED WITH millions of stars. The pond mirrored the brilliance of the crescent moon. Pine trees bordered the fire pit area on three sides, creating a feel of intimacy and giving off a deep woods aroma. Surrounded by her best friends, singing praise and worship songs, Audrey didn't want the night to end.

Pastor Mitchel strummed a chord on his guitar. "I'll take one more request." He played by ear and knew every song the kids named, even the more current secular music that the teens listened to on the radio. His wife was just as talented with her beautiful voice. Audrey thought to herself that they made a great team. She looked over at Trevor, who moments ago had been singing his heart out to "Amazing Grace" along with the rest of the group. She smiled as she looked into her future, envisioning Trevor beside her, completing her, just as the Mitchels completed each other. It was a pleasant thought.

"Lean on Me," Trevor called out.

Audrey's cheeks grew warm; hopefully it was too dark for anyone to notice she was blushing. No one knew that Audrey and Trevor had declared Lean on Me to be their song years ago while listening to music and dancing in the tree house their fathers had built for them.

Trevor winked at Audrey as everybody gathered in close and slung their arms over each other's shoulders, swaying to the music as they sang. She winked back and smiled, swallowing the lump in her throat.

When the fire began to die down and the sugar highs wore off, Pastor Mitchel announced he had important business to take care of. He cued Mrs. Mitchel with a nod of his head. She excused herself and made her way into the house. Pastor Mitchel asked Audrey to stand in front of the group.

"As you all know, Audrey, our sole graduate this year, will be attending Bethel University. As she'll be moving on campus in just a couple of days, I thought tonight to be an appropriate time to give her a proper send-off. Audrey, each person here has prepared a favorite memory of you that they would like to share."

Audrey covered her face with her hands. Everyone was giggling and whispering, excited for their turn to share. Audrey had a feeling that a lot of these so-called memories would be some of her most embarrassing moments.

"I'll start." Pastor Mitchel propped his guitar against a bench and rubbed his hands together. He told about a camping trip to the Boundary Waters when he had shared a canoe with Audrey. It was Audrey's turn to spend one on one time with him, catching fish for dinner. It was a time to discuss her faith and just get to know each other better.

"Being the gentleman that I am, I sat in the back to steer the canoe." He chuckled. "I got us stuck in cattails on the side of the lake. I dug my paddle into the thick mud below the canoe and pushed off with all my might. We didn't budge; my paddle broke in two."

Everyone laughed, envisioning the spectacle.

"Audrey had been quiet, allowing me to maintain my dignity and spare my masculine pride. After watching me struggle for far too long, she gingerly asked if she could give it a try. I gladly obliged.

"She pushed the handle of her paddle into the floor of the lake, releasing the canoe from the mud. She gracefully swept her paddle through the shallow water first on one side and then the other." Pastor Mitchel made sweeping motions with his arms. "The canoe turned to face the open water, and we glided through the grasses out onto clear waters." Everyone clapped.

"Audrey didn't gloat, and for that I was grateful. She caught three fish that day and I caught…none." Pastor Mitchel hung his head.

"We saw the whole thing from the campsite," Jake added, rolling with laughter. "There was Audrey, weighing a hundred pounds soaking wet, paddling the canoe by herself while Pastor Mitchel sat in the bow."

Audrey held her arms up, flexing her muscles.

Mrs. Mitchel was back from the house holding a package behind her back. She heard enough to get the gist of the story. "Andrew, you never told me that story."

"It wasn't exactly a shining moment that a guy brags about to his wife."

"I'm still proud of you." She kissed his cheek and tousled his hair.

Pastor Mitchel playfully flicked her hand away. "That's exactly the reaction I was trying to avoid."

Laughter rang out across the pond as everyone recalled the trip, taking full advantage of the opportunity to harass Pastor Mitchel all over again.

One by one each person told a memory that made people either laugh or cry. Becca sniffled as she told how Audrey has always stood by her side through good times and bad. "Audrey, I'll miss you. I look up to you so much. You're like a sister to me." Becca's shoulders shook as she began to cry.

Audrey pulled her into a hug. "I'll miss you too."

When it was Trevor's turn to talk, everyone sat on the edge of their seat in anticipation of a good story, probably a romantic comedy. He looked up to the sky and scratched his chin. "Audrey... hmm...which memory should I tell?"

"Keep it clean, buddy," Jake teased. "G rated only."

Trevor tossed his empty Mountain Dew can at Jake who caught it in midair and crushed it on his forehead. "Okay, one of my favorite youth group memories of Audrey was when we hung out at the Old Folks' home one Saturday afternoon. That brute of an old lady kept trying to teach Audrey to knit. She thought Audrey was her daughter-in-law." Trevor hunched over. "Any girl good enough for my son will know how to knit an afghan." Trevor laughed. "Audrey was so patient with her. She just played along."

"Is that the best you can do?" Jake cupped his hands around his mouth and booed.

"Okay, there was also the first time Audrey tried wake boarding up at Jake's cabin." Everybody broke out in laughter at the memory of it. "So she did good getting out of the water on only her second try, but then she was so cocky she waved to a boat of guys whizzing past and completely bit it."

Audrey punched Trevor's arm. "That was so embarrassing. Thanks for reminding me—and everybody else."

"Well, that'll teach you not to flirt."

"Lesson learned, thank you very much!" She hit him again, and he pulled her in to a side hug.

Pastor Mitchel cued Mrs. Mitchel to come stand beside him. "Very nice, everybody. Now we have a little something to present to Audrey." Audrey's dad came from out of nowhere with his camera aimed in her direction as Mrs. Mitchel took her position.

Mrs. Mitchel took the package from behind her back and handed it to her. Even wrapped, Audrey could see that it was a canoe paddle. She tore off the paper, and her eyes welled with tears. Everybody had signed it. Camera flashes temporarily blinded her.

Pastor Mitchel beamed. "It's a gift in honor of my favorite memory of you."

"Thank you. I'll put it in my dorm room and look at it whenever I miss you guys." She ran her hand along the smooth wooden handle, beautiful memories flooding back to her of time spent with the youth group. Turning the paddle over in her hand, she noticed writing on the back. *Proverbs 3:5-6 Trust in the Lord with all your heart and lean not on your own understanding; in all your ways acknowledge him, and he will make your paths straight.* It was a verse Pastor Mitchel quoted often, and he made the kids memorize it at the beginning of each school year. She gave everyone a hug and returned to her seat, filled with gratitude.

Pastor Mitchel closed the night in prayer, and then everyone went on their way. Everyone except Trevor.

Audrey and Trevor strolled through the neighborhood they'd grown up in, recounting stories from years past. Trevor put his arm around her shoulders as they walked. Tonight especially, the gesture made her feel safe.

"The campfire was fun. Do you like your canoe paddle?"

Audrey smiled. "It was a perfect gift. I'm really gonna miss youth group. But I'm excited to go to college. Cross-country will be fun." It would be good to get away. To start fresh. She looked at Trevor out of the corner of her eye. She would definitely miss him. "We have to stay in touch."

"I'll call you every Sunday night." He seemed a little embarrassed by his suggestion. "I mean, college-life can get really busy. We might have to schedule time to talk. More than just the occasional text."

"I'd like that. I'll call it T-time. 'T' for Trevor."

"Yeah, I got that." He smiled. As they neared Audrey's driveway, Trevor removed his arm from her shoulder and put his hands in his pockets. "Wanna sit on your porch for a while?"

"Maybe just a couple minutes." Although she cherished every minute with him, she didn't want to talk about last night's party. The longer they talked tonight, the more likely the topic would come up.

They sat on the porch swing, setting it into gentle motion. For a few minutes, they sat in comfortable silence, listening to frogs croaking and slapping at an occasional mosquito. Soon Trevor got all fidgety and released a hefty sigh. "There's something I've been wanting to say."

Audrey felt the blood drain from her face. He was going to bring up last night. She bit her bottom lip, refusing herself to speak of it.

Trevor removed his Twins baseball cap and ran his fingers through his hair. He leaned forward and placed his elbows on his knees, bringing the swing to a sudden halt. "Ok, here goes." He took a deep breath.

Audrey gulped. "You're making me nervous." She giggled lightly, downplaying her fear.

"Remember your ninth birthday party? You know, shortly after you guys moved in next door."

Where was he going with this? "Of course I do. You tried to rescue me from the neighborhood bully. I was handling him just fine on my own. I didn't need a knight in shining armor to swoop in and save me. I had deemed myself Audrey the Brave." She didn't feel so brave anymore.

Trevor chuckled. "You were this tiny little towhead in a pink frilly dress, sword fighting the giant Timmy Windleman—with sticks that really could have done some damage, by the way."

"Yep. And I won the match. I had him pinned up against the fence with my stick resting on his throat. He was holding his hands up in surrender, in case you forgot that part. He didn't stand a chance against Audrey the Brave."

"That brings me to my point." Trevor sat up and rubbed his palms on his jeans. He was looking nervous again. "Do you remember what I said?"

Audrey's cheeks grew warm. "How could I forget? Nobody will ever let us live that down."

"What can I say? I was enamored at your ability to look so pretty, yet be so bold. And tough as nails." His blue eyes twinkled in the moonlight. "I decided right then that I wanted to marry you when I grew up."

"And you announced it to everyone. Kids chanted, 'Trevor and Audrey sitting in a tree, k-i-s-s-i-n-g. First comes love. Then comes marriage. Then comes baby in a baby carriage.' the rest of the party." She punched his bicep. "I was so mad at you."

It had become childhood rhetoric. He repeated those words often over the years. *I'm going to marry you, Audrey Chapman.* Their friends always laughed, remembering the origin of those words, and teased them endlessly about it.

Trevor cleared his throat. "The thing is…I meant it. I still do."

Audrey swallowed, despite that her mouth had suddenly gone dry. Was he serious? He actually had feelings for her? "What are you saying? Are you asking me to run off and marry you?" She laughed to emphasize the sarcasm.

He shook his head, grinning sheepishly. "Of course not. This wasn't meant to be a marriage proposal. What I meant to say is that I really like you. As more than a friend." He took her hand in his. His fingers were shaking—even more than hers. He looked her in the eye. "Would you like to go on a date with me?"

The shock of his words rendered her speechless. She searched his eyes, finding nothing but honesty and humility. She groaned, freeing her fingers from his grasp to cover her face with her trembling hands. This couldn't be happening. Not now. Not with what had happened to her last night. Why did he have to say this tonight?

Trevor stood up and proceeded to pace back and forth on the porch. "That wasn't the reaction I was looking for." He leaned against a pillar and crossed his arms, staring out into the darkness.

"Trevor, I'm sorry. I…" Her feelings were so jumbled up she struggled to articulate them. She had feelings for Trevor as well. They were new for her though. She definitely loved him, but she was still trying to decipher if that love stemmed from friendship or romance. Truly, she couldn't imagine her life without him.

She shifted her weight, feeling the bruises on her hips. The pain served both as a reminder of last night and a precursor of scars to come. The physical scars may heal, but the emotional ones may linger. She had so much to process, and it took all her effort just to get through this night. She wasn't in a good place to jump into a dating relationship.

Besides, Trevor didn't even know that had happened. Would he still want her if he knew she'd been raped? She sat frozen in place, trying to make sense of it all. She could come right out and tell him. *Hey, Trevor. You know last night when you were playing basketball? I was inside getting raped. Actually, I don't remember much. I just woke up in Jake's guest room and...I knew.* It sounded ridiculous and embarrassing even to her. How was he supposed to react to it?

She wouldn't tell him.

He turned and faced her. "Forget it. I thought you knew. I thought maybe you...felt the same way." He smiled, easing the tension. "I'll see you tomorrow morning in church." He put his hat back on.

Audrey's heart pounded raucously in her chest. She needed to say something. "I'm sorry." She looked away from him, hating the awkwardness that had formed between them. She stood beside him. "You're my best friend in the whole world."

"I understand." He hugged her warmly, and this she reciprocated.

He didn't understand. He didn't know that she'd been fantasizing about a future with him. He also didn't know that she was no longer that innocent little girl he'd fallen for. Overnight, she'd become dirty and gross. A liar.

She lingered in his arms, hearing the rapid rhythm of his heart as her cheek rested against his chest.

He kissed the top of her head and brushed the curls off of her forehead. Her skin tingled under his touch. She looked up into his shimmering blue eyes, wanting to tell him exactly how much she cared for him. But this just wasn't the right time.

For now, she hoped Trevor would still want to be her friend.

Chapter Four

❧

AUDREY STEPPED INTO HER DARK HOUSE AND QUIETLY closed the door. She peered out the sidelight window, watching Trevor amble up his driveway until finally he was out of sight. She exhaled, her restraint leaking out along with her breath.

Did that really just happen? She kicked off her flip flops and sprawled out on the front entry rug, staring up at the shadowy ceiling. "Seriously?" She closed her eyes, recounting Trevor Hayes, her best friend since childhood, asking her on a date.

"Seriously what?" The shrill sound of her younger sister's voice, heightened by intrigue, interrupted Audrey's ruminations.

"Honey, what is going on?" Her mom's voice chimed in.

Audrey covered her face with her hands, shielding herself from their stares. This night was only getting worse.

"I've never seen Audrey lose it before," Darcy whispered.

"I'm sure she'll be okay. She's probably stressed out about moving away from home."

Audrey opened her eyes. Her mom and sister, wearing pajamas and holding steaming mugs, hovered above her. "I can hear you guys, you know." She pulled herself up to a sitting position and hugged her knees to her chest. Simba sauntered over to check out the situation, rubbing his head on her shins.

Her mom extended her hand down to Audrey, helping her to her feet. "Come join us at the table. We were just having a midnight snack."

"Mom, cookies and hot cocoa are not going to fix my problems."

"Then it's a good thing we're having strawberry pie."

Her mom's strawberry pie was delicious enough to mask any problem temporarily. She trudged into the kitchen and devoured a slice of pie while recounting Trevor's shocking admission. "I just don't get it." She recalled the bashful expression on Trevor's face. "He said he's had a crush on me since we were kids."

"It's because you flirt with him," Darcy blurted.

Audrey rolled her eyes. "I don't flirt with Trevor." She stuffed a forkful of strawberries into her mouth, savoring the sweet taste of summer. "I can't believe he got all serious and nervous. He's cared about me as more than just a friend all these years." Audrey's stomach twisted, her emotions tumbling about—rolling from shock, to giddiness, to guilt. She dropped her fork onto her plate, regretting the last bite of pie that she'd stuck in her mouth.

Darcy looked all starry-eyed. "Audrey, that's so sweet. He must mean it for real when he says he wants to marry you."

Audrey rolled her eyes and looked to her mom for support.

Her mom leaned forward, resting her elbows on the table. "What did you say to him, honey?"

A pang of guilt stabbed Audrey in the heart. "I was speechless. I mean, how could I tell him that I cherish our friendship so much that I don't want it to change? Plus, everyone knows long distance relationships are difficult." Those reasons played a part in her trepidation anyway. "Eventually, I said... 'I'm sorry.'"

Darcy and her mom shared a similar loss for words. Audrey was afraid they would cry like they always did at sappy movies. She needed to reassure them that the universe wasn't going to fall off its axis. "He handled it really well. He just said, 'See you in church.' And that was that."

The room was silent for a moment.

"You're crazy." Darcy started getting all dramatic. "You think you have to plan out your life minute by minute, but real life isn't perfect and calculated, you know."

"What are you talking about?" Audrey wasn't about to take advice from a sixteen-year-old who looked to teen magazines for wisdom.

Darcy stood up, her chair skidding backwards. "Follow your heart for once. So what if he's your friend? So what if you'll have a long distance relationship when you guys go to separate colleges in the fall?" She spread her arms wide open. So far Darcy's passionate speech wasn't very convincing. "Embrace the time you share." Darcy hugged her arms to her chest.

Audrey gave her mom a look, pleading to make her sister stop. Her mom's mouth twitched in a smile she failed to suppress. "Darcy, for now Audrey needs to let the shock absorb." She patted Darcy's chair, prompting her to return to her seat.

Darcy composed herself and sat back down at the table. "I'm just saying—Trevor is so sweet. And he's hot. Girls are gonna be chasing him down at the U of M, especially once they see how good he is out on the football field. He may not be available anymore by the time you're done sorting out your feelings."

Darcy was probably right about that. But it would be good for him to date someone else. Someone pure and honest who would never deny his love the way she just had. "Why don't you marry him then?"

Darcy wrinkled her nose. "That's so gross. He's like a brother or cousin or something."

"My point exactly. I can't marry my best friend." Audrey crossed her arms.

Her mom smiled. "Honey, I hope you'll marry your best friend."

"Hmm. I've never thought about it that way."

"Did you see Becca's post on Instagram?" Darcy held out her phone. "Check it out. Pictures don't lie." There was a photo of Trevor and Audrey with their arms wrapped around each other, gazing into each other's eyes. Trevor was holding the bouquet of wildflowers, the yellow ribbon floating in the breeze. Becca must have snapped the photo right after Trevor had walked through the gate. She'd typed the caption #bittersweetgoodbye.

Audrey's heart clenched. It was the most romantic picture she'd ever seen in her life. She was a fool to deny this guy. Tears sprang to her eyes, and she was helpless to stop them. Her shoulders shook as soft sobs came of their own accord.

Audrey's mom came to her side and cradled her in gentle arms. Audrey nuzzled into her mom's shoulder, no longer trying to fight the sadness. "Darcy, go on up to bed," she heard her mom say. After a few minutes, the torrent of tears dwindled to a drizzle. She sat up and wiped her face on a handful of napkins.

"Talk to me, honey." Her mom leaned her elbows on the table, allowing Audrey space.

Audrey shook her head. "I'm just sad." Her words came out in a whisper. Simba jumped on her lap as if to comfort her. He rubbed his head under her chin.

"Is this about Trevor? Or is something else bothering you?" Her mom had always been blessed with that thing called mother's intuition. It had always been impossible for Audrey to hide anything from her. That had to change. Now Audrey had a secret so despicable that she'd never tell her mom. She shrugged.

Her mom sighed, leaning back in her chair. "It's hard becoming an adult. Moving away from home. Saying goodbye to everything and everyone familiar. Starting a new chapter of your life." She sniffled. Audrey looked at her mom and saw that she had tears in her eyes. "I wish I could make it easier for you. But my job is to give you wings. To let you go."

Audrey fought the urge to roll her eyes. That sounded so cliché. Her mom was really reaching for some solid advice. "Mom, I'm excited for college. I'm ready. This weekend has just been tough. Graduating from Hope Church youth group makes me sad. And then Trevor went and said all that stuff."

Her mom studied her. "Are you sure that's all? You know you can tell me anything."

It took all of Audrey's willpower to force her head to nod. Deceiving her mom piled more shame on her shoulders. She was already this deep in it, why not just wallow in it. For a split second, she considered telling her mom the truth. That she was miserable because she'd been raped. But the news would break her mom's heart into a million pieces. She couldn't put her through that. "Is it okay if I stay home from church in the morning? I don't feel up to it. I said my goodbyes to church people tonight. I'd rather spend time reading my Bible on my own."

"Sure, honey." She kissed Audrey's forehead. "I love you. I'm so proud of you."

"I love you too, Mom."

She lumbered up to her bedroom and slid between the sheets. Laying in the darkness, thoughts tumbled about in her mind, drumming inside her head like sneakers in the dryer. Her mom kissing her forehead, saying she was proud of her. Trevor asking her on a date. Bitter-tasting beer sliding down her throat. Her toes dragging across carpet. Falling.

She gasped, bolting upright in her bed. Her chest heaved as she sucked in breaths, her heart racing. She flicked on the lamp, reminding herself she was safe at home now, surrounded by her childhood treasures. Little Golden books and The Chronicles of Narnia. Photos of her friends. Birthday gifts from her parents. Her eyes fell on the canoe paddle from Pastor Mitchel and the youth group. She crawled out of bed and held the paddle, letting memories wash over her. Paddling through the still waters up in the Boundary Waters was the closest she'd ever felt to God. She closed her eyes, returning to that place. She recalled the fresh smell of the lake water, the call of loons, and the trees swaying in the breeze. It had seemed as though God's creation was untouched by people. Untainted. Opening her eyes, she read the Bible verse. *Trust in the Lord with all your heart.* "I did trust you, Lord. And you let me get raped." *Lean not on your own understanding;* "Well, I definitely don't understand why you let that happen." *in all your ways, acknowledge him, and he will make your paths straight.* At least that part was promising. Maybe God would straighten out her life again.

She got back in bed, but decided to keep the light on for tonight. With her mind still reeling, she opened her Instagram account and studied the picture of her and Trevor that Becca had posted. They looked good together, she had to admit. She allowed her imagination to pluck him out of the friend zone and drop him into the boyfriend zone. She considered it for a moment. Hmm, not so bad. It seemed a natural progression. And Darcy was right—he was hot. He'd come home from his freshman year at college taller, with more chiseled facial features and muscles that rippled under his shirt. Tall, dark, and handsome.

Even more appealing than his good looks, was the way he made her feel. Closing her eyes, she recalled the feel of being cradled in the safety of Trevor's embrace. His five o'clock shadow brushing against her forehead. The sincere look in his aqua blue eyes when he spoke to her. She breathed in deeply, remembering his scent.

There was no denying, she was falling in love with Trevor.

Chapter Five

THE FIRST DAY ON CAMPUS AT BETHEL UNIVERSITY FLEW
by. Audrey was busy with cross-country meetings and the team's first
practice. She plodded into her dorm room around seven o'clock,
exhausted. She climbed onto the bottom bunk, relishing the peace
and quiet.

Earlier that evening, she'd received a voicemail from Trevor.
A warm feeling had washed over her body at the sound of his voice.
*Hey, how's my favorite girl? You must be out running hundreds of miles
or something. I had a few minutes to call you now, and then we have
another meeting tonight. Give me a call if you get the time. I'll probably
crash around ten.* He paused. *You snuck out of Hastings before I had
a chance to say goodbye.* Another pause. *Talk to you later.* It would be
meeting time right about now.

She tried hopelessly to get lost in a book. She finally closed her
eyes, and her thoughts drifted to Trevor. She pictured him squeezed

into a classroom chair that could barely accommodate his six-foot-four-inch frame, wearing a T-shirt that clung to his rippling biceps and chest muscles.

Most likely he was freshly showered after a day out on the field and his dark hair gelled into place ... or maybe he didn't have time to fix his hair so was hiding it under his maroon U of M baseball cap, worn backwards as he liked to do.

The door tore open, and Audrey's roommate bounded in—a soccer player named Destiny Connors. She was a spitfire of a girl with two bright red French braids dangling behind her back. She plunked herself down on Audrey's desk chair. So much for peace and quiet.

"I was wondering if you're busy because I'm going to the beach with some friends, and I thought you might like to come along." Somehow Destiny managed to speak at length without taking a breath.

"Um," Audrey glanced down at her cell phone and thought about the possibility of missing another of Trevor's calls. She really should talk to him. She decided she'd take her phone with her; she could easily talk to him on the beach. "Sure, that sounds fun."

"Okay, great!" Destiny jumped up from the chair. "Oh, by the way, do you have a car? I saw you parking a car out in the cul-de-sac earlier and none of us has a car so it would be great if you could drive ..."

Audrey held her book up to her face so Destiny wouldn't be able to see that she was rolling her eyes. Why didn't the girl just come out and say they needed a ride? Well, even if Destiny was using her for transportation, a night on the beach would beat sitting around waiting for a phone call any day.

"No problem. Let me get my swim suit on and I'll meet you guys in the lounge."

"That's okay, I'm ready to go so I'll help you get ready." Destiny flung open the top drawer of Audrey's dresser and proceeded to rifle through her more personal articles of clothing. "Is this where your suits are? I'll help you pick one out. Do you wear bikinis—because I'm wearing a one-piece, but I think all the other girls are wearing bikinis. There's gonna be guys there so if you're gonna wear a bikini then I think I'll put one on too, but I don't want anybody to get the wrong idea about me the first time I meet them. First impressions are a big deal, ya know? Here, wear this one." Destiny held up a navy blue one-piece Nike racing swim suit. Very conservative.

Dumbstruck, Audrey sat on her bed searching for what to say now that the girl had finally run out of words.

Destiny tossed the suit up onto Audrey's bed and left the room with the same whirlwind with which she had entered, saying on her way out, "I guess I'll use the bathroom quick before we go cause I'm not sure if there are restrooms on the beach and ..." her voice trailed off.

Audrey dressed quickly, knowing the girl would soon blast through the door again, probably without much warning. The one-piece was a good selection as it covered the bruises on her hips. Before she'd have a chance to give any more thought to that party, she grabbed her car keys and headed out. Audrey smiled, thinking about her new roommate. The girl was just what Audrey needed. Destiny's yammering would drown out all negative thoughts that would threaten to invade her new lease on life here at college. And if Destiny could dribble and shoot a soccer ball as fast as she could talk, Audrey imagined that she was a very decent soccer player.

* * *

Eight kids piled out of Audrey's Toyota Camry at Lake Johanna. They had to sit on laps in order to squeeze everybody in. Apparently, most freshmen didn't have the privilege of driving their own car. Audrey made a mental note to thank her dad for his generosity. Although dusk would soon be descending, the park was teeming with college students. A few were taking advantage of one of the last days of swimming for the summer while others loitered in the sandy area.

A beach volleyball game caught Audrey's eye, and she and Destiny headed in that direction. Audrey didn't recognize anybody from cross-country. Her teammates were probably smart enough to just lounge around for the evening to rest up for tomorrow's practices. Tomorrow would take care of itself. She was here so she might as well have a good time. Plus, it would do her some good to keep her sore legs moving so they wouldn't tighten up.

"Could anyone use a sub?" Destiny called out, as they kicked off their flip flops on the sand.

A tall blonde in a red bikini looked their way. "Sure, you can rotate in after the next point. I'm about to end this game." She winked at them. Staying true to her word, she spiked the ball straight through the hands of an opposing player. "It's all yours." She sauntered over to a picnic table where she high-fived some friends.

Destiny's mouth was agape. "Does Olympian Kerri Walsh Jennings have a little sister?"

Audrey laughed. "I wouldn't be surprised." She stepped onto the court where the winning team was already setting up for a new game. Audrey took an open position in the front row while Destiny joined the team on the other side of the net. Audrey turned to the guy on her right. "I take it that girl plays college volleyball." She motioned to the Kerri Walsh Jennings-looking blonde.

"Yeah, she's pretty good. I'm glad she's sitting this one out. She made the rest of us look bad."

Audrey doubted that. This guy definitely had an athletic look. Chest muscles bulged from beneath his Bethel football T-shirt, and his defined biceps could only be the result of hours spent in a gym. "Well, you don't have to worry about that anymore. I won't be showing anybody up."

He smiled. "That's a relief. It can be tough on a guy's ego."

Audrey laughed. "I'll try my best to make you look good."

"Thanks. I appreciate that."

It didn't take long for Audrey's team to run up the score even without the help of the blonde in the bikini. The guy with the biceps had definitely been humble when he said that girl made him look bad because he had more talent than the rest of the team put together.

The volleyball soon became difficult to see as the sky darkened, driving people to leave the game to cool off in the shallow waters of the lake. Audrey ran into the water, enjoying the feel of it cleansing the sweat and sand from her body. Closing her eyes, she lay back and floated, the cool water soothing her aching muscles.

"Hey," a deep voice boomed.

Startled, Audrey flailed in the water as her feet struggled to find the sandy floor of the lake. She inadvertently splashed water into her mouth and proceeded to cough and sputter. Trying to regain control, she looked up to see the guy with the biceps grinning at her. He reached out and grabbed her arm to help steady her.

"Sorry. I didn't mean to scare you." He didn't even attempt to withhold his laughter. "I was just going to thank you for making me look good out there."

Audrey held up her pointer finger. "I'll be fine. Just give me a minute," she managed between gasps for air.

He patted her on the back in exaggerated motions. His shirt was off now and through her bleary eyes she could see his sculpted six-pack. This guy definitely worked out. "Why so jumpy?"

He wouldn't want to hear the honest answer to that question. It's probably not good etiquette to admit you were raped recently when you've just met the person an hour ago. "I'm okay now, really. And by the way, you're welcome."

"Welcome for what?"

"For making you look good on the volleyball court. I missed all those shots on purpose." She wiped water from her eyes.

"Yeah, thanks. My ego is back intact." He reached out and caught a Frisbee whizzing past his head. "No, seriously, it was a good game." He tossed the Frisbee back to his buddy several yards away.

"Yeah, we really rocked it out there."

"So are you going to Bethel?"

"Yep, I'm a freshman." She could finally talk without coughing up a lung. "You're playing football for Bethel? I mean, I noticed you were wearing a Bethel football shirt."

He smiled. "Uh huh."

"Well, it was nice meeting you. I'm sure I'll see you around." She wasn't in a chatty mood. Her heart was still racing from being scared nearly to death.

"See you." He dove into the water, catching the Frisbee just before it would've splashed directly in front of Audrey.

A picture of Trevor diving on the football field to catch a pass suddenly came to mind. She'd seen him make that move too many times to count over the years. A lump formed in her throat as she thought of him and the distance their lives had created between them. A distance she'd furthered by avoiding him since Saturday night. Maybe he had called. She couldn't stand one more minute without checking her phone.

Toweling off, she announced her departure. Her phone was in her car, beckoning to her. The same group of girls she had given rides to earlier piled back into her car, this time bringing with them wet sand that stuck to their feet and lake water that clung to their hair and clothes. But Audrey didn't mind the mess; she no longer felt used by giving them a ride. She had a good time with these girls and now considered them to be friends.

"Hey Audrey," Destiny said from beneath a fellow soccer player who was sitting on her lap. "I noticed Matt Cook flirting with you tonight. I think he likes you."

"What are you talking about? Who's Matt Cook?"

The other girls simultaneously let out a harmonious squeal at the mention of his name. Destiny looked at Audrey as if she had blasphemed. "Matt Cook is that tall, dark and handsome football player who was following you around like a puppy dog."

"Oh, him." Audrey shrugged. He wasn't tall, dark, and handsome in the same way Trevor was—natural and unassuming. Matt carried himself in a way that suggested he thought he was someone extra special. Audrey wasn't sure if he conveyed confidence or arrogance. He certainly did attract attention. But he wasn't Audrey's type. "Yeah, he's a nice guy."

Destiny pushed aside the girl on her lap to get a better view of Audrey, not noticing that in doing so she caused the girl to bump her head on the window. "He's not just a nice guy, Audrey. He plays running back on the football team. He has his high school's record for rushing yards." Destiny leaned in closer, making eye contact with Audrey, as if saying something very important. "And he's single." She wiggled her ginger eyebrows.

Audrey laughed her comment off. "You can have him. I'm not interested."

"Why not? Do you have a boyfriend?" one of the girls piped in.

Audrey thought of Trevor. "No."

"Who do you keep texting? I see how you're constantly checking your phone."

Privacy was a thing of the past now that Destiny was her roommate. "Oh, that's just a friend. Trevor Hayes."

The girl on Destiny's lap gasped. "Wide receiver for the Gophers? He's your boyfriend?"

"No. He's just a friend."

Destiny sucked in a deep breath, signaling a long speech was imminent. "That's good. My high school sweetheart was two years older than me and he went to the University of Wisconsin Madison. He never called or texted me so I kept texting him, like ten times a day, and you can't tell me that he was never available to answer any of those texts so I got suspicious and drove out to Madison only to find out he was dating some Wisconsin cheese head. In my opinion, long distance relationships are a one-way street to disaster."

Everyone was quiet in the car, not knowing how to respond to Destiny's insensitive comment.

Destiny snatched Audrey's phone from the cup holder and swiped the screen. "Let's see if he called when we were at the beach." She clicked buttons on Audrey's phone, testing Audrey's patience. "He sent you a text. It says, 'Miss you. I hope you are having fun.'"

All the girls oohed and aahed, including Audrey. She parked her Camry in a spot behind the dorms.

Destiny dropped the phone back into the cup holder. "You're so lucky. He sounds like a sweetie. I guess that means Matt is still on the market, right girls?" She looked at the other girls, and they all cheered.

Audrey rolled her eyes again, this time with her face turned to the window.

As they climbed out of the car, Destiny ducked her head back inside. "I'll let Matt know you're taken."

"I told you we're just friends." Did she have to spell it out?

The girls climbed the stairs leading from the freshmen parking lot up to the residence halls. It had been a fun day, and Audrey couldn't wait to tell Trevor all about it. He would get a kick out of hearing about Destiny, but she decided not to mention Matt. She didn't want to hear about girls who were sure to be hitting on Trevor.

Back at the dorm, Audrey showered in the common bathroom where she was unable to find respite from Destiny's constant chatter. Even the sound of the running water wasn't enough to muffle her voice as she showered in the next stall. It wasn't that Audrey disliked the girl. On the contrary, she found her quite amusing, but she simply felt exhausted from the day's events. Listening to Destiny speak took more energy than Audrey could muster.

She retreated to her bed for the night, still not having connected with Trevor. She sent him one last text to tell him goodnight before laying her head on the pillow and closing her eyes for the night.

Sleep easily took her as she nestled under the covers. Her body ached more than ever before. She knew she'd pushed herself hard today. She'd pushed the pace on the team's easy run. The more she hurt, the faster she ran. She was determined not to let what that creep did to her to take away from her running or any other aspect of her life. Playing volleyball with fatigued muscles wasn't the best idea, but it helped to distract her from thoughts of that horrible party and thoughts of missing Trevor. She planned to take it easier tomorrow.

Her mind drifted back over the day's events. Stepping into her dorm room for the first time, meeting the loquacious Destiny Connors. Running with her cross-country team. Playing volleyball and swimming lazily in the soothing water. *Hey!* Matt's voice boomed in her mind. She felt hands grabbing at her waist, digging into her flesh.

Audrey screamed, her body bolting upright in bed. She looked around the room, reminding herself she was in bed. Safe.

"Audrey, are you okay?" Destiny hung her head down from the top bunk.

"I'm fine." The quiver in her voice told a different story. "I had a nightmare."

"Do you always have nightmares? Because I'm the kind of person who needs a lot of sleep."

Audrey rolled out of bed and went into the hallway to get a drink of water at the fountain—and get away from Destiny. Hopefully the girl would be asleep by the time she came back. The hallway was quiet. Everyone else was sound asleep. She sat on the floor, leaning her back against the wall. She pulled her legs to her chest and wrapped her arms around them. The hallway was quiet. *Lord, please help me to put that horrible night behind me. I shouldn't have stayed at that party. I shouldn't have tried beer. I'm sorry. I'll never go to another party again. Please help me to forget it ever happened. In Jesus name, amen.*

Chapter Six

LEAVES SHIMMERED BRILLIANT GOLDS AND REDS, SIGNAL-
ing autumn's return. A cool breeze scattered the few fallen leaves
littering the golf course. Audrey focused her eyes on the red and
white uniform an arm's length in front of her, straining to close the
gap. The opponent weaved in front of Audrey, preventing her from
passing. As the runners turned a corner, ironically on the 18th hole,
Audrey changed her focus from the girl in front of her to the finish
line less than 50 meters ahead. She bore down and leaned into the
wind, feeling a second wind kick in. Her legs took on a mind of their
own as she sprinted to the finish, leaving the red and white jersey in
the dust. Leaning forward, she tore the ribbon that stretched across
the finish line. She struggled to remain on her feet as she moved
through the finishers chute. Her muscles filled with lactic acid and
she kept them moving to prevent cramping. Her lungs burned as she

sucked in the cool air, and her stomach heaved. She half-heartedly wished she were here instead for a relaxing round of golf.

"Way to go, Audrey!" Her mom's voice rose above the crowd. Her parents were waiting at the end of the chute where they finally pulled her into a group hug. She hugged them back with the little strength she had left. "Honey, we're so proud of you." Her mom was glowing.

Tears of pride pooled in the corners of her dad's eyes. "Was that a personal record for you?"

Audrey cheered for a Bethel runner coming down the last stretch before answering. "I don't know. What was my time?" She bent over, her hands resting on her knees as she tried to control her breathing.

Her dad lifted the stopwatch hanging from his neck. "According to my watch, you finished in twenty-one minutes and five seconds."

"Wow, are you serious?" Audrey screeched with excitement. "Yes, that's a personal record. Maybe I can even qualify for nationals this year."

"Is Trevor here?" Her mom shielded her eyes from the sun with her hand, searching the spectators.

Her dad shook his head. "No, the Gophers have a game in Wisconsin today."

Audrey knew this, yet she'd listened for his voice through the cacophony of the crowd, and looked for his face among the cheering fans lining the race course.

"It's too bad he missed it." Her mom gave Audrey a side hug.

"Meanwhile I'm missing his big touchdown catches." She sighed. "But that's alright because I'm going to the Michigan game with Becca in a couple weeks. And tomorrow I'll get to see him. We're visiting a church in the morning and then just hanging out the rest of the day. It'll be the first time I've seen him since school started." She was practically counting down the minutes until she'd see him again.

Goosebumps rose on Audrey's bare legs beneath her running shorts. "I gotta get my sweats on." She hugged her parents and set off for the tent where Bethel had set up camp for the day. She couldn't help but smile. Before today, she hadn't even dreamed about running at Nationals. She plopped down on the tarp and rummaged through her duffle for a T-shirt. One thought that kept chipping away at her happiness about today's race; if only Trevor could've been there to see it.

"You rock!" a guy's voice rang out. *That couldn't be Trevor.* Hope penetrated all reasoning. Strong hands came down on her shoulders, kneading into her muscles.

Audrey turned to identify the mystery masseuse. A grinning Matt Cook stood over her, flanked by a couple of football buddies. Their admiration was palpable as they stared down at her. She stood up, and Matt pulled her into a congratulatory hug. The other guys patted her on the back. "Thanks, guys."

"That was amazing. You won this whole thing!" Matt gestured to the frenzied activity of runners and spectators.

Audrey's heart swelled with pride. "Stop it. You'll give me a big head."

"You deserve it. By the way, are you coming to the game tonight under the lights? We're gonna crush St. Thomas." The guys patted each other on their backs and whooped as if they'd already won the game. Matt pointed behind her. "Is that your family over there?"

Audrey looked over her shoulder. Her dad had his camera aimed in her direction while her mom gazed at her adoringly. They waved animatedly. A combination of embarrassment and pride caused her to break out in laughter. "Yes. They belong to me. C'mon, I'll introduce you. Depending on how my dad's photo turns out, you may have just made it onto his Facebook page. Few moments go uncaptured in my family."

Audrey led the guys over to her parents, grateful that they had filled the void of Trevor's absence.

Chapter Seven

AUDREY WAS SURE THE PITTER PATTER OF HER HEART was audible over the clanking of dishes and chatter of patrons at Snuffies Malt Shoppe. Starry eyed, she gazed at Trevor as she sipped her banana fudge malt and picked at her burger and fries. Trevor was catching her up to speed on all the behind the scenes action of the football team. His love for the game shone through his beautiful blue eyes, and she sat mesmerized by the passion in his every word.

It almost felt like a first date, with butterflies in her stomach and sweaty palms. She had never felt this way around Trevor before. But being reunited after several long weeks apart from him, she realized how much she'd missed him. She had to pinch herself in order to believe she was actually by his side again—well, sitting across from him. A small part of her had wondered if this night would feel awkward from too much time apart—and turning down his offer to start dating. But she was pleasantly surprised to find that today felt like old times, and distance had only made her heart grow fonder.

That morning when he'd picked her up for church, her heart leapt into her throat. His eyes lit up when he met her gaze. Trevor ran to her, seemingly in slow motion like something straight out of a movie. Passersby seemed to disappear as she melted into his embrace. His arms felt strong around her as he picked her up and spun her around, whispering how much he had missed her. She was crazy not to start dating him.

The events of that formidable party were becoming less haunting over time. More of a distant memory. Keeping busy helped the flashbacks to stay at bay for the most part. Maybe soon the memories would feel distant enough that she'd be able to look forward without looking back. Hopefully a day would come when she would forget it even happened. Until that time, she didn't feel ready to start a dating relationship. The sensible part of her told her that at this point, she wasn't in a good state of mind to start a relationship. She was damaged goods.

"Do you like your burger?" Trevor's voice snapped her back to the present.

She looked down at the half-eaten burger in her hand. She was eating like a pig, so hungry she'd felt sick. "Yeah. It's really good. And messy." She licked mayo and ketchup off her fingertips. Good thing it wasn't actually a date. "I'll buy next time."

"If you insist. Otherwise it might feel like we're dating or something." He winked.

Heat rose to Audrey's cheeks. He'd read her mind and was teasing her. Two could play at this game. "I wouldn't want to give you the wrong idea."

"Ouch!" Trevor placed a hand over his heart. He leaned his elbows on the table, becoming serious. He knit his brow together. "Audrey, please clear things up for me. How is it that you really feel? About us, I mean." He locked eyes with hers, waiting for her answer.

Suddenly, her burger felt like a brick in her stomach. How could he put her on the spot like this? Hadn't she made herself clear that she only wanted to be friends? She'd pretty much stomped on his heart when he'd confessed his deep-seated love. Admittedly, once she'd stopped avoiding his calls and texts, she'd been flirty with him as her feelings began to shift. She struggled to come up with a response. She sipped her malt, attempting to appear casual while buying time. Did he really want her to come out and say she was falling in love with him?

"Gotcha!" Trevor laughed. "I had you squirming so bad." He doubled over in laughter, drawing the attention of people at neighboring tables.

Audrey exhaled. "You don't wanna know how I really feel about you right now, buddy." She lobbed a fry at him, and it landed in his lap. It was so like Trevor to joke around like that. She should've known.

Trevor wiped tears from the corners of his eyes. "Let's get out of here before you get us kicked out." He fished cash out of his wallet and secured it under the ketchup bottle.

They drove to a park where they tossed a Frisbee under a canopy of autumn leaves. The hours passed far too quickly and soon the sun began to set. They walked slowly back to Trevor's car, not wanting the day to end, literally dragging their feet. The feelings were undoubtedly mutual. In attempt to lighten the mood, Audrey kicked a small pile of leaves in Trevor's direction. The breeze swept under the leaves, scattering them all over him. Trevor looked at Audrey and raised a cunning eyebrow.

He ran to a maple tree, raking the red and orange leaves into a pile with his feet. Audrey, anticipating his next move, took off running for the car, her laughter mingling with the soft whisper of the breeze. She tried to open the passenger door only to find that it was locked. Trevor dashed behind her, scooped her into his arms and carried her to the leaf pile.

"Let me go," she insisted, trying to wriggle from his grasp.

"Never." Trevor ran for the pile of leaves.

To Audrey's surprise, instead of throwing her into the leaves, he collapsed into the pile himself while holding her in his arms. They flung leaves on each other, wrestling and laughing.

Audrey pinned Trevor to the ground, not sure of her next move. "I told you to let me go, and now you'll have to pay."

Trevor reached up and held her face firmly between his hands. A more serious expression dawned on his features. "Audrey, I'll never let you go."

* * *

Trevor's heart pounded against the wall of his chest, the urge to kiss her almost too powerful to restrain. He'd given up on hiding his feelings for her yet respected her wish to remain friends. Reluctantly, he created a space between them, lying back in the cushion of leaves.

"We should go," he said against his will. "I have studying to do for my physics class in the morning." He pulled himself up, brushing off his jeans. Bending down, he grabbed hold of Audrey's hands, helping her to her feet as well. "Today was fun. I'm not ready for it to end." He watched Audrey out of the corner of his eye, gauging her reaction. He was pretty sure that she was falling for him, but maybe it was wishful thinking.

"I had fun too." She stuffed her hands in her jeans pockets. "You should come around sooner next time. Six weeks was way too long."

"So you were counting the weeks without me, huh?" His voice was teasing, but true hope bubbled inside him.

"I missed you, Trevor." She said it like it was obvious.

They reached the car then, and Trevor unlocked her door. "So you're coming to the Gopher game next weekend?"

"Yep. Get a touchdown for me." She slid into the car.

He closed her door and made his way to the driver's seat. "I'll pump my fist three times in the end zone. That's how you'll know the touchdown was dedicated to you."

"Seriously?" Audrey squealed. "I'd love that."

Trevor hoped to make good on that promise. It's not like touchdowns in Big Ten games were easy to come by.

As they began the drive to Bethel, Audrey's phone rang. She looked at the caller ID, rolled her eyes, and returned the phone to her pocket. "I'll call him back later."

"Him?" Trevor feigned jealousy. "Who is this guy?"

Audrey giggled. "It's just Matt Cook. We're in a study group together."

"Okay. If you say so." Trevor knew she was telling the truth, but he couldn't quell the protectiveness he felt for Audrey. Okay, maybe it wasn't protectiveness. Perhaps it was the slightest bit of jealousy—a reaction to that crazy crush he'd had on her since they were little kids.

* * *

Audrey sauntered into her dorm room with thoughts of Trevor dancing in her head. Their day together had been amazing. He made her feel special and safe and happy. All of her troubles melted away when she was with him. It would be a while before they'd spend time together again, but she was in too much bliss at the moment to worry about that.

She sat down at her desk and pulled out her phone. She swiped the screen and could hardly believe her eyes. *15 missed calls.* Each of them from Matt—today.

The door swung open, and Destiny came crashing through. "Audrey, Matt Cook is downstairs. He asked me to come get you." Destiny scrunched her face up and squealed with glee. "He's so cute!" Then she turned and skipped out the door.

Audrey went down to the lobby and found Matt perched on the side of the pool table, tossing the cue ball in the air while he waited.

"Hey Matt, what's up?"

He hopped down from the table and raced over to her. "Hey, I've been trying to get ahold of you all day. Where've you been?"

Audrey wasn't sure if she should straighten things out with him right then and there. Tell him clearly that she was only interested in a friendship. She decided against it. It would be way too awkward. "I've been around. Just busy. Is there something you need?"

"As a matter of fact, there is." He looked panicked. "We must have gotten our psych notebooks mixed up during our last study group. I have yours. Do you have mine? I really need to study for the exam." He held out her notebook to her. "And I'm guessing you need yours."

Audrey expelled a deep breath. "Oh, I hadn't noticed." She was so relieved she hadn't gone into a speech about just being friends when all he wanted was his notes. "I'll go check. I'll be right back." She took her notebook and ran up to the third floor.

She grabbed a green notebook off her desk and flipped through it. Yep. It was Matt's. She walked toward the door, relieved that she had been wrong about him.

She bumped into Destiny in the hallway. "What did Matt want? He was desperate to see you."

"He needed his psych notebook. Our notebooks accidentally got mixed up."

Destiny raised an eyebrow. "Accidentally, huh?" She put a hand on Audrey's shoulder. "He's so infatuated with you; he probably did it on purpose."

Audrey rolled her eyes. "You have a vivid imagination, Destiny." She pondered the idea of Matt switching their notebooks on purpose. It was preposterous. With his charm, good looks, brains, and athletic ability … he could get any girl he wanted. He didn't need to chase after anybody.

She returned to the lobby and gave Matt his notebook. Feeling uncomfortable, she told him she'd see him in psych class and turned to go up to her room.

"Wait." Matt put a hand on her arm. "Do you have time to study? I promise I won't run off with your notes this time."

"I better not." Confused about Matt's intentions, she needed an excuse to avoid him. "I'm probably more productive studying on my own. Sorry about the whole mix-up. I'll see you tomorrow."

"No problem. See you tomorrow." He headed back to his room.

The whole Matt thing was confusing. Honestly, he seemed innocent of all the rumors. There was a good explanation for his incessant phone calls throughout the day—he had been panicked without his notes. There was no evidence to suggest he had switched the notebooks on purpose.

Maybe she would quit the study group. She really did study better on her own. But then she would just be avoiding him, and there wasn't any reason to avoid him because there was nothing going on.

Destiny was in their room ripe with questions. "So what's going on with you two? I told him you had a boyfriend, but that I know lots of single girls." She pointed to herself and gave a dramatic wink.

Audrey could not believe her ears. "You honestly told him that I have a boyfriend?"

"Yeah. I was trying to spare him from throwing himself at you when it's obvious you have feelings for Trevor Hayes."

"That must've been awkward." Audrey, embarrassed for herself, Matt, and even Destiny, covered her face with her hands. "What did he say?"

"He just looked at me like I was speaking a foreign language. Then he walked away. Maybe he's shy. He's so cute." Another squeal.

"Destiny, please don't talk to Matt about me anymore. You've got it all wrong. We're just in a study group together. That's all. And I don't have a boyfriend—not that it matters." Audrey rifled through her drawer in search of pajamas.

"I was just trying to help," Destiny stomped out of the room, her red hair flying behind her.

Audrey rolled her eyes as she had been doing more often these days. Her bed was beckoning to her. A good night's sleep would help her put things into perspective.

But sleep would have to wait because she had a psychology exam to study for.

Chapter Eight

THE CROWD ROARED AS THE GOPHER MASCOT PREPARED the fans for the team's entrance onto the field while the marching band played the Minnesota rouser. A sea of maroon and gold filled most of the stadium seats, with smatterings of Michigan's blue and yellow.

"There he is." Becca pointed to Trevor running onto the field.

Audrey's heart skipped a beat when she spotted him from her seat in the stands. Her heart filled with pride seeing him out on the field of the crowded stadium, thousands of fans cheering for him and his teammates. She marveled that he was part of something so big.

"He looks hot in that uniform." Becca elbowed her. "Don't pretend you didn't notice."

The ear to ear smile on Audrey's blushing face was enough to reveal her appreciation.

The Gophers won the coin toss and took offense at the start of the game. Audrey held her breath when the quarterback stepped back and thrust the ball in Trevor's direction. Trevor took off running down the sideline. Instinctively, he reached up and caught the ball just as it came into his range. He gained ten more yards, putting the Gophers well into Michigan territory before a defensive player knocked him out of bounds.

The Minnesota crowd went crazy, but the players maintained their focus as they quickly huddled together before lining up for the second play. This time, the quarterback faked a hand-off to the running back before tossing the ball to Trevor. He ran the ball all the way to the end zone for the first touchdown of the game.

Trevor wasn't one to celebrate elaborately after a touchdown, but he did pump his fist three times in the air—just as he had promised. A sign to Audrey that he had dedicated that touchdown to her. Her heart pumped with so much jubilation she thought it might burst. Becca didn't even know he did that for her.

Audrey was on the edge of her seat the entire game. Trevor was good. Before today, she hadn't realized just how good he truly was. By half time, the Gophers had scored three more touchdowns and were in a comfortable lead against the Michigan Wolverines. The Gophers held their lead in the second half and won the game.

Gopher fans celebrated the win as they filed out of the stadium. A triumphant energy buzzed through the streets of Minneapolis as rambunctious college kids dispersed in different directions singing the Minnesota rouser and recalling the most memorable plays of the game.

"So are you gonna celebrate the win with Trevor tonight?" Becca nudged Audrey with her elbow. "You'll have to give him a little somethin'-somethin' in return for the show he put on for you out on the field today."

"Becca, you are a bad girl!" Audrey settled behind the wheel of her Toyota Camry. "Actually, he made plans with the guys. So I was thinking we could make this a girls' night."

"That would be fun. We can hang out at my house. I'll catch you up to speed on all the Hastings dirt. I've got some dirt of my own to share."

"Intriguing. Do tell."

Becca squealed, reminding Audrey of Destiny. "Jake and I are officially a couple." She clapped her hands, squealing some more.

Audrey wasn't sure that this was a good thing, but she congratulated her friend anyway. "That's great news. Especially considering you guys already were hooking up."

"Don't be so judge-y. C'mon. I bet you and Trevor have too."

Audrey shook her head. "Of course not. We're not even dating. Why doesn't anybody believe that?"

Becca laughed. "That doesn't mean you can't be friends with benefits."

"I would never jeopardize our friendship that way. Besides, I decided to wait until I'm married." She felt like a hypocrite. She was no longer a virgin. She looked Becca in the eyes. "You used to say you were waiting for marriage too."

"I grew up, Audrey. That was so unrealistic. Nobody actually waits till they're married anymore. Don't be so old-fashioned." Becca twirled a strand of hair between her fingers. "Besides, Jake might be the guy I marry. I think I might love him, and I'm pretty sure he feels the same way about me."

Audrey rolled her eyes. "That's reassuring."

"New subject. Tell me about college-life."

Relieved for the distraction from their tense conversation, Audrey talked about running for the cross-country team and her hopes of qualifying for nationals. She told Becca about the friends she was making and soon they were doubled over in laughter at Audrey's impersonation of Destiny talking a mile a minute about what a "hottie" Matt Cook was.

* * *

At Becca's house, Audrey sat in an oversized chair facing the flickering gas fireplace in the family room. Becca lounged in a corner of the adjacent sectional. Becca's parents scurried about getting ready to go play Bunko with church friends, including Audrey's parents. Becca's mother poked her head around the corner. "We're leaving, Becca. Don't wait up for us."

"Bye, Mom. Don't get too wild now."

The girls listened as heels clicked across the floor above to the front door, but then got closer again. "Becca, I don't want to come home to a bunch of kids trashing my house. Audrey is the only friend allowed here tonight."

"I know, Mom."

The heels clicked across the floor again and the front door creaked open, then closed with a thud.

Becca twirled a strand of hair. "My mom is so paranoid. Ever since Jake got busted for his party."

Audrey's stomach clenched at the mention of that party. "That's understandable." She had an opportunity to tell Becca what had happened to her. Maybe Becca had heard something about girls getting drugged. Possibly, Audrey wasn't the only one and if enough girls came forward they could catch the guy. But Becca would have brought it up if that were the case.

"What do you want to do on our fun girls' night? Dye our hair? Paint our nails? Play truth or dare?"

Truth or dare was definitely out of the question. Audrey would not be spilling any secrets tonight. "I was thinking we could watch a chic flick. Can't get girlier than that."

Becca grabbed a remote and turned on Netflix. "Okay, we'll do a movie night. But I was really hoping to make you admit that you're madly in love with Trevor Hayes in a game of truth or dare."

They settled on a Nicholas Sparks movie and shared a bowl of popcorn. By the second scene, Audrey's eyelids were already getting heavy. After nodding off a few times, she stretched out on the couch and rested her head on the arm rest, promising Becca she'd try not to fall asleep. Her eyes closed against her will and soon memories of Jake's party filled her mind. Steering her thoughts to positive meanderings, she pictured Trevor playing basketball. But soon her mind took on a life of its own, carrying her down the path she'd tried to avoid. Strobe lights. Loud music. Fingers digging into her flesh. Helplessness.

"Audrey!"

Audrey's eyes flew open at the sound of her name. She could hear the echo of her own screams. Becca was kneeling beside her, jostling her shoulder. Fear emanated from her brown eyes. "You were dreaming."

Audrey sat up. Her heart was beating rapidly and she had to work to calm her breathing. "I…was having a nightmare."

"Are you okay? You were screaming and thrashing. It was freaky."

Tears pooled in Audrey's eyes. "I'm fine." A tear trickled down her cheek. She wiped it away with trembling fingers.

"I've had nightmares before, but I've never cried afterwards. There's something you're not telling me." A scene from The Notebook played in the background, with lulling piano accompaniment.

Audrey stared blankly at the screen over Becca's shoulder.

Becca turned off the TV and sat next to Audrey. "I trusted you with my secret about me and Jake. You can trust me too."

Audrey sighed. "You're right. I do have a secret." The lies and false pretenses were beginning to bog her down. "But I'm not ready to talk about it yet." Another tear ran down her cheek.

Becca crossed her arms. "Is it about school or boys...or running? God?" She raised an eyebrow. "Because I have an answer for all of those things. It is perfectly acceptable to have less than a 4.0. As far as boys are concerned, you should marry Trevor. Running is insane; you should stop that immediately. And...trust in God with all your heart." Becca smiled, pleased with herself. "There you go. All your problems are solved."

"I like that you quoted Proverbs 3:5. Pastor Mitchel would be proud of you." Audrey laughed lightly, although the tears kept flowing. "But my problem remains unsolved. It's not even really a problem. It's just something I need to forget about. Put it behind me. I don't know why I can't just get on with my life." She buried her face in her hands and balled like a baby.

Becca got up, grabbed a tissue box, and set it on Audrey's lap. Then she sat down with an arm around Audrey's shoulder. "Whatever is going on with you is too big for you to keep to yourself. Sometimes you need to talk through something before you can move on."

Audrey shook her head. Becca might feel responsible for what happened since she had suggested they hang out at the party instead of going back out to watch the guys play basketball.

"I'll let you off the hook on one condition. Talk to Pastor Mitchel at church tomorrow morning."

Fear ran cold though Audrey's veins. "Are you giving me an ultimatum? I told you, I'm not ready." She shrugged off Becca's arm. "I'll talk when I'm good and ready."

"I'm trying to help you. That's what friends do. You're being so weird right now—crying and getting all defensive. It's not like you to act that way, so I'm concerned. I don't care if you're mad at me."

Audrey blew her nose into a tissue. She was a hot mess, she had to admit. "I'll think about it."

"No." Becca stared into Audrey's eyes. "Promise me you'll talk to Pastor Mitchel. Tomorrow. Or talk to me right now."

She was desperate to get Becca off her back. "Fine. I'll talk to Pastor Mitchel." It wasn't a complete lie. She would at least consider it.

* * *

"I want a butterfly face," a preschooler screamed at Audrey. The little girl perched on a stool and crossed her arms. "Like at the zoo."

How Audrey got roped into face painting at the church Fall Festival she would never know. To be honest, she did know. It was because she hadn't talked to Pastor Mitchel yet, and Becca was not going to let her off the hook until she did. Audrey had *tried* to talk to him privately, but there hadn't been a good opportunity. The guy was busy on Sunday mornings—teaching the youth Sunday school class and then playing guitar for the worship service. Immediately after the service ended, he was running around, preparing for the Fall Festival. Audrey pointed out the poster of sample face painting designs. "I can make a pumpkin, an apple, a pretty leaf—"

"No! I want a butterfly face."

Audrey held back an eye roll. She didn't have the energy to deal with a tantrum this morning. She was literally sick to her stomach over having to talk to Pastor Mitchel. She'd actually thrown up in the shower. To make things worse, her mom had made homemade cinnamon rolls—Audrey's favorite breakfast. Not wanting to disappoint her mom or let on that she didn't feel well, she had choked one down. Surprisingly, it had made her feel a little better. Carbs always did have tendency to cheer her up.

Audrey peeked around the screaming child to see if the line had died down any. No such luck. For a small church, this congregation sure had a lot of little kids. Becca, sitting next to her, was outlining a heart she'd painted on a little girl's cheek. "How do you get all the easy ones?" Audrey whispered.

Becca shrugged a shoulder, grinning.

"Bu—tter—fly. Bu—tter—fly." The girl was actually chanting.

Audrey dipped a brush in hot pink paint. "Okay. I'll make a butterfly on your cheek." She leaned forward, bringing the brush to the girl's cheek. The girl flailed her arms, knocking the brush out of Audrey's hand and spattering paint on the cement. "No! My whole face."

The girl's mom gasped, looking around to see who had witnessed the outburst—which was pretty much everybody at the festival. "Angel, that was not nice. You tell Miss Audrey that you are sorry."

The girl made a pouty face. "Butterfly."

Her mom giggled nervously. "Can you please paint a butterfly on Angel's face? At the zoo, they painted her whole face to look like a butterfly. She loved it. Here, I'll show you a picture on my phone." The lady had the nerve to take out her phone and scroll through her pictures.

Audrey was starting to feel like she was going to throw up again. Especially since all the kids smelled like pumpkin pie and all the moms seemed to have doused themselves in perfume that morning. The smells were making her more nauseous than she'd ever been in her whole life. "You know what? I'm just not that good of an artist." Spotting Darcy walking nearby, she hopped off her stool. "But my sister is. I'll go get her." She grabbed Darcy's arm. "You're coming with me. You need to work your artist magic on Angel. She wants a butterfly face." Audrey pushed Darcy down onto the artist's stool and pressed a paintbrush into her hand.

"What?" Darcy stared blankly at the little girl.

Angel was grinning ear to ear. "Butterfly face."

Audrey high-tailed it out of there before anyone could protest. She went into the church bathroom to throw up and then washed her face at the sink. Looking at her reflection in the mirror, she wondered how she'd gotten to this place. How did she become this version of herself? A liar and a coward. Throwing up because she was so ashamed to say that she'd been at a party where she'd been drugged and raped. How did she get herself into this mess? What happened to wholesome Audrey?

She smeared lip gloss on her lips and pinched her cheeks to give them a little color. It was time to talk to Pastor Mitchel. She'd feel better after getting this secret off her chest. And he always had words of wisdom.

She took a deep breath, and opened the bathroom door. The church was eerily quiet. All of the action was outside at the festival. Her legs felt like Jell-O as she walked down the corridor leading to the church offices. Pastor Mitchel's door was slightly ajar. She could hear muffled voices coming from inside. She put her hand up to knock, pausing to pray. *God, give me courage.* She reminded herself that she was Audrey the Brave. A little smile worked its way into her heart. *Make me Audrey the Brave again.* When she knocked, the door creaked open further. Pastor Mitchel was standing with his back to her, his hands on his hips. His wife had her arms crossed, and she was crying. They both looked up at her, startled. "Sorry," Audrey said, backing away. "If this is a bad time—"

"No." Mrs. Mitchel sniffed and dried her cheeks with her palms. "Come in. It's fine. Andrew and I can talk later." She picked up her purse from his desk. "I'll see you at home, Andrew." She left the room, patting Audrey's shoulder as she walked by.

Awkward.

"Come in." Pastor Mitchel ran his hand through his sandy blond hair. "Sorry about that. We're just…having a bad day." His eyes were bloodshot.

Clearly, this was not a good time to have a heart to heart with Pastor Mitchel. "Um, I don't know much about marriage, but…I think you should go talk to her."

Pastor Mitchel rubbed the back of his neck. He stood there a beat, staring out into the hallway. "You're probably right." He grabbed his car keys off the desk. "Is that okay? I mean, was there something you needed to talk about?" He was backing toward the door.

There sure was. "Nah. I just wanted to say hi." Lie. "I haven't really seen you since school started. We'll catch up another time."

"We'll definitely talk later." He patted her shoulder on his way out just like his wife had done.

Audrey sat down on the loveseat facing Pastor Mitchel's desk. What was she supposed to do now? Her eyes scanned the library of books shelved behind the desk. There were countless theology books and Bible dictionaries. She wondered if Pastor Mitchel had read all of them. Maybe if she'd read these kinds of books, she'd have the wisdom to handle her current issues. On the other hand, Pastor Mitchel, having read these books, still seemed to be having issues of his own. She sighed. *God, you're just gonna have to help me through this. You need to give me wisdom since Pastor Mitchel is busy at the moment.*

If God were here, face to face, sitting on the other side of Pastor Mitchel's desk, what would he say? Maybe he'd tell her to ask for forgiveness. She closed her eyes, and did so even though she'd tried that before. Her burden lightened some, but she still felt weighed down by shame and secrecy. Then, she thought of her answer. Proverbs 3:5-6. Trust in the Lord. She shrugged her shoulders, not really knowing how she was supposed to go about that. But it was probably the advice Pastor Mitchel would've given, and it was a command from the Lord himself.

So for now, that's what she would do. Trust in the Lord and hope he'd help her to somehow forget that horrible thing ever happened.

Chapter Nine

TREVOR WORKED THE PROBLEM OVER AND OVER, BUT IT never came out right. Physics was one of his favorite subjects. He loved the satisfaction of solving a difficult problem, but tonight he was stumped. Such had been the story of his life lately, with Audrey being the source of his puzzlement.

He hadn't been able to get in touch with her in weeks. She hadn't even answered her phone the last few Sunday nights at their sacred phone time. She was obviously avoiding him. But he wouldn't give up. They hadn't had a fight or even so much as a disagreement. He couldn't think of anything he could have said or done to make her quit speaking to him. He dialed her dorm room number for at least the hundredth time that week. *Please, Audrey. Please pick up.*

"Hello?" It was her roommate.

"Is Audrey there?"

"Hey, Matt. She's not here. I thought she was with you."

"Um, this is Trevor," he said, annoyed.

"Oh … sorry, Trevor. That was awkward." She cleared her throat. "Audrey is at the library with her study group. They have a psych exam tomorrow. She probably has her cell turned off in the library."

"I'll just try again later."

"Okay. I'll let her know you called."

Trevor ended the call.

He shook his head as he went over the phone conversation in his head. *Hey, Matt … I thought she was with you.* Trevor shuddered to think that Audrey could be seeing another guy, even though she had every right to do so. She claimed they were just in a study group together, but Trevor knew what freshmen study sessions were like. They were about twenty-five percent studying, and seventy-five percent goofing off while munching on microwave popcorn and pizza.

An uncharacteristic pang of jealousy coursed through his veins. He threw his phone against the wall of his room and slammed his text book shut. His own studying would have to wait. Right now he had more important things to think about.

He couldn't get ahead of himself by assuming that Audrey was seeing this guy. It made sense that she would be studying tonight. She worked hard to keep her grades up. Matt really was in her study group, along with a few other kids. He knew that much for a fact.

The thing that really bothered him was that she was clearly avoiding him. She hadn't so much as sent him a text in weeks. Then there was the night he drove to her dorm to see her. He was sure it was her peering from behind the curtain as he called her room and finally drove away. Why would she do that?

Maybe this is what people are talking about when they say women like to play games with your head. Maybe this was some kind of hard-to-get maneuver. "Forget it," he said aloud. "I'm not playing any games."

He went out to the kitchen where his buddies were playing cards. "Hayes, grab a beer and come join us. You've studied enough for all of us."

Trevor opened the fridge and grabbed a bottle of water. "No thanks, guys. I'm turning in early tonight."

"Suit yourself, Hayes. I can read your poker face like a book anyway. You're probably better off just going to bed."

Being known for rising to a challenge, Trevor turned on his heel. "We'll see about that." He marched over to the table and pulled up a chair, consciously deciding to dismiss all thoughts about Audrey. She was going on with her life; he could too. Christmas break was just around the corner, and they'd have a couple weeks to work things out. Living next door, it would be impossible for her to avoid him.

* * *

Audrey pulled the Toyota Camry into her parents' driveway. It was good to be home. She couldn't wait to be under the safety of her Mom and Dad's roof, to sleep in her childhood bedroom. At the same time, she was tempted to back out of the driveway and run away. She could drive aimlessly through the night. It didn't matter where she'd end up. As long as she wouldn't have to face her parents and tell them what had happened. In reality, it was impossible to outrun her problems. They would follow her wherever she went. Eventually, her parents would find out.

She looked over at the neighboring driveway. At the sight of Trevor's parked car, butterflies fluttered in her stomach. Flashbacks of all the times she sat next to him in that car ran through her mind. *Forget about him*, she told herself. *He's no longer a part of my life. Just let him go.* Nausea chased the butterflies away.

It was time to stuff thoughts of Trevor deep into the recesses of her mind and concentrate on facing her family. She could only hide what had happened to her that awful night for so long. Audrey was sure her mom knew something was wrong. Her mom had been calling just to check in, just to see how she was doing several times a week. Each time, Audrey promised her mom that she was fine, school was good, and she was looking forward to Christmas. But the lies tasted bitter on her tongue. Up until now, she'd always been truthful with her mom. Until something so gross and horrifying happened that the truth would break her mom's heart, shattering her mom's image of her innocent little girl. She'd simply have to put the ugliness out of her mind and put on a merry smile.

Summoning courage, she closed her eyes and dropped her head back against the head rest. She drew in a deep breath, and then let it out slowly. *God, please be with me.*

A rapping noise on the window made Audrey's heart leap into her throat. Darcy was jumping up and down with excitement outside the car. She opened the door and nearly pulled Audrey out, enveloping her in a tight hug. "I've missed you so much, big sis."

Audrey returned the hug, feeling just as happy to see Darcy. "I've missed you too." Audrey drew back slightly so she could get a good look at her sister. Darcy's eyes sparkled with childlike joy. Her skin shone with the vibrant glow of youth, with rosy cheeks and a porcelain complexion. Not long ago, Audrey had that same vibrancy, but she'd lost it when her innocence was stolen away. She shivered. "It's freezing out here. Help me carry some stuff in?"

Darcy lugged a basket of dirty laundry out of the car while Audrey grabbed a suitcase and a backpack, stuffed with text books, that was nearly bursting at the seams. The front door, adorned with an evergreen wreath and red velvet bow, opened just as they stepped onto the front porch. Audrey's dad greeted her with a warm smile and a tousle of her hair. The aroma of freshly baked sugar and spice cookies wafted out the door. It was like a living Norman Rockwell painting. And she was a smudge—an imperfection that, once discovered, would mar the entire work of art.

"Merry Christmas, Audrey." Her dad slid the backpack off her shoulder. "Wow, this thing is heavy. So this is where all my money has been going." He placed the backpack in the coat closet and then hugged Audrey and kissed her cheek. "We're so happy you're home."

Her mom appeared from the kitchen, wiping her hands on her homemade gingerbread-print apron. Audrey hugged her, savoring the warmth and softness of her embrace. Would her mom be so eager to hug her once she found out what had happened?

Stupid! It was so stupid of her to get in that predicament. Her parents were spending so much money to send her to a private Christian school, and she threw it all away. Her grades had slipped from A's to B's, and she hadn't qualified for Nationals in cross-country. It seemed the harder she tried to put the assault behind her, the more it haunted her and interfered with her life.

The only thing to keep her sane was running. The only time she felt free, almost invincible, was while running. Indoor track season would be starting after Christmas break. She couldn't wait to pound out all her frustrations on the track. That is, if she would be able to run.

Her mom drew back slightly from the embrace and studied Audrey's face. Audrey avoided eye contact, feeling as if her mom would somehow see the truth in her eyes. "Come sit down and have cookies. They're still warm from the oven." Her mom smiled as she spoke, but the smile didn't reach her eyes.

Audrey looked down at her shoes, avoiding her mom's probing gaze. She almost wished her mom would come out and ask what was wrong instead of pretending it was a merry Christmas, just like any other. She would tell her mom every detail, and cry in her arms. Her mom would hold her, and tell her that it wasn't her fault and that everything would be okay. But her mom didn't ask, and Audrey didn't offer the information. Instead, she slipped off her shoes and coat, and then sat down to eat cookies.

The family sat around the white round dining table, creating small talk about the weather and school. When there were nothing but crumbs on the plates, Audrey excused herself. "I think I'll turn in early tonight. I'm exhausted from finals week."

Her mom looked at her dad, hinting that he needed to say something, to keep her up talking a while longer. He held out the plate of cookies. "Want another cookie?" He was so awkward that it was cute.

Her mom stood from the table and protested, "It's only eight o'clock, and you just got here. Stay up and visit for a while." Her moist eyes were pleading.

Audrey's heart ached for her mother, but she couldn't possibly sit here making small talk about the latest snowstorm while a storm of her own was consuming her thoughts. "Mom, we'll have plenty of time to talk." Audrey kissed her mom, dad, and sister on their cheeks before making a hasty exit to her bedroom.

Closing her bedroom door, she let out a long breath. Scanning the room, she noticed what a child she had been before leaving for college. Stuffed animals and dolls sat propped on her bed. Pink curtains, embroidered with delicate yellow flowers, hung daintily over the windows. Her favorite childhood books filled the bookshelves, intermingling with pre-teen romances and mystery novels. She plopped down on her bed and held one of the teddy bears. Why did she have to grow up? She was so blessed to have a childhood filled with beautiful memories.

It wasn't so long ago that she fit into this childhood world. It was only a few months ago, in fact. But now her world was turned upside down. It no longer seemed beautiful and happy, full of promise and love. Now it felt ugly and cruel.

Nausea swept over her. She tightened her grip on the bear, squeezing it to her chest as she had done many nights throughout the years after scary dreams would awaken her. But the bear no longer gave her comfort. It wasn't enough to erase the past, to overturn events of that party. Although she had little memory of what had happened that night, she was still disturbed by it. Somebody had taken advantage of her.

She had always felt in control of her life, believing that she held the key to her own future. She had lived conscientiously; getting good grades, excelling in sports, attending church regularly, and choosing friends wisely. *God, are you punishing me for going to that party? Please forgive me, God. Please.* She sat quietly, her heart searching for an answer. "Lord, I need to know you're here. I'm trying to trust in you."

Her eyes rested on the canoe paddle Pastor Mitchel had given her as a graduation present. She'd lugged it to and from college. She let the scripture etched on the back simmer in her mind. *Trust in the Lord with all your heart and lean not on your own understanding; in all your ways acknowledge him, and he will make your paths straight.* What did the verses even mean? So if she acknowledged God, he'd make her paths straight. That probably meant that if she looked to him for guidance, he would show how to do the right thing. Right?

What would God want her to do right now? She stared up at the ceiling, wishing the answer was written across it in bold letters. She could hear her parents' voices downstairs and clanking dishes. They were probably cleaning up after their little snack. She felt a tug on her heart, wishing she were down there with them. She loved spending time with her family. She especially cherished the late night talks she and Darcy and her mom would share. Now she felt like an outsider, hiding up here in her room.

Audrey gasped. That was it. The answer she was looking for resonated in her heart. The power of God's response swept through her heart. He wanted her to tell her parents.

Her eyes flooded with tears. "Thank you, God. Thank you," she cried, rocking back and forth still clinging to the teddy bear. The God of the universe, the Creator of the world was speaking directly to her. And His voice wasn't punishing, but loving. He knew exactly what had happened that night. He saw it all. He was there when she made the decision to stay at the party. He saw how she was defiled. Yet he still loved her and wanted her to trust him.

Would her parents still love her too? Would they stand by her and help her? Or would they be ashamed of her and angry that she had put herself in a compromising position? Maybe she didn't need to tell them. She could forget it ever happened and just move on with her life. She didn't even remember the rape, so what was holding her back? *Trust in the Lord.* The words rolled through her head.

If God wanted her to tell them, then he would be there to hold her hand through it. She felt empowered by his presence. She made the decision to tell her parents tomorrow. After a good night's rest. But the nausea still lingered in her stomach. It seemed to be there permanently these days. She cracked her door open and peered into the hallway. The voices of her family drifted up from downstairs. She tiptoed to the bathroom, and turned on the shower to muffle the sounds of her vomiting.

* * *

It was still dark outside when Audrey woke the next morning. She tossed off the covers and stretched, contemplating going out for a run before everyone else got up. A chilly draft seeping through the window persuaded her to snuggle back under the covers. Her bed was extra cozy in comparison to the dorm room bunk. She pulled the quilt up to her chin, breathing in the familiar scent of her mom's fabric softener.

Her stomach turned.

A wave of nausea coiled in her stomach, reminding her of the time at the State Fair when she was on the tilt-a-whirl after pigging out on cheese curds. She'd thrown up all over her new sandals.

Stumbling out of bed, she reached the waste basket just in time. Her body heaved violently again and again as she knelt on the floor, staring into the garbage. Finally, her energy depleted, she was able to rest, curling into a ball on the floor. Was it possible that bottling up this secret was making her physically ill? The nausea was intolerable. She needed to tell her mom soon.

Pulling on her running tights and slipping on her pullover, another thought plagued her. She tried to force it from her mind because it was simply too horrific to consider. She ran her hand along her lower abdomen. For a couple months, she'd felt bloated, although her period never came. That happens to runners though. Too much running and not enough nutrition can make runners stop getting their periods. With all of the nausea and vomiting, she definitely wasn't getting enough nutrition. But now, beneath her hand, there was a bulge, like a grapefruit was inside her. She stared at her reflection in the full-length mirror that hung on the back of her door. Despite this so-called lack of nutrition, her belly and her breasts were fuller. There was no denying the notion that she was pregnant. Tears filled her eyes.

God, please don't let me be pregnant.

She wiped her eyes on toilet paper in the bathroom. Crying wouldn't change anything. Running would make her feel better. She crept down the stairs and laced up her running shoes. As she was about to open the door, she noticed her mom curled up in the living room chair. The electric fireplace gave off a cozy glow. Her mom's Bible was on the coffee table; she must've woken up early to do her daily devotions.

Audrey swallowed. This was her chance to talk to her mom privately. As she approached her mom, she saw that her eyes were closed. To Audrey's surprise, her mom wasn't praying; she was sleeping. She tapped her mom's shoulder.

"Mom, are you awake?"

Her mom strained to open her eyes.

The cat, curled up in her mom's lap, sprang from the chair and scurried off.

"I am now." She stretched. "Audrey, is that you? What time is it?"

"Yeah, it's me. It's only six o'clock. Dad and Darcy are still sleeping." She spoke in a whisper, hoping to keep this conversation exclusively between the two of them. She sat on the ottoman next to her mother's feet. "I was on my way out when I saw you sitting down here. I thought maybe you were doing your morning devotions." She fell silent for a moment and then looked down at her trembling hands, willing her nerves to settle. She looked up at her mother through glistening eyes. "Why are you down here? Were you having trouble sleeping?"

Her mom sighed. "Yes. I haven't been sleeping well lately."

"Is it because of me, Mom?" She stared into the fire, her back to her mom.

Audrey felt the delicate weight of her mom's hand rest on her shoulder. "Do you want to talk about it?"

She nodded, fixing her gaze on the dancing flames. Her chest was rising and falling, almost unnaturally as she dug deep for courage to relay the horrific account. Her mom's comforting hand on her shoulder encouraged her to speak. "I made a mistake." Her voice came out in a faint whisper.

Her mom gulped audibly. "Honey, whatever it is, your dad and I will always love you." She gripped Audrey's hand in hers, squeezing her fingers for reassurance. Audrey saw goose bumps raise the delicate hairs on her mom's wrist. Her mom was worried. Justifiably.

She needed to just say it and get it over with. "I went to a party. There was alcohol there. I knew there was serious partying going on, and I stayed anyway. That was my mistake." She sniffed. That part wasn't so hard.

Her mom brushed a loose curl from Audrey's forehead and tucked it behind her ear. "Honey, of course we don't want you drinking when you're underage, but ..."

"That's not all, Mom." She finally looked her mom in the eye.

"What else?"

Audrey shook her head, "I don't know...I felt sick, and I passed out." She hugged her arms to her chest. "I don't remember—"

Footsteps sounded on the steps; she and her mom looked to the staircase simultaneously. Darcy appeared, rubbing her eyes. "What are you guys talking about?"

Oh great. Conversation over.

Audrey stood up, somewhat relieved that she didn't have to tell the worst part. "Nothing, Darcy. I was just going out for a run." She kissed her mom lightly on the cheek. "Thanks, Mom. I feel better now. I won't do it again."

Audrey booked it out the door.

Chapter Ten

⌀

Trevor stood in front of the jewelry counter with his hands propped on the glass, staring into the brightly lit sea of gold and diamonds. The choices were endless.

"How about that one?" Lucas pointed to a gold tennis bracelet. "I don't think Mom has a gold bracelet."

The sales clerk removed the bracelet from the display case and set it next to the gold chain, chandelier earrings, and mother's ring. Her long red fingernails clicked on the glass as she drummed them impatiently. It was the morning of Christmas Eve, and there were many other anxious customers she was eager to help. Trevor and Lucas had been mulling over jewelry for the better part of an hour.

Trevor took off his hat and rubbed his head briskly. "I don't know what to choose."

Lucas was losing his patience now too. "Dude, why can't you make a decision? I vote for the tennis bracelet."

Ready to close the deal, the sales clerk picked up the bracelet. "Shall I box it up for you?"

"Yeah, the bracelet is fine." Trevor's indifference was obvious. It wasn't that he didn't care about his mother's Christmas gift. He was just too preoccupied to make a decision about anything.

Why had Audrey been avoiding him? Was it about that Matt guy who Destiny had mistaken him for on the phone? It frustrated Trevor to no end.

He wished she would've called him and told him that she wanted to see somebody else. Of course he wouldn't have liked the idea, but he would've given her space. It sure would've been easier than suffering the silent treatment.

"Hey Trev, snap out of it," Lucas snapped his fingers in front of Trevor's face as they stepped out of the department store and into the mall.

Trevor unclenched his jaw. He took a deep breath, and then let it out slowly. "Sorry, man. It's time to get my mind on the festivities, huh?"

Lucas gave him a sympathetic smile. "Maybe just for a couple days. It'd be a shame for your whole Christmas to be ruined."

"I'll do my best."

"Have you thought about talking to her?"

"You have no idea how hard I've been trying to talk to her. She won't have anything to do with me. And we never had a fight or anything. I can't think of one thing I did to make her hate me."

"Maybe it has nothing to do with you. Maybe she fell for some smooth talker, and now she feels too guilty to face you."

"You're probably right." Trevor sighed. "I'm ready to forget about it and have myself some Christmas cheer." Trevor forced a smile.

Lucas patted him on the back. "Atta boy."

They picked up a gift card at the golf store for their dad, and then stopped at the food court for a drink.

"Hey, guys!"

Trevor spun around to see Becca and Jake, hand in hand, heading toward him and Lucas. He looked past them, expecting to see Audrey trailing behind them, but she was nowhere in sight. He wasn't sure if he was disappointed or relieved. "Hi, guys. Merry Christmas." He pasted on a smile.

"Merry Christmas to you too," Becca eyed the small shopping bag Trevor held in his hand. "I see you've been doing some last-minute jewelry shopping. Is that a special ring for a special someone?" Becca raised her eyebrows.

Trevor fidgeted with the bag. "Nah, this is a gift for my mom."

Becca frowned. "I thought Audrey was getting a ring on her finger." She nudged Trevor with her elbow. "Or are you just trying to keep it a secret?" She winked at Jake. "Your secret is safe with us."

Trevor, put in an awkward situation, looked to Lucas. The only support Lucas offered was another sympathetic look and another pat on the back. Apparently, Becca was even more in the dark than he was. Had Audrey shut all of her hometown friends out of her life? A chill ran down his spine. Maybe the guy she was seeing was one of those control freaks who tried to keep the girl all to himself. "There's not going to be a ring this year, Becca. She hasn't talked to me in weeks." He tried to act like it was no big deal.

"Me either." Jake shrugged. "She hasn't even been posting on Instagram." The coincidence was uncanny.

"I swear she's avoiding me."

Becca crossed her arms. "It's worse than I thought. I knew something was wrong, but she promised me she'd talk to Pastor Mitchel. Lately, I thought she'd been busy with school and cross-country. I thought that's why I hadn't heard from her."

Trevor stepped over to a nearby table and sat down, mulling over this new information. "Cross-country season ended a while ago." He slapped his hat on the table.

Becca slid on the bench next to him.

Trevor put his hat back on his head and tried to regain control of his emotions. "Is it about a guy?"

Becca shrugged. "She never mentioned a guy...except for Matt something or other." She laughed. "I swear that guy is crushing on her."

Trevor winced. "That doesn't make me feel any better."

"Am I sensing some jealousy Trevor Hayes?" Jake sipped his pop, making slurping noises. Normally Jake could force a smile out of Trevor in any situation. Not today.

Becca patted Trevor on the back. "Don't worry. She didn't seem interested."

Trevor wasn't amused. Everyone knew he had a thing for Audrey, and he didn't care that they knew. Right now he was just worried about her as a friend.

"Dude, you're probably over-thinking this. You know how busy college can be," Lucas said.

"Yeah, probably. I'm so sick of trying to guess what's going on in her head." Trevor stood up. "Time to get home and wrap some presents."

Trevor said goodbye to his friends and headed home with his brother. He wished he could move on from his childish obsession with Audrey. Obviously, she had found somebody else and wanted nothing to do with him. But no matter how hard he tried, he couldn't forget about her. How could he forget a lifetime of memories?

* * *

Audrey and Darcy trimmed the tree with their dad as they did every year. Christmas music hummed in the background and the smell of Christmas Eve dinner wafted through the air. Audrey lost herself in the moment, hunting for the perfect branches on which to hang her favorite ornaments. But when she came across a glittery star hanging from a string of silver yarn, she felt a tug on her heart. She turned it over and read the scrawl, *From Trevor*. She tucked the ornament in the back of the tree.

The doorbell chimed, and Audrey's heart leapt into her throat, helplessly hoping it was Trevor. "I'll get it." She practically skipped to the door.

It wasn't Trevor. She opened the door. "Hi, Becca." She could do little to disguise her disappointment at her unexpected guest. "Come in."

Becca wrapped her arms around Audrey, practically knocking her over. "Merry Christmas! How are you? I've missed you." Her enthusiasm was contagious. So maybe Becca was just the person she needed to see.

"Merry Christmas. I've missed you too."

Becca dangled a shiny red gift bag in front of Audrey's face. "I brought you something."

Audrey's cheeks grew hot. "I didn't get you anything. I mean, we don't usually—"

"We don't usually exchange gifts. I know. But I needed an excuse to see you. It's been too long."

The last time Audrey had spoken to Becca was at the Fall Festival when she'd promised to talk to Pastor Mitchel. Prickles crawled up Audrey's spine. She hoped Becca wouldn't quiz her on why she'd been distant lately. She forced a smile. "Let's go up to my room." Leading the way upstairs, she asked Becca about her senior year of high school.

"School is fine," she sighed. "But youth group isn't the same this year."

Becca sat on the window seat, hugging her knees. Audrey lounged on her bed. "In a bad way?"

"Yeah. It's not the same without you, and Pastor Mitchel is all weird this year. It's like he's detached from us. Like he doesn't want to be there."

That didn't sound like Pastor Mitchel. Audrey's defenses rose. "Are you sure you guys aren't pulling away from him?" Considering the partying and Becca and Jake hooking up.

Becca scoffed. "I don't know. But that's not what I came to talk about anyway."

A pit formed in Audrey's stomach. "What do you want to talk about?"

"Why were you crying at my house that night? What's going on with you?"

There it was. Straight up. She played up the innocent act. "It was nothing. I was just hormonal. It was that time of the month or something."

Becca crossed her arms. "Why have you been avoiding all of your best friends?"

Audrey was dumbstruck by Becca's boldness. She sat with her mouth agape, trying to form a response.

"Jake and I talked to Trevor and Lucas at the mall today. Trevor says he can't get in touch with you." She held up her arms. "Spill the beans, Audrey."

Audrey's heart rate tripled. "You talked to Trevor?"

Becca's demeanor softened. "He looked so sad. His brother was trying to cheer him up. It was kinda cute."

Audrey let Becca's words sink in. "Because of me?"

She nodded. "You're breaking his heart. He asked if you're seeing another guy."

"What? That's absurd." She hadn't meant to mislead Trevor that way.

Becca crossed the room and sat down on the bed next to her. "It isn't another guy, is it?" She'd always been intuitive. "Something is wrong. Please talk to me."

Becca deserved an explanation, and Audrey needed to get things off her chest. She told Becca everything she remembered from the night of the party, ending with waking up in Jake's guest room.

Tears streaked down Becca's face as the story unfolded. "I'm sorry, Audrey. It's my fault. I shouldn't have dragged you in there."

Audrey shook her head, wiping her own tears with the back of her hand. "It's my own fault. I should've been more careful." Audrey wrapped her arms around herself in attempt to suppress a sudden wave of queasiness. "I don't feel so good."

Becca's eyes grew huge as saucers. "Are you...sick?"

Audrey knew what her friend was thinking. "I'm gonna throw up." Audrey pointed to the waste basket, and Becca handed it to her.

As sickness overtook her, Becca rubbed her back and handed her tissues. Audrey was grateful to finally have a confidant.

"Girl, you are pregnant."

Audrey deflated. That comment she could've done without.

* * *

Darcy couldn't believe her ears. Audrey was pregnant! She crept back to her room and closed the door. When she'd heard voices coming from Audrey's room, she'd assumed Audrey and her mom were having a girl talk session. Darcy didn't want to miss out. But just as she was about to knock on Audrey's door, she heard the puking sounds. And then Becca said Audrey was pregnant.

Darcy flopped down on her unmade bed. She couldn't believe Audrey and Trevor had gone all the way. For one thing, Audrey had told Trevor she just wanted to be friends. For another thing, Audrey was saving herself for marriage. They must've slipped up. *I always knew Audrey liked Trevor as more than a friend.*

This was definitely the juiciest girl talk Darcy had ever heard, but it also made her feel sick to her stomach. It had been so important to Audrey that she maintain her purity until she got married, and usually when Audrey made up her mind about something, she followed through. And what about track and field? Would she be able to compete if she was pregnant? Audrey lived for running.

Hopefully, she wouldn't be pregnant. Hopefully, she and Trevor slipped up one time and it would never happen again. This must be the reason Audrey was keeping her distance from Trevor. She didn't want to let it happen again.

There was the possibility that the stomach flu was going around campus. Maybe Audrey just had a stomach bug.

There was one thing Darcy was sure of. This was going to be an interesting Christmas. For the first time in her life, she needed to keep her mouth shut. She stayed in her room the rest of the night except for a speedy trip to the bathroom to get ready for bed.

* * *

Darcy took her time getting ready Christmas morning. The only plans being a few church friends coming over later to visit with her parents. She relaxed in a bubble bath, spent extra time curling her hair, and carefully applied her make-up. With Audrey's secret heavy on her heart, threatening to spill off tip of her tongue, the more time she spent by herself, the better.

She heard the front door open and close. Peering out the window, Darcy saw Audrey jogging down the sidewalk, her blonde ponytail bouncing behind her. It was a beautiful winter day. Large snowflakes floated down, blanketing everything in white. Although travelers wouldn't appreciate the snow, it made for a picture-perfect Christmas.

Darcy eased open her bedroom door, peering into the hallway. No one was in sight. She ventured down the hall, tip-toeing. Her mom and dad spoke in hushed tones in their bedroom. She wondered if they were aware of Audrey's predicament. Her mom had been forgiving when Audrey said she got drunk and passed out at a party. Darcy made a little huff. *Audrey could get away with anything. Let's see how understanding they would be about her getting knocked up.*

She went downstairs and was pouring a bowl of cereal when there was a knock at the front door. Peering out the sidelight window, she saw Trevor pacing on the porch. She gasped and hid behind the door, hoping he didn't see her. What would she say to him? She stood still behind the closed door, willing him to go away.

He knocked a second time. There was a pause. "I saw you, Darcy." He knocked again, more loudly this time.

He wasn't going to leave. Darcy looked upstairs at her parents' closed door. They must be too deep in conversation to notice the knocking. Well, she couldn't just ignore him and leave him standing out in the cold. She took a deep breath and opened the door.

"Hi, Trevor. Long time no see. Merry Christmas!"

The lines etched in his forehead told her that he was not in a joyful mood. "Is Audrey home?"

Darcy folded her arms across her chest to keep warm. She leaned against the doorframe, attempting to act casual in spite of the knot in her stomach. "No."

Trevor glanced over his shoulder at Audrey's car in the driveway. "I know she's home; I can see her car right there. She probably told you to say that, but she can't avoid me forever."

Darcy couldn't help but feel sorry for Trevor. He clearly loved Audrey. He loved her so much that he gave himself to her fully. Darcy wondered if he knew that Audrey was pregnant.

Trevor took off his cap and smacked it on the porch railing, clearly frustrated. He clenched his jaw, trying to maintain control.

"Just tell her I miss her." He put his hat back on his head, and he stepped off the porch.

"She's really not here," Darcy called out to him. "She's running."

Trevor stopped and stared into the falling snow. After a moment, he turned around to face Darcy, his blue eyes intense. "What is she running from?"

Darcy shook her head. "No, I mean she's literally out for a run."

Trevor stomped back onto the porch and stood less than a foot from Darcy. She could see his breath in the cold air and felt it on her face. He wasn't backing down this time. "Please tell me what's going on."

Darcy's heart pounded in her chest. How could she tell him when she wasn't even supposed to know? When she didn't answer, he stepped back, widening the space between them. He pulled himself up onto the porch railing.

"I'm not leaving until I get an answer. I'll wait for her." He looked out at the sidewalk, watching for Audrey to come around the corner, but she was nowhere in sight.

He was leaving her no choice. Darcy had to say something to him. She didn't think it would be a good idea to bring him into the house since her father may or may not know about the situation. If he did, he might not be real happy to see Trevor just yet. "Just a minute. Let me grab my coat." She went in the house and put on her coat, hat, and mittens before heading back outside. Audrey would be home soon. She could at least keep him company while he waited for her to return.

Trevor looked at her expectantly as she leaned on the railing next to him. "So?" He wasn't interested in her company; he just wanted answers.

"Trevor, I don't think it's my place to tell you. That's Audrey's responsibility."

"But she won't talk to me. Just give me a clue. Is she mad at me? What did I do?"

"You know what you did."

"What's that supposed to mean?" Trevor looked puzzled and slightly irritated at her remark.

She expelled a nervous giggle. "Well, I know about you guys."

"What do you know? Tell me because you obviously know more than I do."

Darcy blushed. "I know that you guys went all the way."

"What?" Trevor spat the word.

"Trevor," Darcy looked him squarely in the eyes. "Audrey is pregnant." Oops. She spilled the beans.

Trevor's face turned rosy pink to ashen white, then slowly changed to red, bright red. It was freaky. His right eye began to twitch and his chin began to quiver. He balled his gloved hands into fists.

Darcy's heart rate quickened even more, and she was suddenly afraid that she had said too much. She backed away because she didn't want to be in Trevor's path if he were to explode. She tried to think of something to say to calm him down.

"She might not be pregnant though. Maybe she just has the stomach flu. And even if she is, you guys can get married, right?"

Darcy was trying to help, but the more she said, the more it fueled his fury. He turned and trudged through the deep snow across the yard to his house. Darcy wished she wouldn't have been the one to have to tell him, but she didn't have a choice, did she? He had demanded an answer.

Darcy went back in the house with her heart still thudding nervously in her chest. Hopefully Audrey wouldn't be mad that she told Trevor. Darcy decided that just in case, she'd better retreat back to her room.

* * *

With Christmas behind her, Audrey knew it was time to face the reality of her situation. She and Becca hovered over Becca's computer, searching for a clinic. "Let's try that one." Audrey pointed to the screen. "*Crisis Pregnancy Center. We care about you.*"

"I know where that is. It's downtown. In a little brick building. Looks nice—quaint."

Audrey drew in a shaky breath. "I never thought I'd go to a place like this." She wiped sweaty palms on her pants. "I can't believe this is happening to me."

"You might not be pregnant after all. They'll give you a pregnancy test, and maybe it will be negative."

"Good point." A touch of optimism brightened her outlook. Then she had a revelation. "I can buy a home pregnancy test at the drugstore. I don't need to go to a creepy pregnancy center. I mean, what if they tell my parents? I'd be mortified."

Becca thought about it. "You're eighteen—an adult. I doubt they could legally tell your parents without your permission."

"Hmm. I suppose you're right."

"Plus, I think you should get checked out at the center. You know…in case you have…an STD or something."

Somehow Audrey had failed to think of that. The idea of being pregnant was bad enough. She burst into tears. "That's disgusting," she coughed out between sobs.

Chapter Eleven

A COUPLE HOURS LATER, AUDREY HELD TIGHT TO BECCA'S hand as they waited for the doctor to report the findings. The pregnancy center wasn't creepy as Audrey had feared. It was decorated for the holiday season with twinkle lights and snowman figurines. The waiting area was cozy enough with sofas and plush chairs. However, the leaflets in the waiting area describing gonorrhea and chlamydia served as an unwelcome reminder that she wasn't there for a friendly visit.

Then there was the exam—being poked and prodded, not knowing what the doctor would discover. She shuddered. She couldn't have been more relieved when the exam was finally over. The doctor had told her to get dressed; she'd be back in a couple minutes to discuss the results.

"I'm so scared," Audrey whispered to Becca. She was trembling.

The two of them sat in silence for a minute or two. Becca squeezed Audrey's hand, "Trust in the Lord with all your heart."

A tear rolled down Audrey's cheek and splat on the white linoleum floor. "And lean not on your own understanding." Audrey looked at Becca through blurry eyes. "That's the verse I've been focusing on. I think God keeps reminding me of it."

The door creaked open, and the doctor entered the room with a serious look on her face. She sat down on her swivel stool and began clicking away on a computer.

Come on, lady. Spit it out, Audrey wanted to scream.

The doctor cleared her throat and hesitated before looking up from the screen. "The good news is that you are healthy. There are no signs of disease or infection, although we do need to wait for a few test results to be certain. It would have been better for you to come in right afterwards for a more thorough assessment and preventative measures."

Audrey exhaled. What a relief. Becca hugged her, and the stress of the past couple of hours drained away. She turned to the doctor. "Thank you so much." Audrey could've hugged her too.

The doctor took a deep breath. "Audrey, there was one other test." Bad news was written all over the lady's face.

"What other test? You said I'm healthy."

"You are pregnant." She paused to let the news sink in. Then she stood and opened a cupboard, retrieving a selection of pamphlets and a small bottle of pills. "There are options. I'll give you this information to take home and look over. When you make a decision about how to proceed, give the office a call to make an appointment. In the meantime, take one of these prenatal vitamins daily. Do you have any questions for me?"

Audrey wanted to scream that it couldn't be true, that they should take another test to be sure. But she couldn't find her voice. She looked at Becca who was staring blankly at the pamphlets in the doctor's hand. She was shaking her head, also apparently at a loss for words.

The doctor's eyes softened. "I'll leave the literature here on the desk. Take as long as you like." She stood and left the room, letting the door close quietly behind her.

Becca wrapped her arms around Audrey. Their tears mixed as they streamed onto their shoulders. Audrey clung to her friend, weeping until she finally found the energy to stand up. "I want to go home."

On wobbly knees, Audrey leaned against her friend as they walked out of the clinic.

Audrey slid into Becca's car, moving on autopilot. Numb. Numb to the chill of winter biting her fingertips. And numb to the myriad of emotions whirling through her head.

"Audrey, your phone is ringing," Becca said. She sat behind the steering wheel, breathing warm air onto her hands.

Audrey's phone vibrated in her coat pocket. She read the caller ID through blurry eyes. *Trevor.* Every fiber in her body screamed at her to answer his call. She missed him in a way she hadn't known was possible. She wanted so badly to hear his voice. To hear him say everything was going to be okay. To know he still cared about her.

But she wouldn't answer his call. As much as it was ripping her heart into a million pieces, she had to be strong and resist. He didn't need her with all her baggage. Or maybe he was calling to yell at her for being so rude. Her heart just couldn't take that. The ringing eventually stopped, and she returned the phone to her pocket.

"That was Trevor, wasn't it?" Becca maneuvered the car out of the parallel parking space and onto the street.

Audrey nodded.

"Why don't you talk to him? He's miserable without you."

Audrey couldn't find the words to answer.

When Becca dropped her off at home, she made her promise to keep in touch. "I will. Thank you for coming with me today. I wouldn't have done it without you."

"No problem." Becca smiled.

"Please don't tell anyone about this." Audrey knew she could trust Becca.

"Cross my heart."

Audrey tried to sneak in the house unnoticed but her mom came running to the door, holding the home phone to her ear.

"Just a minute, Trevor. She just walked in the door."

Her mom held out the phone. "Trevor is asking to speak with you."

"Tell him I'm busy."

Her mom continued to hold the phone out, pleading with her eyes. Audrey shook her head and ran upstairs to her room.

She heard her mother's voice. "I'm sorry, Trevor. She can't come to the phone right now." There was a pause. "I'll tell her. Bye, hon."

Audrey lay face down on her bed and put a pillow over her head. Soon she felt the bed sink down as her mother sat beside her. Her mom's gentle hand rubbed light circles on Audrey's back. "Trevor wants me to tell you he'll be home all day if you want to talk."

Trevor's tenacity was unbelievable. After the unfair way she'd been treating him, he still wasn't giving up on her. A part of her wanted to reach out to him. It was possible that she could get through this with Trevor by her side.

She considered calling him back immediately. She'd tell him that she was sorry for shutting him out. But just as quickly, she decided against it. He deserved better than her.

"I can't talk to him, Mom."

"Listen, Audrey. I don't know what's going on with you two, but you need to talk to him soon. He needs to hear that you still care about him. Even if it's just as a friend."

Audrey didn't respond.

"To be honest, I think you'll feel better after talking to him."

"I'll think about it," Audrey uttered under her breath. It was *all* she could think about.

Her mom's hand stilled. "Is there anything you're not telling me? Did you and Trevor have a fight?" Audrey knew that her secrecy was breaking her mom's heart.

"I'm not ready to talk about it."

Her mom sighed. "I'll be downstairs if you need me." Before leaving, her mom kissed Audrey's temple. It was a gesture meant to demonstrate her mom's unconditional love. But her mom didn't have a clue how serious Audrey's troubles were. Would her mom's love be able to stand the test of public humiliation of her daughter's teen pregnancy?

She sat up and took off her coat, removing the stack of brochures she had balled up in her coat pocket. Taking a deep breath, she started to read.

The first brochure briefly explained a medical procedure to remove the fetus. Medical terminology was used to disguise the fact that it was simply describing abortion. Audrey had always been opposed to abortion. God created life and it was up to Him to take it away.

On second thought, did God really create this fetus? God wouldn't use rape to create a baby. Would He? Besides, the brochure didn't use the word baby. It said a doctor would remove the "tissue" from the lining of the uterus. That didn't sound like ending a life. Audrey set the brochure aside, tucking this option into the back of her mind. She would have to think about it more.

She moved on to the next pamphlet, describing the changes a woman needs to make in her daily life to support the needs of a growing baby. There were vitamin supplements to take and foods to avoid. It advised against going in hot tubs and saunas. It suggested taking naps and avoiding carrying heavy loads.

Information overload. The whole pregnancy thing was way too much to deal with.

At this point, the medical procedure to remove the tissue seemed the most logical solution to her problems.

* * *

Trevor slammed his phone down on the coffee table and slumped into the living room chair. It was torture not being able to see or talk to Audrey when she was in the house next door. It bothered him, what Darcy had said about Audrey being pregnant. But he tried not to let it weigh too heavily on his mind. Obviously Darcy didn't have her facts straight. He and Audrey hadn't even come close to having sex.

He looked out the window, past the backyard. The pond was frozen over, and snow was piled knee deep. His mind wandered back to yesteryear, when he and Audrey would shovel a crude ice rink and spend hours shooting hockey pucks or playing broom ball one on one. His head fell in his hands.

Lucas walked up from behind and gave him a brotherly kick in the shin. "Hey, how ya holding up?" Lucas sat on the adjacent chair, a pile of frosted sugar cookies in one hand and a tall glass of milk in the other.

Trevor rubbed his eyes before looking up at his brother.

"Dude, you're looking rough." Lucas eyeballed the phone on the coffee table. "She's still not taking your calls?"

Trevor fixed his eyes on the pond. "Nope."

Lucas followed his brother's gaze out the window. "So what are you gonna do about it?" He bit into a sugar cookie cut out in the shape of a Christmas tree, green frosting coloring his lips.

Trevor rubbed his head. "One minute I'm done with her. She doesn't want me in her life so why waste my time trying? The next minute, I can't live without her, and I'd do anything to get her to speak to me."

"And where are you at right now?"

Trevor sighed and laughed in spite of himself. "I'm desperate, man. Pathetic as that may sound. I'm completely desperate. I'm planning to march into the Chapman's house and pin her to the ground until she gives me answers."

"You might wanna try a more subtle approach." Lucas wiped a hand on his jeans, sending crumbs sprinkling to the carpet.

"Ya think?" Trevor helped himself to a cookie from the pile in Lucas' hand. He stuffed the cookie into his mouth all at once. "Hey, I've got an idea." Bits of cookie fell from his mouth when he talked.

Lucas raised his eyebrows. "Oh yeah, what's that?" He took a swig of milk.

"How about we go out and shovel off the pond? For old time's sake. We could play a little broom ball."

Lucas downed the last of his milk. "That's the spirit! No more moping around, crying over girls."

Trevor didn't tell Lucas he came up with the whole idea while reminiscing about the days of old with Audrey. He grabbed the last cookie from his brother's hand. "Loser shovels the driveway."

Once snow pants, boots, hats, and gloves were on, the guys trudged out to the pond in the deep snow. Lucas tried to keep the mood light with his witty banter, but Trevor's disposition remained as heavy as the snow they pushed to the side of the pond. They piled up snow at opposite ends of the pond for goals, and played an aggressive game of broom ball. It felt good to pour his energy into a game. It was a much needed break from racking his brain about what had happened between him and Audrey.

A biting breeze blew across the ice as the sun began its descent. It was a tie game. Trevor could outrun Lucas on the football field, but their athletic ability was a match on the ice. Lucas had grown up playing hockey, and he could shoot a mean puck.

"Next point wins the game." Lucas charged toward Trevor's goal.

Trevor guarded his snow-piled goal, eyes fixed on the ball, when he heard rustling behind him. He turned around to see Darcy making her way over to the pond.

Lucas took advantage of Trevor's quick glance away, scoring the final goal. "Woo hoo!" He raised his stick in the air. "Undefeated, baby!"

Trevor, ignoring his brother's lack of humility, approached Darcy. "Hey."

"Hey," she echoed, looking down at her boots, buried in the snow.

Trevor waited for her to say more, but when she didn't, he asked if she wanted to join in the broom ball game.

"No thanks. I can't compete with you guys. It just looked like you were having fun out here, and I was bored out of my mind sitting inside." She traced circles in the snow with the toe of her boot. "I wouldn't mind shooting around with you for a while though."

Trevor tried to hide his surprise. Since when did Darcy develop an interest in sports of any kind? He wondered if Audrey had set her up to this. But what harm could it do to play a little broom ball with her? Even if it was some sort of a game Audrey was playing. Or maybe Audrey sent Darcy as a messenger to fill him in on what was going on with her. Or maybe she just wanted to play broom ball.

"Sure. You can use Lucas' stick. He needs a break anyway. He needs time to let that big head of his deflate."

Darcy walked onto the ice and reached for the broom ball stick Lucas extended to her. She squealed as her feet slid out from under her, landing her on her bottom.

"Yeah, you might not be quite ready for a game." Trevor helped her back onto her feet. He showed her how to walk flat-footed on the ice, keeping her weight over her feet. Soon she was able to run with short strides and make feeble attempts at stick-handling the ball. As she approached the goal, she swung the stick back and struck the ball with all her might. Her momentum from the back swing threw her off balance, landing her back on the ice with a thud. Her scream echoed across the pond followed by her laughter, as she rubbed her butt.

Trevor and Lucas couldn't hold back their laughter. This time when Trevor extended a helping hand, she grabbed it and pulled him onto the ice next to her. His stick went flying and sent the ball bouncing into the goal. Soon they were all doubled over in laughter.

Trevor noticed how good it felt to laugh. He looked over at Darcy, silhouetted from the darkening sky. Her frame resembled Audrey's. For a moment, he let his mind wander back to times when he laughed with Audrey over a game of broom ball. He wondered if he would ever laugh with her this way again. He shook his head, shaking his thoughts away. He stood up and dusted the snow off his jeans. He looked down at Darcy, still on the ice. "You're on your own this time. No more help from me."

Darcy batted her frozen eyelashes at him. "Come on. You can't leave a girl on the ground." She dramatically lifted her gloved hand delicately in his direction. "Please? I really need a big strong guy to help me."

Trevor reached for her hand, pulling her to a stand.

Lucas walked over to them, a curious look on his face. "I'm gonna head in. My fingers and toes are frozen." He looked at his brother. "You coming?"

Trevor realized he had his eyes fixed on Darcy as his mind wandered back in time. He had never noticed the strong resemblance Darcy had to her sister. It was almost like looking at Audrey a couple years ago, back when their friendship was untainted. Darcy seemed to squirm under his gaze, snapping Trevor back to reality.

"Yeah, I'm coming. You can head in without me. I wanna talk to Darcy for a minute first."

Lucas gathered the broom ball sticks and walked back to the house. Trevor looked at Darcy who seemed to be squirming more than ever now. "I better go in now too." She turned to leave.

Trevor grabbed her coat sleeve. "No!" He pleaded with her to stay. "Please talk to me, Darcy. Tell me what's going on with Audrey."

"Trevor, I told you everything I know."

"But why won't she talk to me?"

"I don't know, Trevor. That's between you guys." She put her hands on her hips. "It's your own fault, you know. You were supposed to wait until you got married. You got yourself into this mess, so don't keep looking to me to get you out of it."

Trevor took off his stocking cap and rubbed his sweaty hair. "Darcy, we never did it."

"Never did what?" Darcy looked confused.

Did he really have to spell this out for her? "We never had sex. Audrey and I were both waiting for marriage. Anyway, she just sees me as a friend."

"Then she can't be pregnant, right?"

Trevor put his hat back on to cover his ears that were stinging from the cold air. "Not by me."

"That's not possible! You are definitely the only guy she would have sex with." Darcy's face was deadpan as she put the pieces together.

Trevor laughed at the bluntness of Darcy's statement. Soon Darcy was in stitches along with him. "It's true, you know. She totally knows you're the one for her. Any other guy would have to—"

Darcy's laughter stopped abruptly. She gasped and covered her mouth with her hand.

Trevor fought to regain control. "What?"

Darcy's eyes were wide. "I think I figured it out. I bet she was raped."

Trevor felt like the wind got knocked out of him. He clutched his chest, struggling to breathe.

"I've heard date rape happens on college campuses more than people realize."

Trevor's blood ran hot. "Talk to her. Find out what happened."

Darcy nodded. She was stunned, looking like a deer in the headlights. She rubbed her arms, shivering.

"Let's go in." Trevor turned toward their houses. He linked his arm in Darcy's as he carefully guided her off the ice.

"Me and my big mouth. I'm so sorry. I shouldn't have said anything out on the porch that day."

"It's not your fault. I made you talk."

It was time to go their separate ways as they approached the back of their houses. Their arms were still linked as they faced each other. They were each experiencing a new understanding of the situation with Audrey, and sadness filled both of their eyes.

"I hope things work out for you and Audrey." She looked down at the snow now sparkling in the moonlight, before looking up into his eyes. "I really like you."

Trevor pulled Darcy into a hug. It felt good to have Darcy to talk to. He had never paid much attention to her in the past as she always had seemed so young. But she was maturing now. "I like you too, Darcy."

Trevor released her and walked into his house feeling better than he had when he went out. At least he wasn't as worried about Audrey being in love with another dude. He dropped his wet gloves and hat onto the tile flooring just inside the sliding door of the walk-out basement.

Lucas was hanging his coat on a hook. He had a disgusted look on his face. "What's up with you and Audrey's little sister?"

"What are you talking about?"

"You know what I'm talking about—the way you were hugging on her and stuff. Dude, I know you're upset about Audrey and you're all confused, but you better watch yourself." Lucas shook his head as he walked away. "You're losing it, man."

Lucas was right. Trevor was losing it. The whole situation was ridiculous. How did Audrey expect him to react anyway? Was she expecting him to chase after her or did she really want him to leave her alone? Did she really think he could just move on suddenly, forgetting all the years of memories they had made together? Impossible! Especially after he had just poured his heart out to her. How could she ask that of him?

Frustration grew so strong inside of him he thought he would burst. Taking a steadying breath, he pulled the door open and trudged through the snow to the neighbor's house. This time he wasn't leaving until he got some answers straight from Audrey.

Chapter Twelve

ROUNDING THE CORNER TO THE FRONT OF THE CHAPMAN'S house, Audrey's Toyota Camry came into view. She was home. Trying to calm down, he took deep, slow breaths. When Mrs. Chapman answered the door, Trevor faked his best smile, which he guessed she could see straight through.

"Hi, Trevor." Sympathy colored her tone of voice. "You're looking for Audrey, I presume?"

"Mrs. Chapman, I really need to see her."

To his surprise, she opened the door further and told him to come in. "I'll see what I can do. She's up in her room." She started up the stairs. Trevor shook off his wet boots and followed Audrey's mom up the steps. Mrs. Chapman paused in the middle of the staircase and turned to him. "You can wait downstairs, Trevor. I'll send her down."

Trevor didn't budge. "I'm sorry, Mrs. Chapman, but you know just as well as I do that she won't agree to speak to me. Please, let me go up there."

Mrs. Chapman hesitated, but finally moved aside, letting him go up on his own.

He tapped lightly on Audrey's partially open door.

"Come in."

Trevor's heart melted at the musical sound of her voice he had waited so long to hear. Pushing the door open, he saw her sitting on her bed with papers spread out before her. She was busy reading something, so she didn't look up right away. He soaked in the sight of her. Her blonde, curly hair was gathered into a messy bun at the top of her head. A loose fitting T-shirt was draped over her small frame, and she wore a pair of Capri sweat pants. She looked exactly the same as the last time he'd seen her, except that her face was slightly more filled out and he couldn't help but notice that her breasts seemed larger.

Her natural beauty made him so weak in the knees that he had to put a hand on the door frame to hold steady. The anger he had been feeling minutes ago dissipated in her presence. He cleared his throat. "You're not supposed to have to study over Christmas break."

She looked up. Dropping the paper she held in her hands, she covered her mouth, clearly surprised by his unannounced visit. "Trevor, what are you doing here?"

Ignoring her question, he asked if he could come in, but didn't wait for an answer. He entered her room and sat on the end of her bed. If he wasn't forward, he wouldn't get the answers he came for. "I've missed you, Audrey."

"I've missed you too." Her warm response took Trevor by pleasant surprise.

"Did I do something wrong? Because if I did anything to hurt you or make you hate me, I'm sorry."

"No, Trevor. You didn't do anything wrong. I promise."

"Then why have you been giving me the cold shoulder?"

"It's not like that." She closed her eyes momentarily, before continuing. "I just think you're better off without me. You deserve more. You deserve …" She couldn't bring herself to finish the sentence.

"I want to be with you, Audrey. You know that. Nobody is better for me than you." He felt tears well in his eyes and was helpless to stop them from spilling onto his unshaven face. It didn't matter that the world thought of him as strong and tough—a six-foot-four-inch football player. His resolve was completely broken.

"But you deserve…a virgin."

The confirmation straight from her mouth cut him like a knife.

"You don't want me anymore. Look at me, Trevor." Audrey smoothed her shirt over her abdomen, revealing a subtle bulge. "I'm pregnant. I might have to drop out of school and move back home with my parents. You don't want a girl like that. You deserve so much more. Just move on, Trevor. It's over between us."

Trevor wiped his nose with the back of his hand, realizing he was blubbering like a baby. How was he supposed to win her heart back like this? He kept his gaze down as he tried to get a grip on his emotions. Through blurry eyes, he caught sight of the papers she had been studying. They were pamphlets of some kind, something one would get at a doctor's office. He looked more closely and read the heading on one of the brochures. *Your Body, Your Choice,* it read.

"Are you getting an abortion?"

"I don't know. I mean, I don't think so. Let's not talk about this, okay?" She swept the papers into a pile and stuffed them into her bedside table drawer.

"You're pro-life." Maybe she had changed after all. He would address this issue later. Now he needed to get the answers he came looking for. "So who's the guy?" He kept his voice gentle, not wanting to sound accusatory.

Audrey shrugged, "I don't know."

Trevor felt his face flush with heat and his temper began to rise. "You don't know? You're going to sit there and tell me you don't know? All I'm asking for is a simple answer to a simple question." He looked her in the eyes, letting her know he wasn't backing down. "Who is the guy?"

Silence was her answer.

Trevor shook his head in disbelief.

Breaking the silence, her phone signaled that a text message had come in. The phone was on the bed between Audrey and Trevor, where they could both read the name *Matt Cook* displayed on the screen.

Was this his answer? Trevor looked at Audrey. Her eyes were huge as saucers, as if she too couldn't believe the timing of this text.

"It's not what you think, Trevor."

"You don't know what I'm thinking, Audrey. Because I won't know what to think about anything until you tell me what's going on." He picked up her phone. "Tell me what I'm supposed to think about this." He read the text aloud. "Some of us are going to a movie tonight. Wanna come?"

"I've told you that Matt and I are just friends, and that's the truth."

"So how about if you text him back and tell him you'll go, and Trevor's coming with you. I wouldn't mind going to a movie." He was testing her.

Audrey shook her head. "That would be too weird."

That was exactly the answer he'd expected to hear … was afraid to hear. "Why? Because he's your boyfriend and I'm some other guy who's in love with you?" He knew he was jumping to conclusions, but all the signs seemed to be pointing in the same direction. Audrey must have been seeing someone behind his back and it had to be this Matt Cook. He hated using this harsh tone of voice with Audrey, accusing her of things. If only she would be open and honest with him.

Audrey's bottom lip quivered, and she hugged her knees to her chest. She seemed sad, not defensive or angry like he expected. "Matt is not my boyfriend. And you …" she stopped mid-sentence, and a tear left a trail of mascara down her cheek.

"Go ahead. Finish your sentence. I want to hear what you were going to say."

She didn't answer.

"What am I to you?"

Audrey looked down. "I don't know anymore."

She might as well have ripped his heart right out of his chest. But he wasn't giving up that easily. "Do you love him?"

Audrey looked confused. "Love who?" She thought about it for a moment, and then she shook her head. "No!"

"I don't get it." Trevor was honestly baffled. He was getting nowhere.

"I'm disgusting."

Her words caught Trevor off guard. "Because you're pregnant?" He spoke tenderly, finally feeling like he was getting somewhere with her. She was finally letting her guard down.

"It's not that." Audrey shielded her eyes with her hand. "I'm not a virgin anymore. I'm sorry."

Trevor kept quiet, willing her to tell the whole story.

"We all make mistakes, Audrey. You don't have to punish yourself for the rest of your life for slipping up once or twice. Of course I'm upset about it, but I know that we've been apart a lot, and I understand if you fell in love with someone else. I just want an explanation from you so I can have some kind of closure. I know we weren't even dating, but…I just thought…I guess I thought you had feelings for me too."

"I didn't fall in love with someone else. I didn't slip up once or twice either. I was raped."

There it was. The answer he had been searching for. The reason she had withdrawn from him. And now he almost wished she hadn't told him. It was the devastating scenario he hadn't wanted to consider. It was easier to be angry that she was in love with another guy, but to hear that she had been raped was too much to bear. His gut twisted at the thought of some punk taking advantage of Audrey, the girl who'd always occupied a special place in his heart. "He'll pay for this."

"Trevor, I told you I don't know who did it. I never even saw his face."

She told him the whole story, up until the moment she passed out. He knew it was difficult for her to tell him, and his heart ached for her. "We have to find this guy, Audrey. He can't get away with this."

"That's impossible. I've thought about it, believe me. There were so many guys there and I didn't even know a lot of them. I bet Jake didn't even know all of them."

"You have to report it."

"I told them at the pregnancy center. They reported it to the police, but there wasn't any evidence of rape because I waited so long to see a doctor. They said it would be next to impossible to prove it was rape at this point."

"Unless there was a witness." Trevor was hopeful.

"I suppose you're right, but I don't know how to go about finding a witness. It was dark and crowded; I bet no one even noticed." Audrey stretched her legs out and crossed her arms over her mid-section. "I want to just forget about it because finding him seems so hopeless."

"There's a good chance he bragged about it to his buddies, and he's maybe doing it to other girls too. Someone has to stop him."

"I don't know." Audrey didn't appear to have any fight in her.

Trevor thought back to the papers Audrey had stuffed into her drawer. "Are you going to keep the baby?"

Audrey bit her lip. "Honestly, I haven't thought about it much. I was just looking at being pregnant as some sort of disease or something. You know, something bad that happened to me that needs to be fixed." Thoughtfully, she continued, "I've always thought abortion was wrong, but now I'm not so sure. I mean, who wants to know that they were conceived by rape? Is it fair to bring a person into the world under those circumstances? And I can't raise a baby right now. I don't know what to do."

Trevor didn't know either, and he didn't feel equipped to offer advice.

"Do you understand now why I didn't want you to have to get involved in this mess?" she asked.

"I get it. But did you forget the lyrics to our favorite song?" He sang softly, "Lean on me, when you're not strong." He knew it was corny, especially considering how heavy the conversation was, but they had sung that line to each other too many times to count. The cheese factor was what made the song so great. It had never failed to make them smile. And it worked this time too.

Audrey chuckled. "Don't you think that's a bit childish, considering the circumstances?"

"I think there is a lot of wisdom in that catchy little song. Seriously, don't you feel better now?"

Audrey smiled. "Yeah, I do."

"Except now I feel like crap."

"Sorry to break it to you, but you look like crap. Ever heard of a razor?'

Trevor laughed as he rubbed the stubble on his face. "I decided to stop shaving until you talked to me."

"And that's all the further you got?" Her lips curved into a devious smile.

Trevor couldn't help but laugh. He leaned over and rubbed his scratchy face on her cheeks.

"Stop!" She giggled.

Audrey's laughter was medicine to his soul. He kissed her on the cheek. He sat next to her, their arms pressed against each other's. He leaned his head against the headboard. It felt so good to be here next to Audrey again.

"I'm glad you hunted me down. Even though you didn't groom yourself first." She touched his stubbly chin.

Trevor lightly tickled under her arm.

She squealed. Trevor tickled her sides. "Uncle." She screamed and laughed at the same time. Trevor dug his fingers in deeper until she laughed so hard she cried. His fingers traveled to her belly.

"Don't!" Audrey squirmed out from under him and stood up from the bed. She wrapped her arms around her midsection and turned her back to him.

Trevor immediately felt like a complete jerk. "I'm so sorry. I didn't mean to do that. It just felt like old times and I got carried away in the moment."

"It's okay." She sniffed, holding her arms tight around her waist.

There was an awkward silence. Completely at a loss as to what to do or say, Trevor waited for her to break the silence. He sat on the edge of the bed, resting his elbows on his knees.

After several minutes, she sat down next to him. "Do you see now why this isn't going to work?"

Frustration reared its ugly head once again. "You're saying we can't be friends because something terrible happened to you, and you need to survive it on your own? Is it so bad that you laughed for a minute?"

"You need to move on, Trevor. Please just live your life. I don't want to hold you back."

"I can't believe we're back to this, Audrey. Stop being so stubborn!"

Audrey jumped up from the bed. "I can handle this. This isn't your problem. I don't need you." Regret seemed to darken her features the moment the words escaped her mouth.

Trevor knew she didn't mean it, but it hurt just the same. Maybe he had no business being there after all.

Audrey slinked into a ball on the floor, hugging her knees to her chest. "I have too much to figure out." She sighed heavily. "Just because my life is ruined doesn't mean yours has to be ruined too." She looked up. Her eyes were bloodshot. "Please, Trevor. Please leave me alone."

Anger and frustration grabbed hold of Trevor once again. She left no room for negotiation. "If it's really what you want, I'll leave you alone. But only until you figure things out. Don't you get it, Audrey? I love you. I have always loved you, and I always will. I waited my whole life for you. A little more time won't hurt me. I'm not giving up on you, Audrey Chapman." He stood up and walked out the door, not waiting to see her reaction. He was crushed that the conversation had ended like this. Although she wouldn't admit it, he knew she loved him too.

He'd wanted so badly to hold her and tell her that everything would be okay. But truthfully, he couldn't promise that. Only time would tell.

Mrs. Chapman met him by the front door. "I'm glad you came by, Trevor. If anybody could pull her out of her shell, it would be you."

"I don't know, Mrs. Chapman. That is one hard-headed girl you got there."

"*Strong willed* her father and I like to call it." Lydia laughed.

Trevor wondered if Lydia knew what had happened to Audrey. He considered asking her. But Darcy knew about the pregnancy, and no secret was safe with Darcy. Surely she had apprised her mother of the situation.

"Bye, Mrs. Chapman. Merry Christmas."

Back at home, Trevor went into his dad's office and closed the door. He would honor Audrey's request for space while she figured things out. In the meantime he would find the jerk that violated her and get him locked away for good.

But two hours later he found himself at a standstill, having run into one dead end after another. The police department said the same thing that Audrey had told him. It would be nearly impossible to prove that she had been raped because by now the only evidence was the pregnancy.

The officer Trevor spoke with wasn't convinced that Audrey had been raped. "So she's running around partying. Sounds to me like she was looking for a good time. It'd be tough to prove that she wasn't a willing partner." How dare the officer suggest that?

Trevor realized just then how difficult it would be to catch this guy if the police department wasn't even convinced it was rape. Trevor decided he would try to figure things out on his own.

He called Jake and got the names of every guy he could think of who had been at the party. "I have reason to believe that someone at your party used a date rape drug. Do you know anything about that?"

"Are you serious? Not that I know of. I mean, there were a couple of girls passed out on the sofa for a while, but I'm sure nothing happened to them. I sent everyone home after that. It wasn't that kind of party. No drugs of any kind here … unless you consider alcohol a drug."

Trevor talked with him for quite a while, and was well convinced that Jake really didn't have a clue about any date rape drugs or know of anyone who would use them. Trevor's investigation was a complete fail.

Infuriated, he decided a mental break was in order. He went into the kitchen and grabbed a bottle of water from the fridge. Lucas was sitting on the counter top eating handfuls of chips straight from the bag. Trevor slumped against the fridge as he gulped down the cold water.

"So what's the scoop on your girlfriend?"

Trevor clenched his jaw. He wasn't in the mood for joking around. "She was raped."

Lucas swallowed the chips in his mouth with obvious difficulty. He tossed the chip bag on the counter and wiped greasy hands on his pants. "I'm sorry." He jumped off the counter. "Who is he? I'm gonna pound the creep."

"I wish I knew. Audrey doesn't even know. It happened at a party. She was drugged."

Lucas trudged the few feet it took to reach the kitchen table and slouched into a chair.

"It gets worse," Trevor's lower lip trembled. "She's pregnant."

Lucas shook his head in disbelief. "What's she gonna do?"

"She might have an abortion. Can you believe it? I mean, she's always been pro-life and now she might abort her own baby." Trevor hoped his older brother would offer some wisdom.

"I can believe it." Lucas shrugged.

Trevor felt his defenses rise. "But it's her own flesh and blood."

"Her's and some disgusting creep's. Plus, it's not like she would've bonded with it at this point." Lucas straightened. "I'm not saying she should have an abortion. I'm just saying that I get why she's considering it."

Lucas had a point. It's not like Audrey would feel all maternal after something like this happened. Yet for a reason Trevor didn't quite understand, he felt protective of the baby. "I care for Audrey so much. I guess it's just that I love every part of her. No matter what."

A corner of Lucas's mouth lifted into a lopsided smile. "You are so whipped."

Trevor was helpless to stop his own grin. "Yeah, it stinks."

"Nah, it's beautiful." Lucas winked.

Chapter Thirteen

NOTHING GOOD WAS ON TV. DARCY PRESSED THE POWER button on the remote and stood up from the sofa. Being cooped up in the house was making her stir crazy. She needed to get out of the house. A trip to Caribou Coffee was in order. She found her mom in the kitchen and asked if she could take the Durango, which she rarely got the chance to drive.

Having her driver's license less than a year, she hadn't yet fully earned her parents' trust when it came to driving. Darcy assured her mom that she was only going to Caribou Coffee and would be home in less than two hours. After much deliberation with her dad, her mom finally agreed to let her go. But there was one condition. She would need to take Audrey.

"You're not used to driving on snowy roads. Plus, I think it would be good for the two of you to spend some time together."

Darcy didn't argue with her mom. She missed her sister and was sick and tired of all the secrecy in the house. She wanted to have a heart to heart talk with Audrey to get the full story on how she got pregnant.

Audrey also thought it was a good idea and was ready to get out of the house for a while. They each carried their overpriced hot cocoas to leather chairs situated opposite a fireplace. The small coffee shop had an extra cozy feel on the chilly winter day with its woodsy, up-north decor. It was the perfect place for a sisterly chat.

"So what's going on with you and Trevor?" Darcy removed the lid from her cup and slurped some of the whipped cream.

"It's complicated."

"What's so complicated? You've been best friends since forever. He's the perfect match for you."

Audrey shook her head. "It's not that simple."

"Well, I don't know if you'll ever find a guy as good as Trevor Hayes. You'd regret it if you let him get away."

Audrey thought about that for a moment. "I know he's a good guy. That's just it. He's too good for me ... I mean, I don't know if I'm good enough for him. You know ... after everything that happened."

"What did happen anyway? You never told me."

Audrey sipped her drink. Darcy waited.

"I'm in trouble." Audrey stared at the paper cup in her hand.

Darcy thought back to Becca's words she'd overheard. She told Audrey about the night she overheard her and Becca talking. "I figured it was you and Mom having one of your normal girl talk sessions. You know I'm always up for a chat. So I started for your room to join in when I heard Becca say that you're pregnant. That's all I heard. Then I went back to my room." Darcy's cheeks reddened and she shifted in her seat. "I figured you and Trevor had gone all the way."

Her heart thudded in her chest as questions filled her mind. She needed to find out if her sister was in fact pregnant. If so, who was the father? But she was afraid to learn the answers. She couldn't stand to hear that her sister had been hurt in any way. She took a sip of her hot cocoa, stalling. Then she summoned the courage to ask. "That's not what happened, is it?"

Audrey swept her eyes around the room, making sure nobody was listening. There were a few people who had stopped in for an after-dinner cup of coffee, but most seats were empty. No one was in ear shot, but to be sure, Audrey spoke in a hushed voice. "Trevor and I went to a party at Jake's house. We weren't going to stay long."

Audrey blew across her hot cocoa and steam rose into the air. Instead of taking a sip, she set the cup down on the wooden table separating the two girls. Darcy was surprised at how composed Audrey was. It was as if she was talking about someone other than herself. "Trevor was outside playing basketball with Jake and some other guys. Becca drank too much and was puking, so I took her into the house to get cleaned up."

Darcy listened, keeping her thoughts to herself. She was shocked that Audrey had gone to a party like that. She'd never told Audrey that she had tried alcohol a couple times with the youth group kids.

"We joined this dance circle, and soon…I don't even know what happened. Next thing I knew, I felt sick all over—I figure some-one slipped a drug into my drink—and I was dragged off into the guest room. I blacked out before it happened. I woke up early in the morning, and I knew I had been raped. And now I'm pregnant."

Darcy was unable to stop the tears from flowing down her face. People were probably staring but she didn't care. She probably had mascara running down her face too, but she didn't care about that either. Her sister had been raped.

And now there was a poor little baby, her niece or nephew, who would grow up without a daddy. These types of things didn't happen to people she knew, especially not her sister. She watched reality shows about other teenage mothers on TV. She saw how they struggled to raise a baby on their own. It pretty much ruined the teenage mother's life half the time, and it usually even ripped her whole family apart.

This was even worse than what Darcy had seen on TV, because this baby wasn't a result of a boyfriend and girlfriend having unprotected sex or even a one night stand. This baby was a result of a horrible crime.

Darcy felt sick to her stomach. She put her half-empty cup down and excused herself. She went into the women's restroom and sank down into a heap on the cold tiled floor. Sobs racked her whole body. She sobbed for her tiny niece or nephew who was so innocent and precious and was so undeserving of coming into the world this way.

She sobbed for Audrey who worked so hard to do everything right and to the best of her ability. She made bad choices one night and would be punished for them the rest of her life. That didn't seem fair.

And she sobbed for herself. Her world was shaken. Darcy had always looked up to her big sister as a role model. She wasn't jealous of Audrey and all she had accomplished—her good grades, her athleticism, her perfect life. Audrey seemed to have it all and Darcy was nothing but proud. Audrey had set a great example of how hard work and living for Jesus paid off. But now, look where that had gotten her. It scared Darcy that life could be this unpredictable.

Darcy also cried because of the guilt she felt. She knew that the other youth group kids had been partying. She knew first hand because she had gone to a couple parties herself. They weren't big parties like the ones Audrey experienced.

Once a few of the kids had gone to a movie and then hung out at Jake's house for a while. They each had one or two beers, nothing more. Darcy knew it was wrong, but she didn't want to look like a goody-goody, so she went along with everyone else. She had reasoned that there was no harm in drinking one or two beers. She was with church friends after all.

Another time—the time she felt most guilty about—was the night of the Fall Festival at church. Pastor Mitchel had brought them to a corn maze that night, and then the youth group came back to the church to carve pumpkins. It was a fun night. Darcy was proud of the cool designs she had carved into her pumpkin. Everybody complimented her on her artistic flare.

But after Pastor Mitchel went home, the teens lingered in the parking lot for a while. When Becca opened the trunk of her car to put her pumpkin in, she found a case of beer that her parents must have bought. So the youth group kids waited until the end of the festival, and when the last family had buckled their little one into the car seat and pulled out of the church parking lot, Becca started handing out cans of beer.

So there was the Hope Church youth group, sitting in the church parking lot drinking beer. Guilt stabbed at Darcy's chest as she remembered back to that night. She realized at that moment, on the bathroom floor of a coffee shop, why drinking was so wrong. She had never really understood what was wrong with getting a buzz and acting silly with friends. But now it made sense. Bad things happened when people drank that wouldn't happen otherwise. Nothing good came from it.

Darcy wondered if Pastor Mitchel knew that they'd been drinking behind his back. Now she considered confiding in him about it. But for now all she could concentrate on was the situation with her sister. Look where drinking had led her.

There was a knock on the door.

"I'll be out in a minute," she called in the most controlled voice she could muster.

"Darcy, open the door." It was Audrey.

Darcy stood. She wiped her fingers under her eyes and saw black smudges on her fingertips. She looked in the mirror and saw that she had a hopeless case of raccoon eyes from her running mascara. There was nothing she could do to fix that now. She opened the door and saw Audrey in a similar state. Darcy pulled her sister into the bathroom and gave her the biggest and longest hug of her life.

They finally composed themselves enough to walk through the shop and into the parking lot without drawing too much attention. On the way home, Darcy asked if Audrey had told Trevor yet that she was raped. Darcy was relieved that she had. He needed to know.

"So tell me again why you've been brushing him off. I mean… why haven't you admitted you love him?"

Audrey stared at the road straight ahead. She looked emotionally drained. "Because it's complicated."

"Whatever." Darcy knew she sounded sarcastic, and although Audrey deserved sympathy right now, she also needed someone to tell her how stupid she was to turn Trevor away.

"I have too much to work through right now. I'm not in a position to be dating and finding romance. And Trevor deserves to be able to put his heart and soul into school and enjoying college life. He doesn't need to be doting on a pregnant girlfriend. That would be so messed up."

Darcy needed to set her sister straight. "No, your thinking is messed up."

Audrey looked shocked at Darcy standing up to her, but that didn't stop Darcy from speaking her mind.

"You're a smart girl, Audrey, but you're really being stupid. You need Trevor, and Trevor needs you. Plain and simple. Sometimes in life it's better to think with your heart instead of your mind. Sure, maybe it doesn't make sense for you to have a boyfriend when you're pregnant or for Trevor to be dating a pregnant girl, but look how miserable you two are without each other."

She paused, waiting for her words to sink in to her sister's hard head. After a minute she continued, "I know you miss him and I saw how much he misses you. You should've seen the way he looked at me, Audrey. I know he was thinking of you, wishing I were you."

Darcy thought she saw Audrey's eyes glisten with tears, but Audrey quickly looked away. Maybe Darcy was actually getting through to her. She softened her tone of voice. "So what did Trevor say when you told him everything?"

"That he still loves me." Her voice was barely a whisper, but Darcy heard it and she understood how difficult it was for Audrey to accept that he would still love her despite the rape and pregnancy that resulted from it.

"If Trevor loves me as much as he thinks he does, and if he is the man that God has set aside for me to marry, then he will wait for me. We can be together when the time is right. This just isn't the time."

That reasoning made sense, Darcy had to admit. They didn't talk the rest of the way home. Darcy thought about how much she admired her sister. She really was smart. Darcy understood now that she wasn't just punishing herself by keeping away from Trevor. She was doing what was right. There was no need to rush into a relationship. There were more important issues to deal with right now. Their mom had taught them that boys could wait. Darcy just hoped and prayed that Trevor literally would wait for her sister. They were a match made in Heaven. Darcy was sure of it.

"Darcy, Mom and Dad don't know that I'm pregnant. Let me tell them."

Darcy nodded.

Chapter Fourteen

AUDREY LOOKED AT HER PHONE AND REREAD THE TEXT from Matt. She needed to respond. Honestly, she would like to go to a movie. The idea of hanging out with friends who knew nothing about her current situation and getting lost in a fictional story was very inviting.

She thought about Trevor's suggestion of inviting him to come along. She would love to share an arm rest and a bag of popcorn in a movie theatre with Trevor again. He would get along really well with her friends too. For sure he would have a lot in common with Matt since they both played football.

But it would be impossible to hang out with Trevor just as friends, especially after he'd confessed the depth of his feelings for her. As much as she would like him to come along, it just wouldn't work out. It would be better to keep her distance from him.

Plus, if she was honest with herself, she had to admit that it seemed like Matt had a crush on her. It could be awkward having Trevor there even though Matt never flirted or treated her as anything other than a friend. But she could see it in his eyes when he talked to her. Even as they were studying psychology, discussing Pavlov's theories about dogs salivating at the sound of a bell, his eyes would sparkle.

She made sure to never spend too much time alone with him. She didn't want to give him the wrong idea about their relationship, and she didn't want him to fall for her. Her heart was definitely falling for Trevor.

But in his text, Matt made it clear that it would be a group hanging out tonight. It's not like he was asking her to go on a date.

There was no reason not to go.

She texted him back, and soon they had the details worked out. They were meeting at a theatre close to Bethel since that was a central location for everybody. Matt lived about twenty minutes further south of Audrey's hometown, so he suggested that he'd pick her up on his way.

"It doesn't make sense for both of us to drive," he had reasoned. She knew that he was just being logical—not looking for an excuse to spend extra time with her. But she felt uncomfortable about it just the same. She didn't want it to feel like a date. So she invited Darcy to come along.

Audrey looked out the window for what felt like the hundredth time in the past fifteen minutes, watching for Matt's car. She peered over at Trevor's car parked in his driveway next door. She wondered what he was doing at that moment, wishing she were with him, cuddled up next to him on the couch watching TV or down in their game room playing video games. She hoped he wouldn't look out his window to see her climbing into Matt's car. She especially didn't want Trevor to get the wrong idea about her relationship with Matt.

Darcy came bounding down the stairs bringing with her a light scent of perfume. She looked pretty. Her light brown hair fell in soft curls around her freshly made up face. Darcy was an expert when it came to make-up, and she had done a professional job tonight at making herself appear to be at least three years older than her actual age of sixteen. "I'm ready. Is he here yet?" she asked, breathless.

"Not yet." Audrey left the front window to put on her boots and coat. As she buttoned up her coat, she wondered when her growing belly wouldn't allow her to button it up all the way; she hoped it would be a long time. She couldn't hide her baby bump forever. She needed to tell her parents soon, and then she would tell her college friends. She dreaded that day. But this night was all about relaxing and having fun.

Headlights shone into the front window. "He's here."

"Cool. Is he as cute in person as he is in his football picture online?"

Audrey rolled her eyes. Her sister was as bad as every other girl at Bethel. She laughed and then answered honestly. "That picture doesn't even come close to doing him justice."

Darcy squealed and it reminded her of Destiny.

"Now compose yourself. No more squealing." Audrey opened the door and hollered to her parents that they were leaving. They called back telling them to have a good time.

It was freezing outside. Even all bundled up, Audrey instantly began to shiver. She ran to the passenger door and let herself in.

Darcy climbed into the back seat. "Hey, Matt. I'm Darcy." She didn't waste any time on introductions.

Matt grinned at her in the rearview mirror and Audrey noticed how his eyes twinkled. He seemed amused by Darcy. The exchange put a smile on Audrey's face. She glanced over at Trevor's house and was relieved when she didn't see him looking out the window. She was being paranoid. Of course he wouldn't be lurking by the window, watching Audrey's every move.

"Is that where Trevor lives?" Matt seemed to read her mind. He knew all about Trevor. Audrey had told him about how the two of them had grown up next door to each other. There had been a few times that she'd stepped away from their study group on Sunday nights for T-time.

"Yep." She didn't offer too much information and hoped he wouldn't ask for more. Tonight was supposed to be about forgetting her problems with Trevor and just having fun.

"Do you wanna see if he can come with us? Sorry I didn't think of that sooner."

"No, that's okay. We talked about it, but he's not coming."

Matt accepted her answer without probing. The subject quickly changed to football, with Darcy asking question after question about what it was like getting hit so hard or deciding which play to run. She was clearly enamored.

The movie theatre was packed. A lot of great movies had come out over the holidays. It took the group a while to agree on which movie to see, but they finally settled on a comedy. Their group included eight people, five guys and three girls, including Audrey and Darcy. They were all Bethel students, with the exception of Darcy, and Audrey knew them all very well.

She was so thankful for the great friends she had made so far her freshman year. This particular group was an especially easy bunch to laugh with. Besides Matt, Audrey knew two of the guys and the girl from psychology class. One of the other guys also played on the Bethel football team, and the other guy was Matt's roommate. A fleeting and very depressing thought came that she may not finish out the year with them, but she quickly brushed the thought away. Tonight was about having fun.

Audrey found seats a few rows from the back of the theatre. She scooted all the way to the end of the row, and the rest filed in behind her—first Darcy, then Matt, and then the rest. Audrey was sure that Darcy was ecstatic to be sitting next to Matt. She did little to hide her emotions. As soon as they all sat down and were situated, Darcy reached over and squeezed Matt's arm. "I get to share an arm rest with a handsome running back." She wasn't flirting, just being herself, lightheartedly joking around. Matt joked right back. "I apologize in advance if my rippling biceps take up too much room." They all laughed. Darcy fit in perfectly.

The movie started a few minutes later. Darcy leaned over and whispered that she was going to get popcorn and candy. "Do you want anything?

Audrey dug a ten dollar bill out of her coat pocket. "Just a Coke."

"Okay, I'll be right back."

Darcy stood up and shuffled out of the row, squeezing past everyone.

Matt stood up. "I'll go with you, Darcy."

For a reason Audrey couldn't put her finger on, she felt a twinge of jealousy as she watched Matt and Darcy walking off together. They would only be gone a few minutes buying snacks. And what did it matter to Audrey anyway? It's not like Matt belonged to her. Audrey had to admit that in a way it was flattering to have Matt pining over her, although her heart definitely belonged to Trevor. It had to be stupid pregnancy hormones messing with her emotions. She shook her head in an attempt to shake away her irrational thoughts. Soon Matt and Darcy were back, and Audrey chided herself for her fleeting jealousy.

The movie was hilarious; Audrey couldn't remember the last time she'd laughed so hard. It was good to find respite from her dismal problems. It was great to reconnect with her sister too.

Laughter filtered through the hallways of the theatre as the group made its way out to the parking lot. Audrey suddenly realized her bladder would never last the thirty minute drive home. "You guys go ahead; I'll catch up with you." She turned toward the restrooms.

"Wait for me." Darcy darted to Audrey's side.

Matt, continuing to walk with the rest of their friends, called over his shoulder that he would pick them up outside the front of the theatre.

Audrey rushed into the rest room, feeling a sudden sense of urgency, and claimed the nearest stall. She wondered if this was also a symptom of pregnancy.

After washing her hands, Audrey touched up her lip gloss. Darcy stood beside her and did the same.

"Your friends are great." Darcy rubbed her lips together, evenly distributing the shiny gloss.

"Yeah, they're fun."

Darcy crossed her arms and a sly smile crept across her face. "You didn't tell me that Matt has a thing for you."

"What?" Matt had done nothing all night to show any special interest in her. "What are you talking about?"

"Don't act so surprised. This can't be news to you."

Audrey tried to play dumb. "What makes you think he has a thing for me?" She looked at her reflection, combing her fingers through her hair.

Darcy smiled and shrugged. "Because he told me so."

"What? He told you?"

"Well, not in so many words."

So Darcy was reading into things, just like everybody else. Oddly, Audrey felt slightly disappointed. "Okay, what exactly did he say?"

"So when we left to get snacks he asked me if you were okay. I asked him what he meant, and he said you didn't seem like yourself tonight."

Audrey didn't like where this was going. She held her breath, hoping Darcy didn't say anything about her pregnancy. She'd be mortified!

"I said you were fine."

Audrey breathed out a sigh of relief. So far, so good.

"Then he asked me if you're interested in Trevor." Darcy raised an eyebrow. "You know there's only one reason a guy asks that question—when he wants to know if your heart is available."

Audrey's palms became moist with perspiration. "What did you tell him?"

"The truth." She winked at Audrey. "I said you guys are just friends."

Audrey didn't know what to say or how to feel. "Then what did he say?"

"Then a smile spread across his gorgeous face and he said, 'Audrey's a great girl.'"

"Well, it doesn't matter. Obviously, I'm not interested in dating anyone right now."

"You're such a heartbreaker."

"Let's go. He's probably waiting for us."

Matt pulled up just as Audrey and Darcy exited the theatre building. The cold air took Audrey's breath away.

"Shotgun." Darcy raced to the car. She opened the front door and hopped in before Audrey had a chance to respond.

As Audrey slid into the back seat and buckled her seat belt, she caught Matt's eye in the rearview mirror. He smiled, and Audrey caught a glimpse of that familiar sparkle in his eye. "Now I know why you're so competitive. You have to keep up with this pistol of a little sister."

"Is that a bad thing?" Darcy feigned insult.

"Not at all. It's … endearing."

"Endearing? That sounds like a word my grandpa would use."

"That's because I'm so mature." Matt puffed out his chest.

"Whatever!" The girls said in unison.

The night continued with a lot of friendly banter and easy laughter. As Matt pulled into the Chapman's driveway, they all seemed reluctant to let the night come to an end. Matt turned to Audrey. "Do you have any plans for tomorrow?"

Caught off guard, Audrey wasn't sure how to answer. Was he asking her on a date? No, he wouldn't do that with Darcy sitting next to him in the front seat.

"I'll be driving practically right past your house on my way to the Mall of America. My mom needs me to pick something up for her at Nordstrom. I thought maybe you could come with if you're not busy. I mean, I'll feel a little awkward in the women's clothing department. You can help me navigate my way around."

"Oh, um …" Audrey searched her mind momentarily and was unable to come up with a reason not to go. "Yeah, that's fine. I'll be around."

"Well, thanks for the ride, Matt. It was nice meeting you." Darcy unbuckled her seat belt and jumped out of the car. "C'mon, Audrey. It's late, and you need your beauty rest."

Audrey guessed Darcy wanted to get her in the house to ask why she agreed to a date with Matt. She wasn't sure that it was a good idea either, but Matt was a friend. Friends hang out at the mall together. No big deal.

Matt waved. "Bye, Darcy. See you tomorrow, Audrey."

Audrey rushed into the house ahead of Darcy. She wanted to get up to her room before Darcy would have a chance to tell her again how stupid she was.

But Darcy wouldn't let her get away that easy. She stepped between Audrey and the staircase. "You're leading him on, you know."

"Whatever, Darcy. We're going to the mall. It's not a date."

"To him it's a date. He didn't invite me."

She had a point.

"You can't deny that he likes you. He inquired about your relationship with Trevor, and then he asked you to hang out with him again—two days in a row. You need to set him straight. Let him know you're not in the market right now."

"Nice, Darcy. And I suppose you want me to tell him that you are." Audrey regretted it as soon as she said it. She knew Darcy was just being honest. But she didn't want to hear it. "Fine. I'll talk to him tomorrow."

Darcy stepped aside, allowing Audrey to pass. "Thanks for letting me tag along tonight. I had fun."

"I had fun too." Too bad it was time to get back to reality. Audrey turned to go to her room.

"Audrey?" Darcy's voice wasn't more than a whisper. She breezed up the few steps separating the girls. "Did you tell Mom and Dad about…your situation?"

Panic surged through Audrey's veins. "No, and you better not even think of—"

"Calm down. I won't say anything. As long as you tell them soon. They need to know. You need their help."

"I'll tell them when I'm ready." Audrey shot her a warning look.

"I'm only agreeing to keep quiet because they should hear it from you."

Darcy was right. Her mom and dad needed to know. But not tonight. Maybe tomorrow after she'd get home from the mall. Or whenever she had things figured out.

Chapter Fifteen

MALL SECURITY GUARDS DIRECTED MATT TO PARK ALL the way up on the top level of the jam-packed parking ramp. After driving around for ten minutes, dodging shoppers loaded down with bags, they finally found an open spot.

"Don't these people know Christmas is over so they don't need to shop anymore?" Matt had apparently never shopped on December twenty-sixth.

"They're here for the after-Christmas sales."

"You'd think they'd be sick of shopping."

"You'd think." Audrey and Matt climbed out of the car and headed in the direction of the ramp elevator. "Brrr. It's freezing out here. Let's run." She sped to the elevator with Matt following close behind and pushed the down button. "What does your mom need from Nordstrom anyway?"

"A sweater." He pulled a piece of paper from his pocket and read, "Michael Kors chenille sweater."

"Couldn't she order it online?"

Matt chuckled. "That's right, I forgot. You've never met my mother."

"What do you mean?"

"She hates computers and avoids them at all cost. She's completely challenged by all forms of technology. Let me put it to you this way. She's never sent an email in her life."

"Wow."

"Yeah. And she doesn't own a cell phone. My mother must be the last person on the planet to only use a land line."

"That's funny. At least you don't have to worry about her posting embarrassing pictures of you to her Facebook page. So why didn't you order the sweater for her? Or why didn't she call in her order and have it shipped to your house?"

"That would've been easier, but she wanted me to check it for flaws."

Audrey laughed. "You're making this up."

The elevator arrived just when Audrey thought her fingers would get frost bite. They stepped in, and she pushed the button for the ground floor.

She looked up at Matt and noticed his rosy cheeks. Although the cold air could've been the source, she was sure he was blushing. "You are making this up, aren't you?" she said, giving him a playful shove.

"Okay, so I offered to pick it up for her, but she really does hate technology, and she really doesn't own a cell phone, and she really did tell me to check the sweater for flaws." He gave her a light shove back, knocking her into the poster of Nickelodeon Universe hanging on the wall of the elevator.

"So what's your real reason for needing a trip to the mall?"

A sheepish grin lifted the corner of his mouth. "The after-Christmas sales." He winked.

Audrey laughed. So he had really just been looking for an excuse to spend some time with her. She would have to find a way to make it clear that she wanted only to be friends, and she would need to do it soon. It would be cruel to lead him on.

The inside of the mall was bustling with bargain shoppers. Audrey led Matt to Nordstrom, where they asked a sales clerk for help finding the sweater his mom had requested. After carefully inspecting it for flaws, they made the purchase and wandered back out into the mall.

"Your mother has exquisite taste."

"Yeah, she does. Everybody says so. She always looks like a million bucks."

"Aw, that's so sweet."

"I didn't say it was a good thing. I mean, sometimes I think she cares too much about what other people think of her. You know what I mean? Sometimes I wish she could relax and be herself. It's like she thinks she has to be perfect."

"Mmm, does she put those same expectations on you?"

Matt blushed. "You can read me like a book."

Audrey said nothing, letting him know she was listening.

"Yeah, it's been tough living up to her standards, but she's a great mom."

"I'm sure she is."

"I just wish she didn't put so much pressure on herself. Nobody's perfect."

Audrey could sense that he was not only talking about his mother, but also himself. She guessed that would explain why he put so much effort into his grades and even sports. When she really thought about it, she saw the flaw of perfectionism in herself.

They walked side by side, checking out the kiosks on the first floor. Audrey tried on sunglasses and ended up buying a pair. Matt purchased a Twins baseball cap. He put it on and stood back to get Audrey's opinion. "What do you think?"

"I'm not sure it suits you. Maybe we better head back to Nordstrom to find something more sophisticated."

He turned it backward, the way Trevor often wore his hat. "How about now?"

A lump formed in Audrey's throat as she suddenly missed Trevor with every fiber of her body. "It's totally you."

She knew she needed to talk to Matt about just being friends. He had pretty much admitted to the fact that today was more of a date than not. She was afraid of losing his friendship, but that was a risk she needed to take. But before she had time to decide how to tell him, he interrupted her thoughts.

"Do you want to catch a movie?" Matt pointed up to the theater, visible on the fourth floor.

That was her cue. She had to say something now. "Um, I don't think so."

"I know we just saw one last night. You probably don't feel like sitting through another one already. I just thought since we were here—"

"No, it isn't that." Audrey inhaled, held the air, and then blew out slowly.

"Nah, I get it. You're in love with Trevor Hayes, aren't you?"

Audrey shook her head. "That's not it." She sighed. Here goes nothing. "I'm not in a position to be dating anyone right now." Her heart pounded in her chest as she contemplated telling him exactly why. No better time than the present. Soon school would resume and rumors would start to fly. She'd rather that he heard the truth from her.

"C'mere." She took him by the arm, leading him over to a bench that was out of the way of foot traffic. "I have something I need to tell you. I've hardly told a soul, but I can't keep it a secret forever."

"It sounds serious."

"It is." She rubbed her forehead, dreading the words she knew she had to say. "This is so awkward. Okay, um, well, I went to a party with some high school friends back in August." She knew even that much would be surprising to Matt. He didn't drink at all. "It was a really crazy party, and there was a ton of drinking going on."

"Did you drink?"

Shame flooded through Audrey's veins. "A little. It was my first time, and I didn't even want to be there. I was just trying to fit in, as stupid as that sounds. But nobody's perfect, right?"

Matt didn't say anything.

So Audrey continued. "To make a long story short ... I was raped."

Matt was speechless except for an audible gasp. He leaned forward on the bench and let his head fall into his hands. "I don't know what to say."

"Well, there's more. When I was raped, I became pregnant." There. She said it. She had no idea how Matt would respond, and she sat waiting for his reaction. When there was none, his head still in his hands, she nudged him. "Say something."

"I don't know what to say. I'm shocked. I guess I thought you were different."

"What?" His words cut her like a knife, tearing at what was left of her dignity. So he had thought she was different—special. But now what did he think of her? That she was less of a person? "What are you trying to say?"

"I'm saying I didn't think you were like those other girls, running around partying. I thought you were more into school and sports and making something of yourself."

This wasn't the reaction she had expected. She'd expected him to at least say that he was sorry for her and give her a hug. Show some kind of sympathy. He was acting as if this was her fault. Tears sprang to Audrey's eyes and poured down her face.

He picked at an invisible piece of lint on his coat and flicked it on the floor, refusing to look at her. The images of shoppers passing by blurred and the sound of their indistinct conversations became eerily muffled. She wished she were anywhere but here—on a bench in a mall. Why had she chosen this public place to tell Matt something so personal? Why she had told him at all?

"Why did you come here with me today?" Anger colored the tone of his words.

"Because you asked me to come. I thought we were friends." She wiped her wet cheeks with her sleeve, but fresh tears continued to flow.

"You knew I wanted to be more than friends. Everybody else knew it too. And now I look like a fool."

What a selfish jerk! After that huge confession she gave, he didn't show any compassion. He only thought of himself. "You look like a fool? For what? For hanging out with a slut like me?"

Matt finally looked up at her, showing a hint of remorse. "I didn't say that."

"Pretty much."

"Think about it, Audrey. You're in love with Trevor Hayes, you're knocked up with some other dude's baby, and now you're here with me. You have to admit that's messed up." Matt stood up and started to walk. "Let's just go."

Neither said a word as they made their way back to Matt's car up on the roof. The biting cold couldn't even compare to the iciness she felt from him. It was a long, quiet drive home. Audrey could not believe how rude he was acting. She couldn't believe that he had actually said she made him look like a fool.

"So are you gonna keep going to Bethel?" Matt broke the silence.

Audrey's defenses rose. "Why wouldn't I?"

"Soon you're gonna be, you know, bigger, and people will figure out that you're pregnant."

"Of course they'll find out. That's why I wanted to tell you now—in person—before you heard it through the grapevine."

He stared ahead at the road, covered with packed down frozen snow. "Thanks." His voice dripped with sarcasm.

"You know, I thought you were different too." She knew she should hold back and not express her next thoughts, but Matt was being so unfair. "Maybe you're not so unlike your mother, being all concerned with appearances. The apple didn't fall far from the tree."

Matt faced her, his angry eyes saying enough to convey his feelings. He opened his mouth to say something, but stopped himself, and fixed his eyes back on the road. Audrey had a feeling that she wouldn't have liked whatever it was he was going to say. Not another word was uttered until Matt pulled into her driveway where they exchanged a curt goodbye.

Chapter Sixteen

"THERE IT IS," AUDREY SAID TO BECCA, POINTING TO THE brick building tucked between a consignment shop and a law office. The same sick feeling she'd had the last time she'd been here flooded back.

Matt's vile reaction to Audrey's predicament was enough to convince her that she was in over her head. People weren't going to rally around her and support her. They would place blame on her. Matt's icy glare had sent shivers down her spine. She imagined getting negative reactions from more people when she'd go back to school—dirty looks, whispers behind her back, and false rumors. She didn't think she could take that kind of judgment.

And how could she raise a child? She didn't have the know-how, and she didn't want to burden her parents. For the first time, she understood how people could feel backed into abortions. In the least, she needed to get more information on her choices.

Becca parked on the street and cut the engine. "Do you want me to wait here?"

"Are you kidding me? You better not leave my side for one minute."

Becca smiled warmly, "They're not going to do anything today. You're just getting information." She unbuckled her seatbelt. "I promise I won't leave your side."

"Let's do this."

Half an hour later, Audrey felt more confused than ever as she and Becca exited the clinic. Her life felt like a big hopeless mess.

"Audrey?" A man called out to her from the sidewalk. He was running toward her.

Terrified, she looked up to see who this man was that saw her exiting the crisis pregnancy center. She feared it was her dad. Blinking away tears, she recognized the man to be Pastor Mitchel.

He ran to her and placed an arm around her shoulders. "Are you okay?"

"What are you doing here?" She looked to Becca in search of an explanation. "Did you tell him?" she asked Becca, backing away from her friend and shrugging off Pastor Mitchel's arm.

Becca shook her head. "I didn't tell anyone."

"But you're the only one I told about this appointment. How could you tell Pastor Mitchel?" Audrey crossed her arms across her abdomen, widening the distance between herself and Becca. "You promised to support me."

"I texted Darcy. I'm sorry. I was trying to be supportive. I was just…I don't know…scared that you'd have an abortion and regret it.

I got nervous when the doctor asked to talk to you privately. I was starting to feel like an accomplice or something.

"Ladies, we'll sort through all of this later. I'll give you a ride to my house. We'll talk there," Pastor Mitchel took control of the situation.

Audrey looked up at him. She'd never felt so much shame. "Is Mrs. Mitchel there?" She didn't want to have this conversation in front of Mrs. Mitchel.

"She is. Would you rather talk at your house?"

Audrey sniffled. "Are you going to tell my mom and dad?"

"Do they know about the pregnancy?"

Audrey shook her head. "I only told Becca and Darcy and Trevor…and a college friend. Make that *ex*-friend."

"You need to tell your parents. I'll drive you home. I'll stay with you, if you'd like, but you can do the talking."

She'd have to tell her mom and dad eventually. Having Pastor Mitchel by her side would give her courage. Anyway, she didn't really have a choice at this point. She nodded.

* * *

Audrey deliberated between strangling her sister for opening her big mouth and thanking her for the same. Withholding her state of affairs from her parents had become a burden she could no longer bear. Darcy kept a safe distance from Audrey, sitting across the room from her. Wise decision.

Audrey sat in the corner of the couch with her knees pulled up to her chest. Her mom sat next to her, still oblivious to what all the fuss was about. She was worried all the same, rubbing her temples and glancing furtively at Audrey. Her dad was on the couch next to her mom. Pastor Mitchel sat on a chair adjacent to Audrey.

Pastor Mitchel was the first to speak. "Allow me to open in prayer." He bowed his head, and everybody followed his lead. "Heavenly Father," his voice shook. "Where two or more are gathered in your name, you promise to be present. Meet us here today, Father. Fill this home with your Holy Spirit."

Audrey, although her eyes were closed, felt her mom's gaze.

"Let us speak honestly and in love. In Jesus name, Amen."

Everyone looked around at each other, not knowing how to proceed.

"What is this all about?" Audrey's mom asked.

Audrey wanted to tell her mom, but she couldn't find the words. Didn't know where to start. She looked to Pastor Mitchel for encouragement. He nodded at her. "Take your time," he said.

So it was on her shoulders. But she was at a loss for words.

"She had an abortion," Darcy blurted out.

Her mom and dad gasped simultaneously. "Audrey?" Her mom demanded an explanation.

Now Audrey *really* wanted to strangle Darcy. "You have no idea what you're talking about," she yelled at her sister. Audrey covered her face with her hands, sobbing. Her mom knelt in front of her, placing her gentle hands on Audrey's knees.

"Honey, tell us what happened." Her mom's voice was soothing, devoid of the resentment Audrey had expected. "Tom, grab a box of tissues."

Audrey wiped her face, discarding the tissues on the floor. She drew ragged breaths, wanting to tell her parents the truth. "Remember the party I told you about?"

Her mom nodded, still at Audrey's feet. She was trying to be strong, but fear radiated from her blue green eyes. Fear that would soon be justifiable.

"I was raped." The words spilled hastily from her quivering mouth. "I don't know who did it. It was dark, and I figure someone drugged me. A guy was dragging me to another room…I passed out so I don't even remember much. But…I'm pregnant." She covered her eyes in shame. "I don't know what to do." Sobs racked her body again.

Her mom sat next to her on the couch, cradling her, rocking her, crying with her. "Honey, I'm so sorry."

Her dad paced the floor. He was also crying and murmuring under his breath. Audrey didn't know if he was praying or cursing. Or a little of each. He joined Audrey and her mom circling his arms around them. His strength and vulnerability commingled.

"Wait a minute." Darcy stood up. "You said you *are* pregnant. But didn't you have an abortion?"

Audrey pulled away from her parents, mopping her wet face with her sleeve. "No, Darcy. Becca drove me to the clinic to get more information."

Darcy's face paled. "Oh. I assumed—"

"You've said enough!" Audrey didn't want to hear another word from her little sister.

Darcy shrank into her chair.

"You did the right thing, Darcy." Of course her dad would say that. He turned to Audrey. "Why didn't you tell your mom and me about this? We could've helped you."

"You know you can tell me anything." Her mom swept a lock of hair out of Audrey's eyes.

"I'm sorry. I knew you guys would be disappointed so I just wanted to figure it out. I didn't want you guys to worry."

Her dad sat next to her. He regarded her with untainted love. "It was not your fault. We are not disappointed in you." He spoke slowly so that she'd fully grasp the message in his words. And she did. "I love you. We love you." He clutched her mom's hand. "We'll get through this together."

* * *

At one o'clock in the morning, Audrey hugged Pastor Mitchel goodbye. She was finally able to look him in the eye after talking things over with him and her parents over the last few hours. The humiliation and anger she'd felt when he'd first approached her outside the pregnancy center were diminished by a sense of relief. It felt good to unharness the secrets she'd been harboring for so long. "Are you going to tell Mrs. Mitchel?"

"Only if you want me to."

Audrey thought about it. Soon everyone would find out one way or another. She'd rather Mrs. Mitchel heard it from her husband. "I want you to tell her for me."

Pastor Mitchel nodded. "I'll let her know. And don't worry. I'm sure she'll understand. Call me if you ever need anything. Even just a listening ear or someone to pray with you."

She promised to call him if she ever needed someone to talk to. She'd done enough talking for tonight.

As she brushed her teeth, the discussion from the night echoed in her mind. *It was not your fault,* her dad had said. His words washed over her. This was a new concept to her. Of course she knew it wasn't her fault that someone raped her, but it *was* her fault that she chose to attend the party and that she drank alcohol. So, she'd felt responsible for the horrific crime.

But now she saw it through her dad's eyes. His daughter had been hanging out with friends she trusted. Someone had taken advantage of her. Violated her. She remembered the feel of the guy's disgusting hands on her waist before she blacked out.

Her stomach lurched. She spit toothpaste into the sink and rushed to the toilet. Kneeling on the floor, she heaved into the toilet until her stomach was emptied. She didn't know if the vomiting was a result of morning sickness or being grossed out by the repulsive crime that she suffered. She ripped toilet paper off the roll, wiped her face, and lay on the rug, her energy depleted.

None of this was her fault. She had just wanted to spend time with friends before moving to college. She hadn't done anything to justify what that guy did to her. It was completely unfair. She lay on her side, hugging her knees to her chest. Tears streamed down her face, soaking into the rug.

Now her life was completely messed up. How was she supposed keep going to school when she was pregnant? The indoor track season would be starting soon. Could she compete? Would she be able to run at all in a few months? Probably not if she was ginormous, puking all the time.

Audrey pounded a fist on the tile floor. The jerk even stole running from her that night. That made her blood boil. If only she could rewrite the story of her life, deleting the party scene and inserting a relaxing night at home with her family. Then her life would be normal. But her story had been written in ink. Etched into stone. There could be no deleting or ignoring the fact that the party happened as long as this fetus was growing inside of her.

There was a way to undo the pregnancy. Abortion. She let the idea percolate in her mind. After an abortion, she could resume life as usual. She'd always considered herself to be pro-life. But the way she saw it, there was no other choice. She peeled herself off the bathroom floor, splashed cool water on her face, and went to her bedroom.

With her phone in hand, she slid between the sheets and propped herself up in bed, leaning against the headboard. Her hands trembled as she searched for the crisis pregnancy center. She needed to call the 24-hour hotline to set up an appointment for the procedure before she'd have a chance to change her mind. The sooner she had the procedure, the sooner she could get back to being her normal self. She couldn't stand this dismal person she'd become.

She searched for the local crisis pregnancy center and clicked on the link. A photo of the familiar brick building appeared. Below the picture it read *Closed now.* She clicked on the website and searched for a 24-hour hotline number. All she found was a number to call to leave a message. She dialed the number and listened to a recorded voice reminding her of the hours of operation, directing her to leave a voice message, and telling her to hang up and dial 911 in case of an emergency. Frustrated, Audrey hung up. This was an emergency, but she didn't need an ambulance. She needed to make an appointment. Now!

Maybe there was another local crisis pregnancy center that understood crises don't only happen during business hours. A list of women's clinics in Minnesota filled the screen. She skimmed over the results. A place called "Zoe's Place" caught her eye.

Honest information about your health, your baby, abortion, and adoption. Our counselors will assist you by answering your questions, supporting you throughout your pregnancy, and providing aftercare no matter what path you choose.

The part about supporting clients after the pregnancy sent shivers down Audrey's spine. Why would she need support after the baby was out? Wouldn't she just be able to get on with life? She clicked on the word *Aftercare*. Testimonials of women who had undergone abortions were posted. Women talked about feeling sad and guilty because they ended their babies' lives. Some even struggled with depression and suicide.

Audrey clicked on a page titled *Birthmothers*. A picture of a teenaged girl named Camille appeared on the screen along with her testimonial. "The free ultrasound changed my life and saved my baby's life. When I saw my baby's beating heart, abortion was no longer an option for me. "

The other clinic hadn't offered Audrey an ultrasound. She placed her hand on her belly, imagining what her baby might look like at this point. The information from the doctor at the crisis pregnancy center had described it as tissue. But Camille said it looked like a baby.

Audrey read every testimonial on the entire website, and then she re-read them until her eyelids would no longer stay open. She put her phone on her nightstand and snuggled under the covers. Before making an appointment for the abortion, she needed to get an ultrasound. If the results showed nothing more than tissue, she'd get the abortion, move on with her life, and never look back. On the other hand, if the ultrasound revealed an actual baby…she sighed… then God would have to show her what to do. Because she didn't have a clue.

First thing in the morning, Audrey called Zoe's Place. She wasn't sure if anyone would answer since it was Sunday. She held her breath, waiting for someone to pick up. "Zoe's Place. Ally speaking. How may I help you?" The woman's voice was warm and friendly.

"Hi." Audrey's voice was gravelly from just waking up. She cleared her throat. "I need an ultrasound. I mean…I'm pregnant, and I want an abortion. Except if it's really a baby and then I don't know—"

"I'm glad you called. That's exactly what I'm here for. Would you like to come in today or would you like to schedule a time for later in the week?"

Audrey was relieved the lady had interrupted her rambling. She took a deep breath and relaxed a bit. "As soon as possible."

"No problem. Can you be at Zoe's Place in thirty minutes?"

Audrey checked the time on her wall clock. Her family should be leaving for church in just a few minutes. They probably assumed she was sleeping in after the late night talking with Pastor Mitchel. "Thirty minutes will be perfect." Audrey ended the phone call and breathed a sigh of relief. Soon she would see for herself what was growing inside of her and be able to make a decision that would change the course of her life.

* * *

Audrey lay on her back with her shirt pulled up enough to expose her lower abdomen. Ally, a middle-aged woman who was just as warm and friendly in person as she'd been on the phone, squirted a jelly-like substance onto Audrey's belly and began moving a wand slowly over the subtle bulge below Audrey's belly button. The room was dark except for the soft glow of light coming from the ultrasound machine's screen. Audrey closed her eyes, preparing herself for the moment of truth.

A scratchy noise sounded from the machine as Ally moved the wand back and forth. "That sound is like a microphone," Ally said. Gradually, the noise morphed into a steady beating rhythm.

"Is that my heart beat?" Audrey was embarrassed at the fast pace of her heart. As a runner, she'd prided herself on her low resting heart rate. Her nerves must have multiplied her heart rate exponentially.

"That's your baby's heart."

Audrey gasped. Her eyes flew open and she looked at the screen for the first time. The black and white picture was fuzzy and hard to make out; she squinted in concentration. Ally pointed to the screen. "This is the baby's head. Here are the arms, and here are the legs."

"I see the heart." Audrey fixed her eyes on the pulsing spot in the baby's chest, flashing in sync with the sound filling the room. Awestruck, Audrey stared at the screen while Ally took a few measurements.

"The baby is about seven and a half inches long. That means you are almost twenty weeks along. The baby has fingernails and is starting to grow hair. Oh, look. Someone has hiccups."

Audrey saw the baby making jerking movements. "Hiccups already? Wow."

"It's amazing, isn't it?" Ally smiled. "I can print off a picture if you'd like."

"Yes, please." Audrey decided she'd need the picture as proof that this was real. That a baby was growing inside of her. A real baby with fingernails and a beating heart.

Ally wiped the jelly off of Audrey's belly and turned on the lights. Audrey straightened her clothing and sat up. "This is really happening." She was numb. Overwhelmed.

Ally handed her the printed picture of the miniature baby. "Do you have any questions?" She sat down on a stool, holding her folded hands in her lap.

Speechless, Audrey studied the picture. One of the baby's arms was extended, almost as if the baby were waving. Tears welled in her eyes. "I have so many questions. I just don't know where to start."

"Take your time."

"For now, I just need to go home and think about everything."

"I understand. Is it okay if I call you tomorrow?"

Audrey nodded. "I would appreciate that." She hopped off the exam table and put on her coat. She slipped the ultrasound picture in her coat pocket.

Ally led her to the door. "Was the ultrasound helpful?"

Audrey fingered the picture in her pocket. It took her a moment to sort through her thoughts enough to answer. "To be honest, I came here looking for proof that an abortion was my best solution. I didn't expect to see a cute little baby hiccupping and waving at me." She expelled an incredulous laugh. "Abortion is no longer an option."

"I'm glad it was helpful. Feel free to call me anytime. Day or night."

Audrey thought back to last night when she was making a phone call in the middle of the night. "You might regret telling me that."

They exited the building, and Ally locked the door. "Can I give you a hug?"

Audrey was amazed at Ally's genuine interest in her case. So far, this pregnancy center's care far surpassed the other center. Audrey accepted the hug and thanked Ally for everything.

On the drive home, Audrey thanked God that she hadn't killed the cute little baby rapidly developing inside of her. She never would've believed it was already a baby had she not seen it for herself. She also thanked God for Ally. The sweet gentle woman was exactly the confidante Audrey needed. However, the morning's events were taking her on an emotional rollercoaster that made her sick to her stomach. Now that abortion was ruled out, Audrey had to face the fact that she was a mom. An eighteen-year-old, unwed, college-bound mom.

"Trust in the Lord," she reminded herself in effort to ward off a panic attack. "Lean not on your own understanding. In all your ways, acknowledge him, and he will make your paths straight."

Chapter Seventeen

~

EXCITEMENT TWIRLED IN AUDREY'S STOMACH AS SHE drove back to campus. She was relieved that winter break was over and was anxious to see her cute little dorm room, her teammates, and even her chatty roommate. A warm fuzzy feeling washed over her as the campus came into view. She turned onto Bethel Drive and flashed her ID at the security guard. He smiled and waved her through. It felt good to belong here. To be just another student. Coming back to college would serve as a welcome distraction from her problems and restore a sense of normalcy to her life.

Loaded down with her bags and a basket of freshly laundered clothing, she managed to open the door to her dorm room. "Audrey!" Destiny barreled toward her, pouncing on her with an enthusiastic hug. "Let me help you with all this stuff." The hyperactive roommate grabbed the laundry basket and proceeded to hang the articles of clothing in the tiny closet. "How was your Christmas? I didn't hear from you all break. I had so much fun in Colorado. The snow was perfection—like powder. Nothing like the ski hills around here. Do you snowboard?"

Audrey dropped her bags on her bed and unbuttoned her coat. "Um, yeah. I love snowboarding."

"We should go sometime. I mean, it won't be anything like Breck, but maybe we could go up to Lutsen. Those slopes are pretty sweet, for Minnesota anyway."

"Maybe." Unlikely. Audrey squeezed past Destiny to hang her coat in the closet.

Destiny stood back, looking Audrey up and down. Audrey held her breath, hoping Destiny wouldn't comment on her weight gain. She decided to beat her to it. "I think I gained like ten pounds over Christmas. My mom makes the best Christmas cookies. I need to get back to running."

Destiny laughed. "You can afford to gain ten pounds."

Phew! Bullet dodged.

Destiny checked her own reflection in the full-length mirror, straightening the collar of her emerald green sweater and fluffing her red hair. "Anyway, I've been dying to tell you that I signed us up on a broomball team. Everybody plays broomball in January so I knew you wouldn't mind. I know you'll be great."

"I love broomball!" Happiness bubbled inside Audrey, spreading a huge smile across her face. "I bet you're good too. I've seen you play soccer."

"I hope so. I've never played. I guess it's like hockey but with a different stick and a ball instead of a puck. B-T-W, I have a surprise for you."

Audrey sat on her bed, her giddiness dampened. "I don't like surprises."

Destiny held up her phone and snapped a selfie, her lips pursed. "You only have to wait until our team practice tonight to find out."

Audrey groaned. "This better be a nice surprise." She lay back on her bed and closed her eyes. "I can't handle anything drastic."

"It's a very nice surprise."

A few hours later, Audrey was driving herself and Destiny to the ice rink off campus for their first team practice. The snow covered roads sparkled under the full moon's light. Audrey's feet were sweating in her boots and two layers of socks. Good thing it was a short drive.

Destiny was in the passenger seat, munching on Flamin' Hot Cheetos that matched the shade of her hair. "How's the neighbor boy?" she asked before licking red-orange salt off of her fingertips.

Audrey's heart squeezed. "We're not talking right now."

"That's so sad. What happened? I mean, he was like your best friend, right? Oh, turn here." She pointed a Cheeto toward a parking lot.

Audrey veered into the lot, thankful there wasn't much time for further discussion. "I'd rather not talk about it."

Destiny turned the corners of her orange-stained lips down into a dramatic frown. "That bad, huh? Well, my surprise will cheer you up." Her frown transformed into a gleaming smile. She pointed—a finger this time—to the ice rink. "Ta da!"

It was a surprise alright. In the middle of the rink, under the bright lights stood Matt Cook. He was holding a clipboard in his gloved hands, studying it. A couple other guys ran past him, racing to shoot the ball, sticks in hand. "You've got to be kidding me. Matt is on our team?" Audrey groaned. "I should've known that was the surprise."

"He's team captain. He'll be so stoked that I brought you. We needed one more girl. Our team is going to dominate!" Destiny grabbed her stick from the back seat and ran out of the car. She joined Matt in the middle of the rink, leaving Audrey in the car, suddenly shivering.

Her escape from reality had been brief. It had been nice for a few hours to pretend that she was a regular college student, but seeing Matt—who knew her dark reality—brought everything back into perspective. She was living this fantasy life on borrowed time. Soon everyone around campus would know her secret. Soon she'd be big as a beluga whale. Soon she wouldn't be just a college student. She'd be a mom.

Her throat swelled with emotion. She shook her head. There would be no crying tonight. Tonight, she would play broomball and have fun doing it. She had nothing to be ashamed of. She grabbed her stick and joined Matt and Destiny out on the ice.

"Hi. Matt." Audrey held her head high.

Matt stared at her, a confused look on his face. He wasn't as cute as Audrey remembered. His sour personality somehow dimmed his beauty. "Are you sure you should play?" He flicked his eyes down to her abdomen. "In your state?"

Destiny put her hands on her hips. "What are you talking about? Aren't you so excited to see each other? Do you know how hard it was for me to keep this a secret?"

Matt scoffed. "For one day? Good job, Destiny."

Destiny squealed. "I know, right?" Matt's sarcasm had somehow eluded her.

A couple other players ran over. "Hey, Audrey's on our team. Sweet!" A guy from Audrey's and Matt's psych study group high-fived her.

"Matt doesn't think she should play. Why shouldn't she play, Matt?" Destiny said in a whiny voice.

Audrey gave Matt a look meant to convey that if he spoke a word about the pregnancy he'd be sorry. To her relief, he didn't answer, so she did. "Matt is worried about me getting hurt before the indoor track season starts. Don't worry, though. My coach encourages her athletes to play broomball. To stay in shape." It was a lie that tasted salty on her tongue. Saltier than those Flamin' Hot Cheetos. Truthfully, she was pretty sure her coach wouldn't want her to play.

Of course track hadn't been Matt's concern. She knew his comment was in reference to the baby.

"Then what are we waiting for? Let's practice," the guy from study group said.

Matt shook his head, "Whatever." He listed off all the positions he wanted everyone to start in. Matt, Destiny, and the guy from study group would be forwards. He listed positions for all the remaining players except for her. Everyone ran to take their place as they would for a game.

"What about me?" Audrey glared at Matt.

"Oh, you can be an alternate in case someone gets hurt or something."

She wanted to punch him. "I know what an alternate is." She trudged across the ice to the outside of the rink and propped her elbows up on the wall, watching her teammates practice.

A van pulled into the parking lot, dispensing a team of broom-ball players sporting various shades of neon green. A second vehicle followed suit. "You guys ready to scrimmage?" one of the green players asked Audrey.

"Yeah, sure."

A guy carrying a girl piggy-back sidled up next to her. "We're short a player. Mind playing with us, just for tonight?"

Audrey's spirits lifted. "I'd love to."

The game started out pretty low-key. A couple kids could barely stay on their feet, and the worst player on the green team turned out to be a ball hog. As Audrey stood her ground as right wing, she considered Matt's question. *Are you sure you should play?* Ally had said it was safe to run. Audrey hadn't thought to ask about playing broomball. A hard fall on the ice probably wouldn't be good for the baby.

No worries. She'd grown up playing broomball and was solid on her feet. The rest of the scrimmage, she surrendered to the game. Well, the game wasn't much to surrender to, but she put all thoughts of the baby, the party, Trevor, and Matt out of her mind. She scored the only two goals for the green team, but they still lost by three points.

They wrapped up practice with a team huddle. Matt announced new positions for next week. Audrey was pleasantly surprised when he named her as right winger. She mouthed the word "thanks" to him, but he pretended not to notice. The cold shoulder act was getting old. Her blood ran hot; she felt her face flush. She waited until the huddle closed with a cheer, shouting their team name—*The Psychos*, since most of them had been in psych study group together—and then she called out to Matt. "Hey, Matt. Did you drive?"

Caught off guard, he answered, "No."

"You can ride with me." She flashed him a sappy smile. "Destiny, do you mind catching a ride with someone else?"

Destiny complied. "Sure, I get it. You two look like you could use a little alone time. You need to kiss and make up." She winked, instigating laughter and whistles from the rest of the team.

Matt agreed to ride with Audrey, but he looked like he wanted to kill her. She let the engine idle so the car could warm up and because she was too angry to drive. As soon as they were both situated with their equipment tossed in the backseat and their seatbelts buckled, Matt started ranting. "Did I not make myself clear? I'm not interested in you anymore so quit stalking me."

Audrey was glad she was sitting on her cold hands to warm them. Otherwise, she would've slapped him across the face. "Stalking you? Really?"

"First you join my team, and then you corner me into riding back to campus with you."

"Look, buddy. I didn't know Destiny set me up to be on your team. Stop being such a narcissist."

"I'm a narcissist? You're the one risking the life of your unborn baby to play a childish game of broomball."

"Childish? You were taking the game pretty seriously out there when you checked that girl who is half your size."

Matt stared out at the rink, shaking his head. "So you dragged me into your car to call me a narcissist. Is there anything else?"

The other players had left the park, heading back to campus. A tingle of fear ran down Audrey's spine. She was alone with a fuming Matt Cook. She decided to calm things down a bit. "I'm sorry I called you a narcissist."

"And?"

This guy was really a piece of work. "And I want us to act amiable with each other."

"I was trying. I put you at right wing."

"I appreciate that." Audrey sighed. "Here's the thing. Stop treating me like crap. I trusted you enough to tell you something deeply personal. Because I thought we were friends. I thought you'd support me. Instead, you're treating me like a disease. It's not fair." She unfastened the top button of her coat. The heater seemed to have kicked up the temperature to one-hundred degrees. She turned the fan down a notch.

"The whole story sounds far-fetched. Am I really supposed to believe that you were drugged?"

"Yes!"

"It's far more likely that you got so wasted that you don't remember what happened. Maybe you wanted it."

His words were so hurtful that her heart physically hurt. Tears threatened to spill from her eyes, but she blinked them back. She put the car in gear and drove out of the parking lot. She could hardly tolerate another minute with this guy. "It doesn't matter if you don't believe me. All I ask is that you treat me with respect, and please don't tell anybody. I'll tell them when I'm ready. Fair enough?"

"In return, all I ask of you is that you stop associating with me. I'll let you play on the broomball team, but that's it." Matt made a big huffy breath. "People might think it's mine. You know how everyone talks about us. It was no secret that I had a crush on you."

It was hard to believe she'd actually been friends with this self-centered jerk. "Don't worry, Matt." She patted his knee, seething underneath her syrupy exterior. "I made it clear that I was never interested in you."

She parked in the student lot, turned off the ignition, and waited in the car until Matt was in his dorm, out of sight. Then she allowed the tears to rain.

* * *

Audrey woke with a horrible ache in her back. With her eyes still closed, she stretched, slamming her knee into something rigid. Straining to open her eyes, she tried to remember where she was. It definitely wasn't her comfy bed. A streetlight hovered above her, shining through the windshield of her car. She rubbed her eyes, feeling the salt of dried tears on her fingertips. She'd fallen asleep in her car, and the bone-chilling cold of January had stiffened her every joint. She checked the time on her phone. Ten-thirty. She'd only slept about thirty minutes. Good thing she woke up. She could have frozen to death out here.

Shivering, she started the car and turned the heater on full blast. She anticipated the scenario that would likely ensue when she entered the dorm. She would tip toe around, avoiding Matt. Once safely in her room, Destiny would bombard her with questions. Audrey couldn't fathom living out that scenario. Not now. Not ever. Exhaustion was getting the better of her—physically and emotionally.

Maybe she could just sleep out here in the car tonight. She could wake up and run the engine for a few minutes every couple of hours to warm up.

She rolled her eyes. That idea was pathetic.

Who was she trying to fool? As long as she was pregnant, the college-scene was too much to handle. Picking up her phone, she decided there was only one thing to do. She needed to make a phone call. As the phone rang, she restrained herself from crying again.

"Hello?"

A quiet sob escaped Audrey's throat. "Mom, I'm coming home."

Chapter Eighteen

ALTHOUGH DARCY DIDN'T HAVE A BOYFRIEND, SHE wasn't about to sit around pouting about that fact on Valentine's Day. She had invited her single girlfriends over to her house to eat snacks and watch a romantic comedy. It wouldn't be as romantic as a date with a cute boy, but it was the best she could do.

Darcy filled a red paper plate with candy hearts and chocolate-dipped strawberries that her mom had helped her prepare for the party. Squeezing between two girls on the sofa, she put her feet up on the ottoman and pushed *Play* on the remote control. As the previews played, Darcy thought about how happy she was to have made the decision to invite friends to her house tonight. Her church friends were getting together at Becca's house, but that would be a different kind of party. They had continued to drink even after learning about the horrible tragedy that had happened to her sister, but Darcy never wanted to touch alcohol again.

A phone rang in another part of the house, and Darcy heard her mother answer it. Soon, her mom rushed into the room and tapped Darcy on the shoulder, motioning for her to come into the next room.

Darcy followed her mom into her dad's office. Darcy's father, who was sitting at his desk paying bills online, swiveled in his chair to join the conversation. "What's going on?"

Her mom's forehead was creased with worry lines. Darcy had seen that expression on her mom only one other time—the day she found out Audrey was pregnant. A lump formed in Darcy's throat.

"I have some bad news. We need to pray."

Darcy's mouth went dry and her fingers trembled. Audrey was working at her nanny job. Darcy panicked at the thought that something may have happened to her sister or the baby. "Is it Audrey?"

"No, Audrey is fine. But Pastor Mitchel was in a car crash."

Darcy and her dad simultaneously gasped in horror.

"He's at the hospital in a coma. Apparently, he hit his head pretty hard." Her mom brought her fist to her mouth, stifling a soft cry. "They're not sure if he's going to make it."

Darcy's heart sank, and she was at a loss for words. She thought about what an amazing role model Pastor Mitchel had been for all the teenagers at their church. Then she thought about how most of the youth group was partying at that very moment, ignoring his warnings about teenage drinking, while he lay in a coma.

"Darcy, are you okay?"

She tried to process the situation. "I'll be ok." An idea formed in her mind. She would gather the youth group kids together to pray. It was something Audrey would do. Darcy needed to stop relying on her sister to be the leader. It was time for her to step up. "I know what I need to do." Then she told her parents her idea.

* * *

Audrey drove straight to the hospital as soon as she could get away from her job. The mother of the children she babysat for arrived home from work moments after Audrey received Darcy's text that Pastor Mitchel was in the hospital. Darcy had sent out a group text to all of the youth group kids, asking them to meet in the emergency room. Only family members were allowed to visit him, but the kids could still gather to pray.

Audrey rushed into the ER waiting area and found Darcy, Jake, Becca, and Gavin in a quiet corner, seated in a circle on the floor. They were holding hands and had their heads bowed in prayer. Audrey squeezed in between Darcy and Becca, sitting cross-legged with her back against a wall for support. Sitting on the floor was not an easy thing to do these days with her belly the size of a basketball. But she wouldn't miss joining this prayer circle for anything. She closed her eyes.

Darcy prayed, "Dear heavenly Father, please save Pastor Mitchel. Heal his brain and wake him up from the coma. We need him. He's taught us so much, and we still have so much more to learn. And Mrs. Mitchel needs him. They make such a cute couple. We know you can do anything, Father. Please let him walk out of this hospital completely healed."

Kids took turns praying as they felt led. Despite the dire situation, Audrey's heart soared. The same kids who had meant to spend the night consuming profuse amounts of alcohol were instead pouring their hearts out to their Savior. And she was so proud of Darcy for organizing the prayer meeting.

A long silence followed Becca's turn, signaling closure to their prayer time. Audrey peeked open her eyes just enough to take inventory of all those present. Jake was the only person not to have prayed. She waited a moment, and just when she was about to close in prayer, Jake finally spoke.

"Dear Lord." His voice cracked. "Pastor Mitchel doesn't deserve this. He's a good guy." An awkward silence followed while Jake tried to compose himself enough to continue. Audrey peeked around. Becca put her arm around Jake. Tears were breaking free from his eyes, despite his obvious attempt to hold them back. "Don't take him, God. You don't need him up there." He coughed. "We need him down here. Amen."

Everyone stood up and hugged. Except for Audrey. She remained in prayer, thanking God for this circle of friends she had the privilege of growing up with. She silently prayed that they would stay close forever. She also prayed that her friends would listen to Pastor Mitchel's advice and stop partying so much. She shuddered at the thought of gathering at the hospital to mourn the loss of a friend after a drunk-driving accident.

Darcy sat next to Audrey, wrapping her arm around her shoulders. In the comfort of her little sister, Audrey balled like a baby. She had become close to Pastor Mitchel over the last several months. He called to check in with her regularly to ask how she was doing, often times on Sunday nights—her former T-time. He mostly just listened to Audrey vent, offering advice only when she asked for it. She told him about how the pregnancy was taking over her body in weird and frightening ways—without going into too much detail. She talked about the flashbacks that kept her awake at night. She even told him about her feelings for Trevor. She couldn't imagine Pastor Mitchel being ripped from her life right now. She laid her head on Darcy's shoulder. "He can't die, Darcy. He just can't." Her body shook with grief and fear.

Darcy stumbled over words, struggling to express encouragement that he would survive. But she came up short. She couldn't promise that. She sighed. "Trust in the Lord, right?"

A smile tugged at Audrey's lips. "Definitely."

The group stayed at the hospital for quite some time, reminiscing about the years gone by with Pastor Mitchel as their leader. A mingling of laughter and tears filled their time until late into the night when cell phones began to ring with parents beckoning their teens to come home. Audrey hated to leave, but she was hopeful that God would answer their prayers.

* * *

As she climbed into bed late that night, her body ached. Six months into the pregnancy, the baby was growing like crazy, making her feel heavy and fatigued on a normal day. This day had been downright exhausting. She was relieved to finally lie down, but her enormous belly made it difficult to get comfortable. She rolled onto her side and tucked pillows behind her back, between her knees, and under her belly for support. Once settled into her cocoon, she grabbed her phone off of her nightstand to check the Hope Church Facebook page for updates on Pastor Mitchel. A post from Maggie Mitchel popped up—a selfie of her and Pastor Mitchel at a restaurant, their heads tipped together, smiles lighting up their faces. The caption read, "Hard to believe that a few hours ago we were celebrating

Valentine's Day at our favorite Italian restaurant, and now he is in the ICU. Please pray."

Dozens of people had already *liked* the post and left comments. Most people promised to pray; some quoted Bible verses. Audrey decided to write some words of encouragement but was unsure what she could say that hadn't already been said. Nothing profound came to mind. She rubbed her eyes; they burned from all the tears she'd shed. After much deliberation, she conceded to borrow advice from Pastor Mitchel himself. She typed *Trust in the Lord with all your heart.*

Instantly, someone *liked* her comment. Her heart warmed with all the love people were showing Pastor Mitchel. With all of Hope Church praying, he would definitely pull through. Curious, she checked who had reacted to her comment. Her eyes lit up at the sight of the name. *Trevor Hayes.*

Chapter Nineteen

A FEW DAYS AFTER PASTOR MITCHEL'S ACCIDENT, AUDREY and her mom browsed through a store, choosing items to fill a gift basket for Maggie Mitchel. Pastor Mitchel had shown little improvement, so Audrey hoped a care package would lift Mrs. Mitchel's spirits. The cart was filling up fast with a pair of comfy slippers, a crossword puzzle book, Debbie Macomber's latest novel, and snacks—both healthy and unhealthy.

"That should do it," Audrey tossed a box of Little Debbie's into the cart for herself. Her feet were screaming at her to sit down. "Let's check out."

"Just one more thing." Her mom veered in the opposite direction from the registers. "I have a coupon for diapers. We should start stocking up as long as we have a coupon. Diapers are so expensive these days."

"Seriously, Mom? Isn't it a little soon to be buying diapers?" Even though the ultrasound had made the whole baby thing seem more real, it was still hard to believe that an actual baby would appear in a few months.

Her mom just kept walking as if she was going to pick up something ordinary like a carton of milk. "The baby will be here before you know it." She stopped in front of a rack of bibs, receiving blankets, and teething toys. "Oh for cute. Look at this." Her mom held up a pink bib that read, 'Grandma loves me'. "Of course, we don't know if it's a girl or a boy." She hung the bib back up on the display. Audrey breathed a sigh of relief. She was already struggling with the idea of purchasing diapers. Bibs were taking it to a whole new level.

"Here we go." Her mom led the way down an aisle that smelled like baby powder. Audrey's stomach turned at the powerful scent. "Now I'm getting excited." Her mom reached for a package of diapers.

A lady pushing a cart with a drooling baby strapped into the seat grabbed a package of the same brand of diapers. "These are the best deal, and they never leak. Well, except for those blow-outs the first few months. Nothing can contain those." The lady laughed. Then she kept walking.

Audrey failed to see the humor. "What's a blow-out?" The toddler she nannied for never had a so-called blow-out. All this baby stuff was making her feel that she was in over her head.

Her mom smiled and placed the mom-recommended diapers in the cart. "You'll find out soon enough. Trust me; ignorance is bliss."

Audrey rolled her eyes. This moment did not feel like bliss. "Can we please go now?" She turned the corner to a wide aisle where she finally escaped the powder fresh scent. A couple of girls she recognized from Becca's class were shopping in the junior's section. They were having fun, holding dresses up in front of mirrors. It reminded her of shopping with Becca or Darcy. She couldn't wait for this pregnancy to end so she could be carefree like that again.

The cashier was a cheerful woman with silver hair and bifocals dangling from a chain around her neck. When she scanned the diapers, she did a double-take of Audrey's belly. Then she turned to Audrey's mom, "Are you the lucky grandma?"

"I sure am." A smile lit her mom's face.

"Bless your heart. You don't look old enough to be a grandmother."

Her mom didn't state the obvious fact that her daughter was a teen mom. Instead, she accepted the compliment. "Thank you, dear. This is my first grandchild."

"Well, you are going to love every minute. You get to spoil the grandkids, you know." She perched her glasses on her nose and announced the total of the bill.

"Mom, I'll wait for you in the car. Can I have the keys?" Audrey held out her hand.

"Sure, honey." Her mom fished her keys out of her purse. "Are you alright?"

Was she alright? Hmm…no. She was a pregnant eighteen-year-old college drop-out who wanted nothing more than to just be a regular girl shopping for dresses with her friends—from the junior's section, not the maternity department. Meanwhile, her mom was dragging her around the store to find the perfect package of diapers while daydreaming about being a grandma. Not to mention that the person she looked to for advice was in a coma. "I'm fine. I just need to sit down."

When would the lies stop?

* * *

Basket in hand, Audrey tapped on the glass door of room one in the Intensive Care Unit. "Come in." Mrs. Mitchel's voice was raspy, as if she'd been sleeping, even though it was mid-afternoon.

Audrey slid open the door and stepped inside, bracing against the shock of what she was about to see. Mrs. Mitchel was curled up in a recliner, wrapped in a thin white hospital-issued blanket. A plush blanket would have been a nice addition to the gift basket. "Hi, Mrs. Mitchel." Audrey handed her the basket, maintaining her focus on Mrs. Mitchel and off of Pastor Mitchel. The antiseptic smell and beeping machines were unsettling enough. She wasn't ready to see Pastor Mitchel lying lifeless in the bed. "We brought you something." She handed Mrs. Mitchel the basket.

Mrs. Mitchel looked over the contents. "I'll put these to use right away." She put the slippers on. "Thank you so much."

Audrey's mom walked to Pastor Mitchel's bed. "How is he doing?"

Mrs. Mitchel sighed. "Not much change. They were hoping he would've come out of the coma by now. The sooner he does, the better his prognosis."

Audrey forced herself to look at him. Her gaze followed the tubes and wires up to the machines lit with digital numbers and squiggly lines. She drew in a deep breath and looked at his face. Tears instantly blurred her vision. Pastor Mitchel, a pillar of strength, was now vulnerable and weak—unable to even breathe on his own. A bloody bandage was wrapped around his head, and a tube was literally taped to his mouth.

The world seemed to be spinning off its axis. She'd always believed the world to be good. She had believed that through her unshakable faith in Christ, all things were possible. Live, laugh, love could have been her motto. She used to pride herself as being smart, strong, and brave. She was Audrey the Brave after all.

She had been wrong about all of that. Her faith was shakable. And her new motto was *live, cry, and puke.* She sat on a couch under the window, her knees feeling wobbly.

Her mom seemed to be holding up okay. "Hi, Andrew. It's Lydia Chapman. Audrey and I are here to see you." Her voice was rich and steady. How did that woman stay so calm? Why couldn't Audrey have inherited that trait? "You look good." Pffft. Apparently Audrey had inherited the *liar* trait. He looked horrible. "We're praying for you." She rested her hand on his shoulder and bowed her head. When she looked up again, her eyes were red.

Audrey cued her mom to sit beside her by patting the couch. Her mom sat down, folding her hands in her lap. It was quiet for a few minutes, sadness filling the room like a living, breathing thing.

"We were on the mend." Mrs. Mitchel spoke softly.

Audrey's mom nodded as if she understood what Mrs. Mitchel was trying to say.

"Andrew gave me a dozen red roses after the first grade Valentine's Day program. He does that every year, but this year it meant more after everything that's happened."

"Valentine's Day is a perfect day for a relationship to get a fresh start." Her mom always knew what to say.

Mrs. Mitchel dabbed at the corners of her eyes with a tissue. "After the program, I got in my car and noticed a sticky note from Andrew on my rearview mirror." She almost smiled. "He sent me on a scavenger hunt that eventually led me to the Italian restaurant where he'd proposed to me. He could have just said he was sorry. But he went out of his way to make me feel special." Mrs. Mitchel sniffed. "I took him for granted all that time."

"You can't think like that. Every relationship has its ups and downs. You came through it and were stronger for it in the end."

Audrey sat quietly listening. She had no idea that the Mitchels had been having problems. She felt like an idiot for venting all her problems to Pastor Mitchel while he was having troubles of his own.

"Lydia, I just can't understand why God would take him from me after bringing us through those hard times. What was the point of all that?"

Her mom fidgeted, twisting her wedding band around her finger. "In the worst case scenario," she cleared her throat, "you'll have closure to that difficult time. You loved each other through it. You won't have any regrets. That sweet scavenger hunt and romantic dinner will be your last memory of him."

Audrey stiffened. Her mom was implying that Pastor Mitchel might die.

"Or…God plans to heal him and wants all that negativity to be in your past so you can concentrate on the beautiful future the two of you will share."

Audrey breathed a sigh of relief. "That has to be it."

Mrs. Mitchel smiled. "I prefer option number two as well."

Audrey's mom stood up. "We better not overstay our welcome." She hugged Mrs. Mitchel, and Audrey followed suit.

"Thank you for coming. It really helps to have visitors. When it's too quiet, I get all inside my head."

The visit had been good for Audrey as well. It had helped her to look outside herself. She'd been so focused on herself ever since that party. "Mind if I come back tomorrow? I've been spending too much time inside my head too."

"I'd like that."

* * *

The next evening, when Audrey stepped onto the Intensive Care Unit, there was a bustle of activity at the nurse's station. Mrs. Mitchel was leaning her elbows on the counter, speaking rapidly to the nurse on the other side. She was wearing the new slippers. Audrey ran to Mrs. Mitchel's side, trying to grasp what was happening. The nurse didn't appear concerned.

"I saw his lips move. Like this." Mrs. Mitchel demonstrated a slight grimace.

The nurse followed Mrs. Mitchel into the room. She studied the monitors and then Pastor Mitchel. "I'm not seeing any changes. Are you sure he moved?"

"Yes." Her eyes were pleading with the nurse to believe her. She picked up Pastor Mitchel's hand cradling it in hers. She gasped. "He moved his finger. Did you see that?"

The nurse bent over the bed to get a closer look.

Audrey blinked, focusing so she could see the slightest movement. Her gaze traveled from his hands to his face. His eyelashes made a discreet flutter. "He's trying to open his eyes." Her heart danced with hope.

The nurse was underwhelmed. She explained that involuntary movements were common with coma patients. She bent down close to Pastor Mitchel's face. "Andrew, how are you doing?"

No response.

"Can you open your eyes?"

No response.

"Andrew, move your fingers if you can hear me."

No response.

The nurse straightened. "I'll let the doctor know what you saw. We'll cross our fingers that he does it again. Keep talking to him. He may be able to hear you, and you may be able to coax him out of this coma." She looked over the monitors again before leaving the room.

Mrs. Mitchel continued to stare at Pastor Mitchel, watching for movements. Audrey was torn between sharing Mrs. Mitchel's hopefulness and embracing the more realistic speculations of the nurse. She took off her coat and laid it on the couch. It was warm in the hospital room. She pushed up the sleeves of her pink maternity sweater. Then she joined Mrs. Mitchel at the bedside. "I don't think it was involuntary movements."

Mrs. Mitchel tore her eyes from her husband to look at Audrey. Her light brown eyes were filled with desperation. "Audrey, will you pray with me?"

"Of course." Audrey bowed her head.

"Dear Lord," Mrs. Mitchel began, "Thank you for saving Andrew's life. Thank you for giving us a second chance at our marriage. Lord, please continue to heal him so that we can live a long life together." She sniffed. "Please let him remember me."

Audrey was taken back by Mrs. Mitchel's prayer. She hadn't considered the fact that Pastor Mitchel could have amnesia. Overwhelmed by the dire situation, her palms began to sweat. "God, we need a miracle. We beg you to restore Pastor Mitchel to complete health. With his memory intact. His dorky sense of humor intact. And his love for Mrs. Mitchel intact. We trust in you, Lord. You are the divine healer." As she prayed, her confidence in his recovery increased. God was capable of anything. He created the universe, after all. So healing Pastor Mitchel would be cake. "In Jesus name, amen."

Mrs. Mitchel giggled, wiping tears from her cheeks with a tissue. "Audrey, you already made me feel better."

"Sorry I asked for his sense of humor to be restored. I should've asked for a less dorky sense of humor." Audrey was glad they were able to joke a little bit. She sensed Mrs. Mitchel needed the laughter even more than she did. She sat on the couch. It was firm and covered in vinyl or something. Poor Mrs. Mitchel had been sleeping on this.

Mrs. Mitchel sat on the recliner. "Let's talk about you. How are you doing?"

"I'm good." She placed a hand on her ever-expanding middle. She felt a little kick from the baby.

"Really?" Mrs. Mitchel opened a bag of chocolate covered pretzels that Audrey had packed in the gift basket. She offered some to Audrey, and she gladly accepted. Then Mrs. Mitchel nibbled at one.

Okay, so Mrs. Mitchel wasn't just making small talk. She was settling in for a heart to heart conversation. "The baby is healthy. I'm healthy."

Mrs. Mitchel nodded. "You have that pregnancy glow."

"I guess that's a real thing. My hair is extra shiny. I guess that's a perk of pregnancy. Who knew?"

"Have you been sleeping well?"

Audrey knew she was asking about the nightmares that had been keeping her up at night. Flashbacks of the party would fill her dreams as soon as she'd fall asleep. "Now the baby keeps me awake, kicking as soon as I lay down in my bed. It has its days and nights mixed up."

"I've read that babies do that in the womb. All day when you're up walking around, the baby is rocked to sleep. When you lie still, the baby wakes up and thinks it's playtime."

"That makes sense."

"How are the nightmares?"

Audrey sighed. "They come less often. I'm hoping that eventually they'll stop coming altogether. I've been talking to Ally at Zoe's Place about it."

"I've heard good things about Zoe's Place." Mrs. Mitchel replaced the bag of pretzels in the basket. "Do you have any leads on who your attacker was?"

She shook her head, dropping her gaze to the floor. She hated thinking that the guy was still out there. "I don't have the energy to invest in searching for him. I'm just trying to survive this pregnancy for now. I feel guilty knowing he might be doing it to other girls, but—"

"You have nothing to feel guilty about, Audrey. The guilt belongs to the one who violated you."

"I know."

"Besides, I know someone who is looking for him as if his life depends on it."

Audrey snapped her focus back on Mrs. Mitchel. "Who?"

"Trevor Hayes." Mrs. Mitchel smiled coyly.

"Seriously?" Audrey's stomach did a little somersault. "What do you mean?"

"He and Jake have been collecting names of everyone at the party. Trevor calls them, asks them for names of kids that were there, and then he questions everyone on the list. The girls too."

"Wow. I had no idea." She should've known Trevor would do something like that. He was the most caring person she'd ever met.

"He's been researching date rape drugs and trying to figure out where a kid in Hastings might get them. He's a good guy to have in your corner fighting for you."

Heartburn crawled up Audrey's throat. She wasn't sure if it was from the chocolate pretzels or the guilt of turning her back on Trevor. Add *guilt* to her new motto.

There was a rapping on the door, and Jake Preston entered the room. His eyes were red and puffy. "Mrs. Mitchel, I'm so sorry." He crossed the room and gave her a hug. "I've been praying nonstop ever since I heard about the accident, but I just had to come see him. I hope you don't mind." He spoke quickly, almost erratically. Fear emanated from his eyes. "Is he going to be okay?"

Audrey's own heartsickness doubled, seeing her friend so distraught.

"Thank you for coming, Jake. Andrew is…" Mrs. Mitchel gestured to Pastor Mitchel. "…still in a coma. We're waiting for him to come out of it. You can talk to him. He may be able to hear you."

Jake stepped up to the bed. "Hi, Pastor Mitchel. It's Jake. I just wanted to let you know that everybody's praying for you." His voice was shaky. "You have to get better. I'm not ready to say goodbye."

Mrs. Mitchel inhaled sharply.

Audrey's heart broke for Mrs. Mitchel, having to witness people voicing goodbyes to her husband. She hoped there wasn't a need for goodbyes, yet she understood Jake's sense of urgency. Andrew's condition was serious. And although she didn't want to admit it, there was a chance that Andrew wouldn't recover, on this side of Heaven.

Jake held a fist to his mouth, stifling a cry between clenched teeth. He released a quiet sob, and then began again. "I need you." Jake's voice cracked, and a tear slid down his face, dripping onto the white bed sheet. "You mean more to me than you'll ever know. Well, I wanted you to know that. That's why I'm here tonight. I needed to tell you how much you mean to me. And I wanted to thank you for being there for me."

Jake's words took Audrey by surprise. Not because she doubted Andrew's positive influence in each of the youth kids' lives, but because Jake had seemed resistant to Andrew's influence. He'd let his grades slip over the year and he'd continued drinking, despite what had happened to Audrey at his party.

Maybe Pastor Mitchel had been mentoring Jake the same way he'd been mentoring her. Pastor Mitchel had a way of making each person feel special, as if that person were his biggest priority. Tonight was proof that Pastor Mitchel had made a big impact on Jake.

The nurse entered the room and logged onto a computer. She entered numbers from the monitors into the computer. Then she began listening to Pastor Mitchel with her stethoscope. Audrey put her coat on and hugged Mrs. Mitchel. "I better go now." She patted Pastor Mitchel's shoulder. "Bye, Pastor Mitchel. Get better soon." She gave Jake a hug, and he reciprocated with a hug tight enough to take her breath away. She never would've guessed that Jake Preston was such an emotional guy. "He's going to be okay. We need to have faith that God will heal him. I need him too."

"He doesn't look so good," Jake whispered in her ear. He pulled back from his embrace and sucked in a ragged breath.

"Trust in the Lord with all your heart." Audrey managed a smile.

She walked away with her hope dangling by a thread. Jake had put a voice to her feelings that she was afraid to face, and it was difficult to hear. He was right. Andrew looked awful. Scary awful. Blood had soaked through the bandage on his head, and he had a black eye. His body was unnaturally still, except for the rise and fall of his chest. She wanted so badly to take her own advice and believe that God would heal him, but by the looks of it, only prayer could save him now.

Chapter Twenty

AUDREY TOOK A SEAT IN THE WAITING AREA OF ZOE'S Place. The Christian music playing softly in the background helped to soothe her anxieties. The song was by Jamie Grace—one of Audrey's favorites. But no distraction could disguise the fact that Audrey's pregnancy was soon to be over, and she needed to come up with a plan.

Audrey's long talks with Pastor Mitchel had sustained her through the second trimester of her pregnancy. Now as she entered the third trimester, she needed support more than ever. With Pastor Mitchel in a coma, Audrey turned to Ally at Zoe's Place for advice.

"Audrey?" Ally's voice rang out into the waiting area.

Audrey greeted her with a hug. They walked down a short hallway to a cozy room housing a loveseat, piled with cute decorative pillows, a coffee table, and a comfy chair. Audrey took the loveseat, settling into the nest of pillows and putting her feet up on the ottoman.

"Would you like a drink? Tea? Water? Coke?"

"Coke, please." Audrey suddenly felt parched.

"Sure thing. I'll be right back."

Ally left the room, leaving Audrey alone with her thoughts. She looked around the room. It was decorated in a shabby chic sort of fashion with gauzy curtains filtering sunlight that shone through the corner window. A painted bookshelf held an assortment of items: books, a tissue box, plush blankets, and packages of saltine crackers. Audrey knew what the crackers were for—morning sickness. She was thankful that this room was pretty, comfortable, and welcoming. Unlike her obstetrician's office that was decorated with pictures of pregnant women or mothers and babies. Even this far into her pregnancy, it was difficult for her to identify with images of mothers. Which was what brought her here today.

"Here you go." Ally came through the door, popping open a can of Coke.

Audrey took a drink of the ice cold beverage, enjoying the refreshing fizz sliding down her throat. "Thank you. I didn't realize I was so thirsty."

Ally relaxed in the comfy chair, crossing her legs. She held a steaming mug by the handle and took a sip. "Me either."

Audrey braced herself for a barrage of questions. But none came. Ally appeared relaxed, as if she was just hanging out with Audrey as a friend.

"I heard about your pastor. I'm sorry."

Audrey sighed. "Thanks. He's still in a coma. I really think God will save him." Audrey thought of Jake, crying at Pastor Mitchel's bedside. "I don't think God is finished with him yet."

Ally smiled. "I hope you're right. From what I've heard, he's an amazing man."

"He is." Audrey set down her Coke. It was time to talk about what she came for. "I wanted to discuss something with you."

"Of course."

Audrey placed her hands on her belly. She could feel gentle stirrings inside. "Zoe's Place does adoptions, right?"

Ally nodded. "We do. We help match birth mothers with adoptive parents if that's what they choose."

Audrey took a deep breath, preparing to voice her most inner thoughts she'd been safely guarding in recent days. "I'd like to learn more about that."

"Sure. You don't need to be ashamed, Audrey. I see the guilt in your eyes. Giving your baby up for adoption is a selfless gift. You'd be giving your baby a chance to be raised by two loving parents whom you would choose. Parents who share your faith in the Lord."

"That's what I've been thinking about. I'm not a mom. I mean…I am, but…" She struggled to put her thoughts into words. "I want this baby to have a mom and a dad. I want the baby to have its own room, all decorated with cutesy baby stuff. I can't give the baby any of that." She gained confidence as she spoke her heart. The most difficult part would come next. "I'm not excited about the baby. I mean…I love it. I know God has a purpose for it otherwise he wouldn't have created it. But, I want someone else to be the mom." A tear trickled down her face. She felt like a horrible person for saying that about her precious little baby. Ally would probably kick her out of the office.

Ally stood up.

Audrey held her breath.

The woman sat on the loveseat next to Audrey and hugged her.

Audrey exhaled.

"It's brave of you to be honest. I can tell you've given this a lot of thought. Have you prayed about it?"

"Every day. I pray that God will make me excited about the baby the same way that my mom is excited."

Ally nodded, patiently listening.

Audrey grabbed a tissue from the box on the coffee table. "When I daydream about the baby growing up, I picture her or him in a different family. I see a mom kissing the kid goodbye before sending him onto the school bus. I see a mom and dad kneeling at the child's bed at night, saying prayers, and then tucking her in for the night." She looked into Ally's eyes, craving her genuine reaction. "It's like I forget that *I* am supposed to be the mom."

Ally's eyes remained compassionate. "What do you see when you look into your own future? Of course, no one truly knows our future, except for the Lord. But what do you envision?"

A smile came to Audrey's face. "I see myself going back to college. I want to be a social worker. Like you."

Ally's eyes welled with tears and creased at the corners with a tender smile. She put a hand over her heart.

"I want to run on the cross-country team again, and I'm hoping my friend Becca decides to go to Bethel with me. That would be so fun." A vision of Trevor came to mind. Someday, she saw herself marrying him. But she decided to keep that idea to herself. "I'm impatient for this pregnancy to be over, so I can resume my normal life. But then I remember. Oh yeah, I'm going to be a mom. I don't know if I can go to school or run on a team ever again. I'll have to keep working as a nanny. But then who will take care of my baby? My mom? She wants to be the type of grandma who spoils the grandkid, not be the one to raise and discipline it. I don't want to do that to my mom." Audrey covered her face with her hands. She took a moment to compose herself before continuing. "Somewhere there is a mom and a dad praying for a baby. Maybe this is their baby."

"I agree."

"What?" Audrey had been expecting Ally to tell her that God gave her the baby because she was capable of raising the child, especially with the support of her parents. That she should stop being so selfish.

"I agree. Maybe God has been preparing you all along for giving the baby up for adoption. Maybe that's his plan for this child. God will give you the desires of your heart. As long as you are praying about your decision, God will show you what to do."

"I really do love this baby." She wanted to make herself clear on that.

"I understand. It's because you love the baby so much, that you want the very best life for him or her."

"Yes." Audrey's heart seemed to burst with relief that Ally understood her point of view. "That's exactly it. But what if the baby doesn't get that? What if the baby feels that I rejected it some day?"

Ally shook her head. "If you feel God leading you to give the baby up for adoption, then you have to believe that his will is the best way. Entrust the child to his care. He loves this baby even more than you do. Keep praying throughout the child's entire life. Ask God to help him or her to understand your decision."

Audrey felt as though a weight had been lifted off her shoulders. "I'm pretty sure I want the baby to be adopted, but can I think about it for a while?"

"Of course. We, at Zoe's Place, will support whatever decision you make. I can pray with you now if you'd like."

Audrey folded her hands and bowed her head. She listened as Ally prayed a beautiful prayer of thanksgiving for the child in Audrey's womb. She begged God to show Audrey what decision to make about raising the baby or giving him or her up for adoption. Then Audrey prayed, first thanking God for Ally, and then echoing Ally's request to lead her to the right decision. "And please, God, show this baby that I love him or her. More importantly, help this baby to know your love. In Jesus name, Amen."

Audrey left Zoe's Place feeling light as a feather. She could sense the Holy Spirit walking with her. She was pretty sure that God had a plan for a different family to raise her baby. She could live with that decision, even though it would be difficult to say goodbye. But there was one person she feared would not be able to live with that decision.

Her mom.

The February sun beat down on the road, reflecting off the melting snow. At the first stop light, Audrey took her sunglasses from the front pocket of her purse. Her phone chimed, signaling a Facebook update.

She lifted her phone from her purse and saw the blue blinking light, affirming that there was a Facebook update. Possibly news about Pastor Mitchel's condition. Or a maybe just a food picture from a distant relative. Or another picture of her fifth grade teacher's sleeping cat. In a mere ten minutes, she would be home and could safely check her phone. She dropped it back in her purse just as the light turned green.

Facebook could wait. The biggest thing on her mind was telling her mom she was considering placing her baby for adoption. As she continued the short drive home, she considered her mom's possible reactions. There was a possibility that her mom would be happy that Audrey would be able to finish her education. Plus, her mom maybe felt too young to be a grandma. She didn't even have gray hair yet.

Audrey was fooling herself. Her mom was excited to be a grandmother. To her, the baby was something positive that came from the experience. She talked about how the baby was proof of how God works through evil situations, making good come from them. To be honest, her mom would be heartbroken about placing the baby for adoption. She would consider it another loss.

How could Audrey do that to her?

She pulled into the driveway, and shut off the engine, no longer feeling light as a feather as she had back at Zoe's Place. "God, please give me the words." She grabbed her purse and made her way into the house.

"Audrey!" Her mom smiled, her eyes lighting up like a Christmas tree. She dropped a mug into the dishwasher she'd been loading and drew Audrey into a hug. "Did you hear the good news?"

Audrey plopped herself down on a stool at the island. She didn't think she could take the wide swing of emotions she was going through today. "No. What is it?" She prayed it was good news about Pastor Mitchel.

"Maggie Mitchel sent out a post on Facebook. He's awake. Pastor Mitchel is awake." Her mom bounced on her toes, doing a little happy dance.

Audrey's heart filled with relief. She checked her own phone, wanting to see proof with her own eyes. There was a picture of Pastor Mitchel, still looking horrible, but his eyes were open. He mouth was tipped into a sideways line. Quite possibly, he was trying to smile. "Are you sure he's okay?"

Her mom settled down a bit and sat next to Audrey. "Did you read the post? He's been coming-to slowly. It doesn't happen all at once like in the movies. But he has said a few words, and he recognizes Maggie. He doesn't remember the accident, but his memory is intact otherwise."

"I'm so happy. Mom, I wasn't sure if he was going to live." It finally felt safe to openly acknowledge her concern to the contrary.

"We'll keep praying for his full recovery." Her mom jumped off the stool, too excited to stay seated. "I wonder if Victoria heard the news yet." She went to another room to call Trevor's mom, her best friend.

Audrey wondered if *her* best friend had heard the news. Under the Facebook post, there was a list of people who had reacted. There were many people from church, some names she didn't recognize, and finally…the name she was searching for. Trevor Hayes.

She would love to call Trevor so they could rejoice together over the phone. There was so much she would say. She'd tell him how bad Pastor Mitchel had looked in the hospital. How she had feared he wouldn't survive. She'd tell him about the unsettling conversation Mrs. Mitchel shared with her mom about their troubled marriage.

An ache filled her chest. A physical pain from missing her best friend. She needed him more now than ever before, but keeping her distance was imperative. Truly, she was keeping her distance for Trevor's sake, even if he didn't understand that. She was not girlfriend material at the moment. She may never be. Trevor would be better off finding someone else. A girl without all the baggage she now carried. She stood up and slid her phone into her back pocket.

It was lunch time so she opened the fridge and pulled out fixings for a lettuce salad. She wondered if Trevor had dated anyone this school year. The ache in her chest doubled. There had to be girls interested in him. He was undoubtedly good-looking. A gorgeous, modest, nice guy was a rare find. And Trevor possessed all of those qualities.

"Why do you have that dorky look on your face?" Darcy strode into the kitchen, catching Audrey by surprise.

"I don't have any look on my face. Aren't you supposed to be in school?"

"You look like you want to make out with that head of lettuce. And we have the day off. Teacher convention or something."

Audrey had to admit she'd probably been starry-eyed when thoughts of Trevor had sashayed through her mind. "Whatever." She ripped pieces of lettuce from the bunch, piling them onto a plate. She sprinkled shredded cheddar on the greens and drizzled ranch dressing on top. "Have you heard from Trevor lately?"

"Ha!" Darcy laughed. "I knew you had a dreamy look in your eyes." She got a plate of her own and began shredding lettuce onto it.

Audrey shrugged, not denying it. "So? Have you heard from him?"

"No. Nothing other than an occasional Instagram post."

Audrey hadn't noticed him on Instagram lately, although she hadn't been checking it much with everything else on her mind. She sat on a stool and stabbed a fork into her salad. While she chewed, she opened Instagram on her phone and viewed Trevor's profile. There was a photo of a tree covered in ice crystals, the sun shining through it. Audrey giggled. Since when did Trevor become a nature photographer?

The next picture made Audrey's stomach turn. "Who's that?" She angled the phone for Darcy to see the selfie of Trevor and a college-age girl sporting matching U of M hats at a Gopher basketball game.

"Oh, that's Esme. Some girl Trevor is friends with. I don't think it's a big deal. Her Facebook profile says she's in a relationship. There are lots of pictures of her with a guy named Henri." Darcy patted Audrey's back. "I creeped on her Facebook page and Instagram to be sure. Her hometown is in Iowa. She's an art history major. She's five foot, eleven inches tall and plays intramural basketball. She has a cat named Cupcake, and she voted for Donald Trump."

"Thank you for the extensive biography." She'd expect nothing less from Darcy. But Audrey still wasn't convinced there wasn't something more going on. She breathed a sigh of relief nonetheless. "If you say so."

"I warned you that other girls would be crushing on him."

"I know."

"He only has eyes for you." Darcy smiled.

"Yeah, well, he hasn't seen me like this." Audrey patted her belly, puffing out her cheeks.

Darcy burst out in laughter. "All the more to love."

Audrey laughed too. Something she hadn't done in far too long. She and Darcy ate their salads, rinsed their dishes and put them in the dishwasher. "Darcy, are you excited about the baby?"

"Of course. I love babies. I can't wait to be an aunty."

Audrey had been hoping Darcy would say something along the lines of having a baby around would be a little weird, but that somehow they'd get used to it. However, she hadn't sensed the least bit of trepidation from her sister.

But Darcy's life wasn't going to get turned upside down by becoming an aunty. She would just get a cute baby to play with and cuddle.

Darcy crossed her arms and narrowed her eyes. "Are you excited to be a mommy?"

She hesitated. "Sure." Her brief silence had said it all.

"That's good because this baby is coming in a few months."

Audrey looked around the corner, making sure her mom wasn't in ear shot. "What if I'm not ready to be a mother?"

"I'm sure you're not. But that's not the point. This baby is coming whether you're ready or not." Darcy cupped her hands around her mouth and in a baby voice said, "Ready or not, here I come." She laughed at her own joke.

"I'm thinking about placing the baby for adoption."

Darcy's jaw dropped.

"I'm still praying about it. Don't tell Mom and Dad yet."

Darcy rubbed her forehead. "Why do you always do this to me? I hate keeping secrets."

"This is serious, Darcy. Don't tell anyone. I wanted to run it by you before I bring it up to Mom. I know she'll be sad. She'll probably try to talk me out of it."

Darcy nodded. "She's been buying tons of baby stuff. She ordered a crib on Amazon this morning."

Audrey's heart dropped. "I don't want to disappoint her again." She toyed with her running watch. "I'll let her enjoy the good news about Pastor Mitchel while I pray about this decision."

Darcy crossed her arms. "I have to admit that Mom isn't the only one who will be sad." She turned her lips into an exaggerated frown. "I was super excited about being an aunty. But I get it." Darcy made a zipping motion across her mouth. "I won't tell anyone. Not even Trevor. Cross my heart."

Chapter Twenty-One

~

Trevor opened the door to the Vic's Pizza Shoppe on campus at the U of M. The wooden booths, red and white striped aprons of the servers, and the juke box stationed in the corner gave the impression of stepping back a few decades in time. From the outside, the place looked like a dive with a faded green awning perched over a door with a little bell that jingled every time a customer arrived. That this restaurant hadn't changed from its original form was exactly what brought in customers. The food was delicious, and the service was just as friendly as it had been back when Vic himself was baking the pizzas.

Trevor spotted Jake Preston, wearing a black beanie over his short, dark hair, at a table by the front window. "What did I tell you? Isn't this place great?" Trevor shed his coat and slid into the seat opposite from Jake. He breathed in the aroma of baking pizza dough.

Jake lifted a plastic drinking glass filled with ice water. "Very retro."

"Thanks for meeting me for lunch. So you have the day off of school?"

Jake shrugged. "Yeah. Teachers have a convention or something." The bell jingled and a trio of guys walked in with back packs slung over their shoulders. "It's pretty cool being on campus. College sure beats high school."

Trevor opened his own menu, although he already knew what he wanted. "Do you know where you're going to college?"

Jake took the black beanie off his head and flung it onto the booth next to him. "I haven't made a decision yet. My dad wants me to follow in his footsteps and become a lawyer, but I have no interest in that."

"You've had recruits interested in you. Are you thinking about playing college football?"

"Yes. The Gopher coach has been practically harassing me to play here at the U of M."

"That's great, bro! You can get a big fat scholarship, and it's only a short drive home on the weekends to get laundry done and eat a home cooked meal. You can't pass that up. I'll show you the ropes around this campus."

Jake's eyes lit up in excitement but soon dimmed. "It's ideal, right?"

Trevor set his menu down and leaned in, letting Jake know he had his full attention.

A silver-haired woman approached the table, a pad of paper and pen in hand. "What can I get for you boys?" She looked at them over a pair of colorful reading glasses.

"Can you give us a minute?" Trevor tapped the menu. "Too many good choices."

The kind, older woman nodded, poking her pen into a bun secured at the base of her neck. "Take all the time you need, honey."

Trevor turned his attention back to Jake. "So you said playing at the U is ideal. I heard a "but" coming on."

"But… I have no desire to be a lawyer. I don't want to be anything like my dad."

Trevor knew that Jake's dad had disappointed him on countless occasions. His work often trumped his fatherly obligations, leaving Jake to feel less than important. Like parent night for Hastings High School football. His parents didn't show up, so when Jake's name was called, he found Pastor Mitchel in the bleachers and delivered the yellow carnation to him. And that was just one example. "I get it. But you don't have to be a lawyer. You can major in whatever you want."

"Yeah. My dad's really pushing me to go to the U because that's where he got his bachelor's degree. I guess I wanna go somewhere else just for spite." Jake took a long pull of his water. "Maybe Baylor."

"Baylor is cool. Texas, huh?"

"Maybe."

The waitress returned to their table, and Trevor ordered hot wings and a large sausage pizza with extra cheese. She scurried off to the kitchen. "Did you hear that Pastor Mitchel came out of the coma? Mrs. Mitchel posted on Facebook this morning."

"Yeah, I heard. Becca texted me. It's good news. The dude had me worried. Senior year is supposed to be a blast, but I've been stressing big time. First there was the whole Audrey-thing…that happened at *my* house. And then Pastor Mitchel almost kicks the bucket. Crazy."

"You can say that again." Something Jake said stuck in Trevor's mind. "Hey, Jake, you know it wasn't your fault that happened to Audrey."

Jake looked off into the distance, his light brown eyes pensive. "It never would've happened if I hadn't had that party. So yeah. It kinda *was* my fault."

"She doesn't blame you."

"Well, I wish I could find the guy who did it. It's creepy that someone like that was in my house and did that to my friend. Audrey is, like, the sweetest person ever." Jake gritted his teeth. "I wanna pound the guy."

"I know the feeling." Trevor had to work to stay calm whenever he thought about coming face to face with Audrey's attacker. He took a couple deep breaths. "Jake, I'm starting to doubt we'll actually catch the guy. Even if we figure out who did it, proving he raped her would be next to impossible."

"Are you saying we should just give up?"

Trevor ran his fingers through his hair. "I don't want to let Audrey down." There didn't seem to be any other option. Then an invisible lightbulb dinged above his head. "Your dad is a lawyer. Have you asked him about any of this?" Why hadn't he thought of this earlier?

Jake laughed humorlessly. "No. He turns red in the face every time the subject comes up. So I avoid the topic. I was hoping we could figure this thing out without his help."

The waitress delivered wings to the table. "Roberto made these extra hot for you. My eyes are watering just from carrying them to your table." She dabbed her eyes on the sleeve of her shirt. "Enjoy!"

Jake picked up a wing dripping with sauce and sunk his teeth into it. "It's not that hot." He licked sauce from his fingers.

Trevor sat back, waiting for the heat to hit. It wouldn't be much longer. He waved the waitress back to the table just as Jake's face turned bright red and his upper lip began to sweat. "Can you bring a glass of milk, please?"

The woman nudged Jake's shoulder. "I warned you." She disappeared into the kitchen for just a minute before bringing back a tall glass of milk.

Jake chugged the milk. "Is this your idea of hazing? I'm not officially a freshman here yet."

Trevor laughed. "I call it a rite of passage. By the way, do not rub your eyes. I learned that the hard way."

Jake coughed a few times; his eyes were red and watering. "So if I can survive the hot wings at Vic's, then I suppose I can survive talking to my old man."

"That's very insightful." Trevor smothered a wing in ranch dressing before taking a bite. "It wouldn't hurt to run it by him before giving up altogether."

"I'll do it for Audrey…and Pastor Mitchel."

"What does this have to do with Pastor Mitchel?"

"Before his accident, he was always telling me to try to find common ground with my dad. A way to connect with him. You know? My dad isn't into football or anything I'm interested in. I don't even know how to begin asking him about his job. But this could be a way for us to relate to each other."

"Cool. You'll do Pastor Mitchel proud."

Chapter Twenty-Two

AUDREY PULLED A T-SHIRT OVER HER HEAD AND stretched it over her rounded belly. Then she put on a pair of shorts and stood before her full-length mirror, examining her reflection. From the back she could almost pass for any normal eighteen-year-old girl. But from the side, she looked like an eighteen-year-old girl who had swallowed a beach ball. Now eight months into the pregnancy, she didn't see how her body could expand any more than it already had. And she still had a couple weeks to go.

The changes that had warped her body over the past few months had been terrifying. The skin over her abdomen was stretched so thin that it was taut, she suffered random nose bleeds, and constipation and heartburn plagued her day and night. There were days she felt angry and so depressed that her mom had to coerce her out of bed. But once in a while, she would have a day where she felt hopeful and even mesmerized at the idea of a baby growing inside of her. Today was one of those days.

The house was quiet as she padded downstairs. Her dad had left for work a few minutes earlier, and her mom was out buying flowers with Trevor's mom at the local nursery. She plopped down on the chair in the entryway to put on her running shoes. Reaching around her belly to tie them was getting more difficult each day. Running in general was becoming more difficult each day. Her body felt heavy now, and the baby bounced on her bladder with each step. In spite of the discomfort, she was determined to run up until the day she delivered. Without running, she thought she might lose herself entirely. A moan escaped her lips as she pushed herself to a standing position and waddled out the door.

Warm May sunshine kissed her cheeks. She breathed in the scent of freshly cut grass. Closing her eyes momentarily, she relished the newness of spring. It had been a long, cold winter and this spring in particular was a welcome sight.

She set her Garmin watch, which reminded her how slow she was these days, and headed out. Passing by Trevor's house, she said a prayer for him. It had been nearly five months since they'd talked up in her bedroom. He had honored her wish and hadn't tried to contact her, but a perpetual ache in her heart didn't allow one day's passing without her thinking of him.

She prayed for him whenever he came to mind. She prayed that he was getting along fine without her, and she prayed that if God wanted them to be together one day that He would give each of them patience for when the time was right. She also boldly prayed that if it wasn't in His plan for them to be together that she would be able to let him go.

Her talks with Pastor Mitchel had been helpful. He'd resumed calling her every Sunday night since discharging from the hospital. Only Pastor Mitchel would be thinking of others while recovering from a near death experience. He prayed with her and encouraged her that God had a plan in all of this. As well as a plan for him and Mrs. Mitchel.

The first few minutes of the run felt awkward as Audrey adjusted her gait to accommodate her growing body, but soon her legs found a natural rhythm as she ran through the neighborhood she had run through too many times to count. She had the sidewalks memorized, down to each crack. She could accurately anticipate the bark of each dog behind the fences. Her feet knew the route without her having to tell them where to go. Not a day had gone by without her running, with the exception of Sundays. Running was the one consistency in her life.

She loved being in the sunshine and fresh air, getting the exercise her body craved. But mostly she loved that running gave her time to think and to pray with no interruptions. And she'd had a lot of thinking to do lately. There were important decisions to be made and time was running out. She needed to decide what to do once the baby was born. She pondered the options.

The first option was that after giving birth, she and the baby would continue living with her parents. Her mom volunteered to watch the baby while Audrey worked. Audrey would do her best to save up money in hopes that one day she would be able to move out and be self-sufficient in raising the child. In addition, she would commute to school. But that was asking a lot of her mother.

Audrey leaned toward option number two. Adoption. This would allow Audrey not only to return to school but also to live on campus. Her mom and dad would be able to enjoy being empty nesters once Darcy would graduate. The baby would have mature, financially stable parents. It seemed to be the obvious choice, except for one thing. It would break her mom's heart.

Not that placing her baby for adoption would be easy for Audrey either. The idea of handing over her baby to strangers was pretty scary, but not as much if Audrey was able to choose the family herself. Ally said that waiting couples put together an autobiography in scrapbook fashion. The scrapbook page would give Audrey a good picture of the home her baby would be raised in. Audrey would even get to meet the couple before the baby was born, so they really wouldn't be strangers.

Even so, it would be difficult for Audrey to say goodbye to her child. What if, after the baby was born, she would fall in love with him or her—only to never see her baby again? She put a hand on her belly and was surprised at the gut wrenching tug on her heart. This baby was a part of her, after all. She couldn't just give it away.

There was no good option.

Overwhelmed by the weight of her decision, Audrey stopped dead in her tracks. Her paralyzing emotions refused to let her body take another step. A young boy, who had been approaching on his bicycle, swerved onto the grass to avoid hitting her. "Hey, be careful, lady!"

She stood, unmoved.

Above her, a breeze rustled the leaves on a tree branch extending over the sidewalk. She looked up. Through the leaves, she saw a robin perched on the side of her nest. Audrey watched as the bird rose into the air and circled above her before landing on a nearby fence post.

If only I could be a bird, Audrey thought, *without a care in the world*. It reminded her of a Bible passage that talked about how God takes care of even the smallest sparrow. The point was that as God's children, we shouldn't worry. If He takes care of the birds, of course He will take care of His children. Something like that.

Staring into the bright blue sky she begged aloud, "God, show me what to do. Make your plan clear. I promise to be obedient, just show me what to do." She stood still, her prayer resonating in the spring air.

She sucked in a deep breath and exhaled slowly. Amazingly, as the air seeped from her lungs, a peace washed over her and settled her racing heart. She felt her shoulders rise as the load of her burdens miraculously lifted. She knew that God had taken the burden from her, and in time He would reveal His plan. She just needed to trust Him and His timing.

Feeling renewed, she began to move her feet again. For the first time since that awful night last fall, Audrey felt free. Free as a robin soaring through the sky. She experienced freedom from the guilt that had rested so heavily on her conscience, freedom from the responsibility of deciding how to handle her pregnancy, and freedom from the fear of her unknown future. It was all erased in a matter of seconds.

It was what Audrey called a "God moment." It was the kind of moment she could never put into words because no words could do it justice. It was a moment where God spoke clearly and unmistakably to her heart. She still didn't have the answer to her dilemma, but she knew that God did.

Her footsteps gradually quickened and soon she was bounding down the sidewalk, a smile spreading across her face. The vibrant colors of the tulips bordering the sidewalk seemed brighter than ever before, and the scent of lilacs had never seemed so lovely. For that moment, all seemed right with the world, all because God was in control.

She ran two more miles, enjoying the newness of spring and basking in the Lord's palpable presence. With just a couple of blocks to go, a reference to a Bible verse came to mind: 2 Corinthians 12:9. Only she couldn't remember the words. All she remembered was learning it at church camp years ago and feeling power in the words like she'd never experienced from the Bible before. It was her first God moment. She hadn't experienced that same power since, until today.

What were the words to that verse? She'd never been good with memorizing scripture. Never retained them much more than a week. With the exception of the verse Pastor Mitchel had pounded into her head.

She raced home and ran up to her bedroom, out of breath, her heart pounding. Paging through her Bible, she finally found 2 Corinthians. Her anxious eyes scanned the pages until they fell on chapter twelve, verse nine. The words were highlighted in red, showing that they were words spoken by Jesus. It read, "My grace is sufficient for you, for my power is made perfect in weakness."

Chills ran down her arms. He wanted her to be reminded of the verse again today, didn't He?

His grace was sufficient.

That was where the peace had come from that she experienced standing under that tree. No matter how bad her mistakes, God would extend His grace to her, His forgiveness and His mercy. And at her weakest moment, when the weight of her problems became too much to bear, His power overcame her weakness.

In His power, she was able to move one foot in front of the other and continue her run. Not just finish her run, but run with her head held high and joy in her heart. In the same way, God would empower her to walk through this difficult time in her life.

Audrey closed her eyes and spoke to the Lord. "Thank you for your grace. Thank you for taking care of me." She put her hand on her belly. "Thank you for taking care of this little one. I give this baby to You, Lord. I will do whatever you lead me to do for this child. You know what is best for her ... or him. If you want me to be a mom, I will. And I will love this baby with all my heart. But if you have another family chosen for her ... or him, please help me to find them. And please give me the strength to let my baby go."

The infant squirmed under Audrey's hand. She opened her eyes to see something that could've possibly been a miniature foot glide across her abdomen. She giggled, amazed by the truth that a little person, alive and well, was being formed inside of her. She rubbed her belly, where she guessed the baby's back to be. And speaking straight from her heart, she quietly said, "I love you, baby."

It was true. She did love this baby. She loved the baby so much that she was at peace with whatever God would want her to do. She had enough love to care for her child and to be the mother God would equip her to be. But if led in a different direction, she also had enough love to give the child to another loving home.

God promised to take care of the littlest sparrow. Likewise, He would take care of Audrey, and He would take care of her baby.

Audrey showered and lay down on her bed, sinking into the downy softness. Running took a lot more out of her these days.

A nap would be nice, but her mind was wide awake. She brought Facebook up on her phone and scrolled through the entries. There were food pictures, snapshots of pets, vacation photos, and then a post that caught her attention. A middle-aged woman from church was posing with her elderly grandmother in a botanical garden. The caption read, *Early Mother's Day celebration.*

This Sunday would be Mother's Day. It was a tradition for Audrey and her sister to bring their mom breakfast in bed. Each year, they placed a corsage on the breakfast tray that their mom would wear the rest of the day. Something to make her mom feel special. Something to show everyone she came in contact with that day that she was someone special. That she was loved.

In that moment, a realization dawned. Mother's Day was for her mom. It wasn't for her. She wasn't going to be a mom.

She'd felt all along that her baby belonged to someone else. Yes, she would always be the birth mother. She'd always have that connection to the child, and nothing could change that. But someone else would raise the child. Like Ally had said, God had been preparing her to place the baby for adoption. Now she recognized that beyond a shadow of a doubt. It was time to let her mom know.

Audrey's mom was seated at the table, paging through her Bible. "Hi, Mom."

Engrossed in her study, her mom didn't answer. That's okay. It allowed Audrey a few more minutes to prepare how to break the news.

Her stomach growled. She rummaged through the refrigerator and then the cabinets. It was difficult to make any decision with her mind preoccupied by her anticipated conversation with her mom.

Empty-handed, she came over to the table and sat down next to her mother.

Her mom looked at her. "Couldn't find anything good?"

"Actually, everything looks good. I need a minute to decide." Audrey put her feet up on a chair and leaned back, lengthening her torso to make more room to breathe.

"I'll heat up a cinnamon roll for you." Her mom rose from her chair. She placed the roll on a pretty plate warmed it in the microwave. "Would you like butter?"

"Yes, please."

Soon the aroma of cinnamon and warm butter filled Audrey's senses. Her mom placed the roll in front of Audrey, along with a tall glass of milk. "I'm happy to see you've got your appetite back. I have to admit I was worried about you not getting enough nutrients for a while."

"It's back with a vengeance." Audrey took a bite and licked gooey cinnamon off her fingers.

Audrey had always loved when her mom made homemade rolls. As a little girl, Audrey would sit at the counter watching her mother knead the dough. Her mom would break off a piece of it so Audrey could mold it like Play-dough.

Her mom folded her Bible closed, tucking her worksheets neatly between the pages and set it aside. "It won't be long before the baby will be here."

"Funny you should mention it." Audrey sighed, picking at crumbs on her plate. "I've been thinking about that." She looked up from her plate and out the window facing the pond. "I don't feel ready."

"You don't feel ready for the baby to come? There is a lot to do. We could go out and do some shopping today. We need an infant bathtub and baby shampoo—"

"That's not what I mean." She looked her mom in the eye. She had to just hurry up and say it before she'd chicken out. "I mean…I don't feel ready to be a mom."

"What are you trying to say?" Her mom's fingers were trembling.

"I've decided to place the baby for adoption. I've prayed about it a lot."

Her mom didn't say anything, but the expression on her face told Audrey that she was deeply saddened. She placed her hand on Audrey's belly and closed her eyes. Maybe she was praying for her grandchild. Or maybe she was memorizing the feel of the little kicks.

"Mom, I've always wanted to be a mother … and I still do. But not now." She wanted her mom's approval so badly. "Is that selfish of me?"

Her mom withdrew her hand from Audrey's belly. She touched a strand of Audrey's hair, still damp from her shower. "No. It's not selfish."

Audrey breathed a sigh of relief. "You have no idea how much I needed to hear you say that. I mean, I love this baby. But keeping it just doesn't feel right. I want my baby to have a good life with a mom and a dad. I know we have a good home, but I want more for my baby. Know what I mean?"

"Yes. I'm sad, but I understand." A tear slipped down her face.

"I've already talked to Ally at Zoe's Place about adoption. She'll walk me through every step."

Her mom hugged her. "Honey, are you sure this is what God wants?"

Audrey didn't have to hesitate. "I'm sure."

Chapter Twenty-Three

THE HOPE CHURCH YOUTH GROUP GATHERED AROUND
the television in Pastor Mitchel's living room. Audrey collapsed into
a recliner and elevated her feet. The other kids occupied the couch
and loveseat, and sprawled out on the floor. Although the Mitchel's
home was modest in size, it was just big enough to accommodate
the group who had gathered to congratulate the graduates. Pastor
Mitchel slid a DVD into the machine, and the boisterous crowd
immediately hushed.

A baby picture of Jake filled the screen, sending oohs and aahs
bouncing around the room. Next was a picture of Jake as a toddler,
perched on Santa's knee. Elementary and middle school pictures followed. Jake wasn't one to embarrass easily, but his face was flushed
bright red. Finally, more recent photos of Jake, taken during youth
group events, flashed on the screen—wakeboarding, flaunting a

walleye he'd caught in the boundary waters, and playing broom ball on the Chapman's frozen pond.

Similar slideshows of Becca and Gavin followed, set to the tunes of their favorite songs. It wasn't until a sappy song called God Gave Me You by Dave Barnes played that the viewers were reduced to tears. Accompanying the music were group photos of the kids throughout their years at Hope Church. Trevor's face appeared on several images, melting Audrey's insides to mush.

Audrey looked around the room, capturing the reactions of her friends. Becca had her head resting on Jake's shoulder, her face stained with tears. In contrast, Gavin and Darcy had dry eyes and smiles on their faces.

But it was Pastor Mitchel's response that struck Audrey the most. Pride emanated from his eyes, almost as if the kids were his own. And in a way, Audrey supposed, they were. He had played a big part in raising the youth group kids. This year had been especially important. Pastor Mitchel's accident had profoundly impacted the teens and had taught them that there were more important things in life than partying.

When the DVD was finished, Pastor Mitchel said special words he had prepared about each of the graduates as he had done the previous year when Audrey had graduated. Then he presented each of them a unique gift.

Becca received a compass. Pastor Mitchel described Becca as a leader, saying that a compass symbolically would guide her in the right direction. Gavin was given a rock, symbolizing that he stood firm in his faith. And Jake was presented a football with everyone's signature and favorite Bible verse inscribed on it.

The night brought back memories for Audrey of the gathering around the campfire to celebrate her high school graduation, when she was so eager to start a new chapter of her life. The baby rolled in her belly, reminding her of all that had happened since that night.

With the DVD and the gift presentation finished, people dispersed throughout the house, some going back to the kitchen for snacks and some retreating to the basement for a game of ping pong. Audrey heaved herself out of the recliner and headed straight for the bathroom. Her bladder seemed to be the size of a pea these days.

Making her way down the hallway, she admired the framed photographs hanging on the walls. Audrey paused to look at a picture taken on the Mitchels' wedding day. Mrs. Mitchel was radiant in her white gown, and Pastor Mitchel looked equally handsome. There were more pictures of people Audrey didn't recognize, probably family. At the end of the line of pictures hung an aged-looking photo of a beautiful woman in striking resemblance to Mrs. Mitchel. The woman's eyes were gentle and kind. Audrey felt oddly comforted just looking at the woman's photo.

"She's my mother," Audrey heard a voice say behind her.

Looking over her shoulder, she saw Mrs. Mitchel. "She's beautiful. She looks just like you."

"Thank you. This picture was taken when she was about my age."

"I've never met your mother."

"She passed away several years ago."

"I'm sorry. I didn't know." Audrey couldn't imagine life without her own mother. "Do you still miss her?"

Mrs. Mitchel crossed her arms over her chest and leaned against the wall. "I miss her with every fiber of my body."

"I guess that was a stupid question." Audrey didn't know what to say in these situations. She'd never lost anyone close to her.

"No, it wasn't." Mrs. Mitchel had a pensive look in her eyes. "They say time heals all wounds, but I would disagree."

Audrey felt bad for making Mrs. Mitchel sad, but she seemed to like talking about her mother. "Is your father still living?"

Mrs. Mitchel shrugged. "I never met him. My mom raised me all on her own."

"Wow, she must have been amazing." Audrey put her hand on her belly, thinking of the choice she had made to give her baby up for adoption in order for her child to have a two-parent family. Mrs. Mitchel, although raised by a single parent, turned out perfectly. Second thoughts crept into Audrey's mind about the adoption plans, but she immediately dismissed them, knowing that she had prayerfully made the right decision.

Pastor Mitchel came from the kitchen with a handful of pretzels. He leaned against the wall next to his wife and popped a pretzel into his mouth. He read the serious expressions on their faces. "Am I interrupting something?"

Audrey pointed to the picture of Mrs. Mitchel's mother. "I was just looking at the photographs."

"Ah." Pastor Mitchel nodded in understanding. He nudged his wife's elbow. "Did you give Audrey her gift yet?"

Mrs. Mitchel shook her head. "Not yet. I'll go get it."

Although touched by the idea of a gift, Audrey thought about her bursting bladder. She looked at the bathroom door longingly but decided she could wait a couple more minutes.

Mrs. Mitchel opened the door to their guest room and removed a package about the size of a shoe box from a drawer. It was covered in lavender paper with a delicate floral pattern; a tag dangled from the lid by a matching satin ribbon. What caught Audrey's eye the most was not the box, but the room from which it was retrieved.

Once simply decorated with neutral tones and housing only a bed, a dresser and a nightstand, the room was now transformed into a nursery complete with a crib and rocking chair. Pale yellow walls complemented the Winnie the Pooh theme covering the crib sheet, a baby quilt draped over the rocking chair, and the curtains framing the corner window. Audrey had always wondered if the Mitchels would ever have kids. Maybe there was something she didn't know.

Mrs. Mitchel must have seen Audrey's bewilderment at the room. "Do you like the nursery?"

"Yeah, it's adorable."

"Come on in and look around."

Audrey stepped into the cozy room, admiring the sweet touches that had been placed around the room. A framed photo of Pastor and Mrs. Mitchel sat on the dresser next to a baby book picturing the lovable red-shirted bear on the cover. No detail had been overlooked. Baby hangers hung in the closet. A basket of diapers, wipes, and ointment sat on the changing table next to a second basket filled with shampoo, lotion, washcloths, and hooded towels.

Audrey sat in the rocking chair. Closing her eyes momentarily, she imagined rocking her own baby in such a cozy room. "It's so cute. Are you guys expecting?"

"No, no. We decorated the room last fall. I don't know if Pastor Mitchel ever mentioned it to you, but I had a miscarriage."

Audrey gulped. She hadn't even known that Mrs. Mitchel had ever been pregnant. Overcome by a strange feeling of guilt, she folded her hands across her abdomen, as if hiding her pregnancy. "I'm so sorry."

Melancholy colored her features, yet Mrs. Mitchel smiled. "Thank you."

"So are you guys trying again? To have a baby?"

Mrs. Mitchel ran her hand along the rail of the crib and then straightened out a wrinkle in the sheet. "We're praying about it." Just then she remembered the gift that she had tucked under her arm. "Oh, this is for you."

Audrey took the box and read the tag. *Dear Audrey, Fill this box with treasures of your precious little one. May you experience blessings as rich as the blessings you are providing this dear child of God. Love, Pastor Mitchel and Mrs. Mitchel*

Tears sprang to Audrey's eyes. It was the perfect gift. She could fill it with items such as hospital photos, footprints, and the baby's first pacifier. The Mitchels knew exactly how precious these items would become. Audrey wondered if they had a similar box of their own to commemorate the baby they had lost. "Wow. Thank you so much." Audrey sniffed, overcome with emotion. "So you guys have had a pretty tough year too, huh?"

Pastor Mitchel put his arm around his wife's shoulders, giving her a light squeeze. "More than you know."

The Mitchels had been through so much with a miscarriage and a horrible car accident that easily could have taken Pastor Mitchel's life. "How do you stay so strong?"

Mrs. Mitchel's eyes lit up. "By the grace of God. It wasn't easy. A struggle with infertility and then a miscarriage challenged our marriage. We each dealt with the grief differently."

Pastor Mitchel kissed Mrs. Mitchel's cheek. "But God was the glue that held us together. In fact, our marriage is stronger now than ever before."

"My grace is sufficient for you, for my power is made perfect in weakness." Audrey quoted the verse God had placed on her heart recently. "I think God has been teaching me about grace." She said the word to herself, letting the meaning percolate in her mind. *Grace.* Through the events of the last year, she had experienced God's grace in so many ways. "You know, if I have a girl, I'm going to name her Grace."

Mrs. Mitchel clutched her hand to her chest. She looked as if she might fall over. Grace was a pretty name by anyone's standards, but Mrs. Mitchel's reaction was greatly exaggerated. By the look in Pastor Mitchel's eyes, he seemed to be experiencing a similar reaction. Obviously, the name held some sort of significance for them.

"What? Was that your baby's name?"

"No." Mrs. Mitchel self-consciously dropped her hand from her chest and regained composure. "Grace is my mother's name."

Pastor Mitchel kissed his wife on the forehead. "It's the perfect name."

"If you guys want to use that name for your kid someday, I'll find something else. Really, I don't mind."

The pair shook their heads dramatically, insisting that wouldn't be necessary.

Audrey hoisted herself up from the rocking chair, knowing she needed to get to the bathroom urgently now. "Suit yourselves." She hugged first Mrs. Mitchel and then Pastor Mitchel. "Thanks for the gift, you guys. I'll treasure it always."

Chapter Twenty-Four

FIREFLIES FLICKERED IN THE TALL GRASSES BORDERING the pond. Audrey watched them from her window, contemplating catching a few in a jar like she had done as a little girl. But that would just be procrastinating. She needed to look through the album of adoptive family profiles. It was a daunting task, but the baby could come any day. Time was running out.

She sat on her bed and carefully lifted the cover of the album. She turned the pages slowly, absorbing every detail on each page. Each family was uniquely special and so deserving of a child. There were couples turning to adoption after years of unsuccessful fertility treatment. Others had biological children and now wanted to share their loving home with a child in need of a family. Some couples were older and settled while others were young and adventurous.

How would she ever choose? She lifted her eyes from the book and gazed heavenward. *God, show me who to choose. Make it clear; I don't want to make the wrong choice. Show me your will.*

She flipped several pages ahead, skimming through the various profiles. Suddenly, her heart skipped a beat. She turned back a page, not believing her eyes. Scrolled across the top of the page was *Proverbs 3:5-6. Trust in the Lord with all your heart and lean not on your own understanding; in all your ways acknowledge him, and he will make your paths straight.* The verse Pastor Mitchel had instilled in her heart. Her breath caught in her throat as she examined the pictures. The couple's eyes shone with love. A love that also emanated from the words that beautifully spilled from their hearts onto the page. They possessed the qualities she had been looking for—a dedicated marriage and an unmistakable love for Jesus. This was the couple who would raise her child.

With trembling hands and a heart surging with joy, she picked up her phone and made possibly the most important call of her life.

"Zoe's Place. Ally speaking; may I help you?"

Audrey froze, too consumed with emotion to speak.

Ally spoke again, more impatiently this time. "Hello? Is anybody there?"

"Yes. I'm here. This is Audrey Chapman." She strained to speak, her words a faint whisper.

"Hi, Audrey. How are you?" Her voice was gentle again and now rang with compassion. She knew Audrey well, as she had mentored her through the pregnancy and now guided her through the adoption process.

Audrey took a deep breath before speaking the next sentence. "I've made my decision."

"That's wonderful. Would you like to come to the office so we could talk about it?"

Audrey inhaled deeply, and let the air out slowly. "Yes. I'm ready."

They made plans for Audrey to come to the adoption agency first thing in the morning. Audrey would reveal the family she had chosen for her child, and they would make plans for her to meet with the couple as soon as possible.

Audrey ended the call and released a sigh as she collapsed onto her down comforter, her heart filling with peace. She knew she was doing the right thing. God already had a home prepared for her baby.

Chapter Twenty-Five

TREVOR TURNED UP THE VOLUME ON HIS CAR STEREO, singing along to the music. He'd just completed his last final exam of his sophomore year and was ready to celebrate. With his bags packed for a long weekend at home, he pulled out of the driveway of the house he shared with his college buddies. Donning a Twins baseball cap and a Joe Mauer jersey, he commenced the drive home where he would pick up Lucas before heading to Target Field. He checked his wallet for the tickets—for at least the third time. Yep. Still there. The seats were great and the weather was perfect for outdoor baseball.

As he neared his parent's house, the familiar melancholy overcame him. Whenever he came home, he couldn't escape the painful reminders that Audrey was no longer a part of his life. Since Christmas, he'd stayed away from home as much as possible, keeping in touch with his family mainly by phone calls and texting. His mom gave him frequent updates on Audrey. She was still living at home, working as a nanny, and nearing the end of her pregnancy.

His mom said she was giving her baby up for adoption and had recently chosen the adopting couple. Trevor had mixed emotions about that. He was happy that Audrey was able to make such a brave decision. Knowing Audrey and her tender heart, it must be hard for her to relinquish her child. She probably decided the baby would be better off in a home with a mom and a dad. But Trevor also felt a twinge of sadness that he wouldn't get to know Audrey's baby. Maybe it would be a strong-willed, curly-haired pixie like Audrey. Trevor grinned. That would be too cute.

Audrey's car was parked in the Chapman's driveway; she must be home. He wanted so badly to knock on the door and give her a big hug. He bet that she probably needed one right now as her due date neared. But with respect to her wishes, he resisted.

"Well look what the cat dragged in." Lucas welcomed Trevor home with a firm slap on his back.

Trevor set down his laundry basket towering with dirty clothes on the front entry rug. Then he shrugged off the bag draped over his shoulder. Lucas was dressed in a pair of red gym shorts and an old T-shirt with the sleeves ripped off. Anxious about the time, Trevor checked his watch. "Dude, get dressed. The game starts in less than two hours."

"Relax. I was just on my way up to shower." Lucas tipped off Trevor's hat as he breezed past him.

"You don't have time to shower." Lucas was already upstairs, turning on the faucet. Left with no choice other than to take his brother's advice and relax, Trevor carried the laundry basket into the laundry room and loaded the washer. As the machine filled, Trevor hoped Lucas was getting doused with a blast of cold water. Then maybe he would get out of the shower sooner.

Ten minutes later, Lucas showed up looking more like he was going to a baseball game and less like he had just finished playing a game of pick-up basketball. He slipped on his shoes and grabbed his keys off of a hook next to the front door. "Whatchya waitin' for?"

Trevor had to admit that Lucas had gotten ready in record time, so he let his irritation slip away. Stepping outside, he put on his sunglasses. The sun was bright with just a few lazy clouds hovering in the light blue sky. Movement next door caught his attention, and Trevor looked over to see Audrey. She was locking her front door, a large bag slung over her shoulder as if she might be going away for the weekend.

Trevor's heart rate quickened at the sight of her. All the months apart hadn't dampened his feelings for her one bit. He was deeply in love with her, and knew he always would be, no matter what the future held. *I'm gonna marry her one day.*

When she turned from the door, Trevor was shocked at the size of her belly. If he hadn't known better, he'd have thought she was carrying twins.

Lucas nudged Trevor with his elbow, and then he called out to her, "Hey, Audrey."

She looked up then, her eyes instantly locking with Trevor's. It didn't matter that she was pregnant; she still made him weak in the knees.

Looking just as shocked to see him, her feet stuttered temporarily. She gave a quick wave as she practically waddled to her car. But just as she was about to open the door, she grabbed her midsection and winced.

Panic coursed through Trevor's veins. "Are you okay?" He ran across the yards to her. She was hunched over with her hands on her thighs. "Audrey, what's wrong?"

When she didn't answer, he tucked her hair behind her ears so he could see her face. Her eyes were squeezed shut. She sucked in a deep breath and blew it out slowly. "I'll be fine." She straightened, looking much better. "I just need to get to the hospital."

Lucas was also at her side then. "Is the baby coming?"

Audrey nodded.

Of course the baby was coming. Nothing was wrong. She was going to have the baby. A new sense of urgency flooded Trevor's mind. He grabbed her bag and threw it into the backseat of her car. "We'll take you."

Audrey hesitated but not for long. She slid into the backseat.

Trevor thought about the Twins tickets in his pocket. He had really been looking forward to the game. But there would be many more games. Although disappointed about missing it, he was mostly relieved that he could be here for Audrey. He hated to think of what could've happened had she tried to drive herself to the hospital.

Trevor took the driver's seat, and Lucas sat in the front next to him. As he drove, Trevor kept an eye on Audrey in the rearview mirror. A few minutes later, she cradled her belly with her arms and groaned.

Lucas noticed also. "Hurry up, dude. There she goes again."

Trevor checked the speedometer. He was already violating the speed limit. "I'm going as fast as I can. I don't wanna get in an accident."

"Well I don't want her to have a baby in this car."

The contraction slowly let up and gradually Audrey began to relax again. "Trevor, you don't have to speed." She was short of breath. "Just get us there safely. My doctor said I'll be in labor for several hours since it's my first time."

Trevor tried to slow down but his racing heart wouldn't let him. He was terrified to be responsible for getting a woman in labor to the hospital. At the same time he was elated to have this time with Audrey. He had missed her more than he had ever thought possible. A protective feeling came over him. He would do anything to keep her safe right now, and he wished he could take away her pain. But right now his job was to get her to the hospital, so he focused his attention on the road like a man on a mission.

Finally they reached the hospital, and Trevor pulled up to the front doors. Audrey needed to wait for a contraction to pass before getting out of the car.

Trevor looked to the front doors, expecting to see medical personnel running out to assist them, but no one seemed to be alarmed or rushing over to help. A girl in scrubs pushed a wheelchair holding an older gentleman through the automatic double doors. The man held a vase of flowers on his lap. Trevor couldn't help but think that the poor guy looked worse for the wear. Trevor looked around for someone else to help but when he didn't see anyone, he called to the girl in scrubs. "I have a woman in labor. I need help."

The girl smiled, evidently unalarmed. "Go in and talk to the lady at the front desk. She'll direct you where to go."

Although the girl was friendly and slightly helpful, Trevor was appalled at her calm demeanor. Couldn't she see that this was an emergency? "Can you get us one of those wheelchairs?" Trevor helped Audrey out of the car.

Audrey patted his arm. "I can walk."

Trevor was skeptical about that. He needed to take control of the situation since everyone else seemed to have a laissez faire attitude. "Lucas, you park the car and meet us inside. I'm gonna stay with Audrey."

The lady at the front desk had silver hair tied up in a bun on the top of her head. Her long painted nails clicked on the keyboard as she entered Audrey's information into the computer. She, too, was in no hurry. Finally, she looked up from the computer. Pointing over her shoulder, she directed them to a bank of elevators. "Go up to the third floor and take a left. They'll be expecting you."

Trevor grabbed Audrey's hand and started for the elevators before the woman had a chance to finish her sentence.

"Thank you," Audrey called as Trevor dragged her away.

Trevor pushed the "Up" button three times before a set of elevator doors finally opened, revealing a mother toting three young children. One of the kids was crying because he didn't have a turn to push a button so was refusing to exit the elevator. A second child was whining that he was hungry, and a baby girl in a stroller had dropped her pacifier on the floor. These people could take all day to get off the elevator so Trevor decided to help. He picked up the pacifier and popped it into the baby's mouth. At least one of the children was happy now.

The mother, however, chose that moment to reach her boiling point, and took out her frustration on Trevor. She pulled the pacifier from the baby's mouth, causing the little one to scream loud enough to drown out the voices of her brothers. The woman glared at Trevor. "Do you know how many germs are on this floor? Would you eat off of this floor?"

Just in the nick of time, another set of elevator doors opened behind them. "Sorry, ma'am." He pulled Audrey by the hand into the empty elevator.

Leaning his back against the wall of the elevator, he exhaled. Then he looked at Audrey. She had her eyes shut tight again and had a hand bracing her lower back. Trevor looked up at the digital numbers illuminating the floor they were on. How long could it take to go up three floors? Finally the doors opened on the third floor. "We're here, Audrey." He pulled on her hand, but she didn't budge.

She shook her head. "I can't. It hurts too bad."

Bending down, he tried to pick her up. One way or another, he was getting her to labor and delivery.

Audrey punched him square in the face. "Don't touch me!"

Stunned, Trevor backed away from her, wedging his foot between the elevator doors threatening to close.

Slowly, the contraction receded, and Audrey relaxed. She looked up at Trevor, noticing the dazed look on his face. "Oh no. I'm so sorry I punched you. I really didn't try. It just hurt so much." She giggled.

Trevor smiled, rubbing the sting from his cheek. It was pretty funny, he had to admit. He remembered then about hearing of women's erratic behavior during labor. "It's okay. I should've known better. Now let's get off this elevator already."

Audrey took a step forward and then gasped. She looked up at Trevor, her eyes wide open. "My water just broke." A trickle of water pooled at her feet.

The lights dimmed. Trevor's body went numb. That's the last thing he remembered before falling to the floor.

Chapter Twenty-Six

꒕

DRESSED IN A HOSPITAL GOWN AND HOOKED UP TO MON-
itors, Audrey rode out the contraction one painstaking breath at a
time. This was it. The day her baby would be born. She'd planned a
dinner for next week to introduce the adoptive parents to her mom
and dad. Instead, the meeting would take place today in the hospital.

The door to her hospital room opened and her mom entered
the room. "Mom, I'm so glad you're here."

Her mom came to her side and held her hand. "Sorry I didn't
come sooner. I forgot to turn my phone back on after Bible study.
I went to the grocery store and when I was standing by the limes I
remembered to turn my phone on, and then I saw all of your texts."

"It's okay, Mom. Trevor and Lucas drove me here so I wouldn't
be alone." Truthfully, she hadn't thought she'd last another minute
without her mom.

Her mom brushed a loose curl off of Audrey's forehead, tucking it behind her ear like she used to do when Audrey was little. "How are you doing?"

Audrey sighed. "Oh, I'm fine. But it hurts really bad."

As if on cue, a contraction started. Audrey drew in deep breaths as the nurse had instructed, exhaling slowly through pursed lips. She trained her eyes on the machine at the bedside, watching the numbers climb as pain gripped her abdomen and back. Finally, the numbers steadily decreased again, and Audrey relaxed.

"Honey, you can get an epidural so it won't hurt so much."

"I already got an epidural. The nurse said that it shouldn't take away all the pain. She said it will be easier to push if I can feel more. Plus, my labor is going really fast for a first-time mom. I guess that makes it hurt more."

"So where is Trevor? I didn't see him when I came up."

"He and Lucas are in the waiting room. It was too awkward having them in here when the doctors and nurses keep doing stuff to me."

"That makes sense."

"Yeah, well Trevor probably couldn't handle all the medical stuff anyway. He already fainted once."

Her mom laughed. "That's why women have the babies. Men couldn't handle it."

"That's what the nurse said." Audrey would laugh too if it weren't for the constant ache in her lower abdomen.

"Is he okay?"

"Actually, he got a pretty big goose egg on the side of his head. They gave him an ice pack, a Tylenol, and a Sprite. They told Lucas to keep a close eye on him. I think he'll be alright." Talking took great effort at this point, but it helped to keep her mind off the pain.

"The poor guy." Her mom stifled a laugh.

There was a light knock on the door and her dad and Darcy walked in. "What's so funny?" Her dad kissed her mom lightly on the lips.

Her mom shook her head. "Absolutely nothing, dear."

Her dad kissed Audrey's cheek. "How are you, honey?"

"Don't ask." Another contraction was tightening her belly.

This contraction was longer and more intense than any other. It seemed it would never end. She looked to her dad for strength and saw tears welling in his eyes. He locked eyes with her until the pain let up.

"Well, honey, you sure did a number on Trevor."

Her mom laughed. "So you heard about him fainting?"

He chuckled. "Yeah, and I also heard about Audrey slugging him."

Her mom looked at Audrey quizzically.

"I forgot to mention that part."

"I'll fill you in later," her dad told her mom. "I told Trevor and Lucas they could go, now that you're mother and I are here."

Audrey moaned, tightening her grip on her mother's hand. "It hurts so bad, and I think I have to go to the bathroom."

"I remember that feeling." Her mom jumped to her feet. "Usually that's the baby telling you it's time to push. How dilated did they say you were?"

Audrey couldn't answer right away. She bit the inside of her cheek and moaned. Through clenched teeth, she answered with all her strength, "like eight or something."

Her mom pressed the nurse call button.

The pain was unbelievable. Just when she thought it couldn't get any worse, the next contraction would make the previous one feel like a picnic. Pushing was hard. She didn't know if she was doing it right. All she knew was that it hurt. *Toughen up*, she'd tell herself.

While she was incredibly thankful for her parents' arrival, they were quite possibly making her more anxious. Her mom kept rubbing her temples between contractions. And then when the contractions came, she would squeeze Audrey's hand so hard that it gave her a second reason to moan in pain.

Her dad remained calm, but he couldn't hide the tears in his eyes. They were tears of love and concern but also of regret and sorrow. Audrey didn't want to think about the bad thing that had happened to get her where she was today—laying in a hospital, painfully birthing a child she would have to say goodbye to. For now, she just needed to think positive thoughts so that she could survive each contraction. Her sister was a quiet source of comfort, mostly keeping to herself.

The best distraction from the pain was the anticipation of her family meeting the adoptive parents. It was disappointing that the dinner plans hadn't work out, but it would possibly be more fun for the meeting to take place here in the hospital. Audrey had called Ally at the adoption agency as soon as she was in labor. Ally said she would contact the adoptive parents and tell them it was time to go to the hospital.

It was Audrey's choice whether or not she would invite them into the birthing room. She decided to invite them in after she'd had a couple of minutes to hold the baby. Ally said that she would poke her head into the delivery room to let Audrey know when they had arrived. So when the pain wasn't too consuming, Audrey fixed her eyes on the door, watching and waiting for Ally.

Finally, after pushing for an hour, Ally entered the room. But with her presence came something that took Audrey by surprise. Sadness. She had been so looking forward to Ally's arrival, yet with it came the reminder that she would have to say goodbye to her baby, almost as soon as she said hello.

Audrey watched her mom go to the door and introduce herself. Her mom promised Ally that she would send a nurse to let her know when the adoptive parents were welcome in the room.

Half an hour later, the doctor told everyone to get their cameras ready. A shrill cry filled the room as the baby breathed for the first time. The sound roused emotions in Audrey she'd never felt before. Awe and wonder washed over her. Nothing could have prepared her for the overwhelming feelings of joy and love that consumed her with the sound of that first cry. Tears streamed down her face as she gave one last push, her chin to her chest and her eyes squeezed shut.

The doctor placed the squirming infant on Audrey's abdomen. Audrey wanted to open her eyes to see her baby, but overcome by exhaustion, she laid her head back onto the pillow. Reaching a hand down, she felt the baby's soft cheek. Slowly, she summoned the strength to lift her head and look at her baby.

"She's beautiful," the doctor said. "Congratulations."

"Thank you," Audrey whispered, overcome with emotion. The doctor was right. The baby girl was the most beautiful thing Audrey had ever laid eyes on.

A nurse stepped in and rubbed the baby vigorously with a blanket, causing her to cry louder. A protective instinct kicked in and Audrey wanted to order the nurse to be gentle. As if reading her mind, the nurse explained that crying helps to clear her lungs.

Audrey touched the baby's miniature fingers, marveling at the perfection of each one. She cupped the baby's delicate hand in hers. "Shh, baby Grace. You're okay."

The nurse placed a pink hat, topped with a pom-pom, on the baby's head. Then she wrapped her in a dry blanket and placed her in Audrey's arms. The baby instantly quieted and struggled to open her eyes. "Hi, sweet girl. Welcome to the world."

Audrey's family gathered around the bed, hugging, snapping pictures, and oohing and aahing. But no photo could capture the bittersweet emotion welling in Audrey's soul. She had never experienced a greater love in all her life than at that moment, gazing into her daughter's eyes. "I love you, Grace." She kissed a downy cheek and breathed in the fresh newborn scent.

Darcy captured the moment with a click of her phone's camera. "She's so cute!" Darcy snapped a couple more pictures. "And I'm not just saying that because I'm her aunty. She is honestly cute."

Audrey's mom leaned in to get a closer look at the infant. "She looks just like her mother." Nostalgia shone in her eyes.

The nurse offered to take a picture of the entire family gathered around the head of the bed. Everyone posed, soaking in the joy of the moment. Capturing it on photo as well as in their hearts. "One big, happy family." The nurse handed the camera back to her dad.

The nurse's words stung. If only it were true. If only Audrey could take baby Grace home. They could be one big, happy family. The nurse was well aware of the situation, and Audrey wished she had been more sensitive. Truthfully, the family was incomplete, so far. The other members were outside the room, praying and waiting for Grace's arrival. It was only fair to include them in this beautiful moment.

But first, Audrey took a moment to memorize each detail of her daughter's face, smoothing her delicate eyebrows, kissing her soft pink cheeks, and nuzzling her button nose. Then with eyes spilling over with tears, and a heart overflowing with a mingling of sorrow and joy, she nodded to the nurse. It was time to introduce the adoptive parents to their new baby girl.

"Are you sure about the adoption? You think you can say goodbye?" Worry creased her mom's brow. Although she supported Audrey's decision, she was unconvinced that it was God's plan.

"Mom, I promise you that I found the perfect couple."

Her mom nodded weakly.

"Would you like to hold her?"

"I'd love to."

Carefully, Audrey handed the baby to her mom. Grace's eyes were wide open, and she made gentle cooing sounds. Her mom smiled at the baby. "Hi, little girl. We love you so much. You're mommy did a great job bringing you into this world." She held the baby to her chest. "Jesus loves you, precious girl."

The door creaked open. Audrey held her breath.

Pastor Mitchel and Mrs. Mitchel walked in.

Her mom greeted them, cradling Grace in her arms. "What a nice surprise. Audrey didn't tell me you were coming." She positioned Grace so they could see her face. "Meet my new grandbaby."

The Mitchels stared at Grace in wide-eyed wonder. Then they looked at Audrey.

Audrey lifted her hand in a dainty wave, hoping the Mitchels would be as excited as she was about the arrangement.

Mrs. Mitchel clutched her chest as joyful sobs overtook her. Pastor Mitchel wrapped his wife in his arms, also crying like a baby. It was a better reaction than Audrey had even imagined.

Her mom struggled to put the pieces together. "What's going on?"

Audrey giggled. "Mom, I would like you to meet Grace's new mommy and daddy."

Ally, from the adoption agency, stepped into the room behind the Mitchels, a sly smile curling her lips. She winked at Audrey, and Audrey winked back. They'd pulled off the surprise. Audrey sat back, watching it all play out.

"Yes!" Darcy ran to Pastor Mitchel and threw her arms around his neck. "This is so awesome!" She hugged Mrs. Mitchel next.

"Thank you, Darcy," Mrs. Mitchel returned her hug. "We feel very blessed."

"And incredibly grateful," Pastor Mitchel added.

Audrey's mom was speechless, her mouth agape. Her dad strode across the room and shook Pastor Mitchel's hand, and then hugged Mrs. Mitchel. His eyes were glistening when he released her. "*We* are also blessed ... and incredibly grateful."

Finally, Audrey's mom embraced each of the new parents separately, holding Grace in the crook of one arm. "My heart is bursting with joy." She stood back, soaking in the site of the adoptive parents—her friends. "Audrey was right. This adoption truly has been orchestrated from Heaven above."

Audrey smiled. "Now do you believe me, Mom? They're the perfect parents, right?"

"Hold on a minute," Pastor Mitchel chimed in. "Those are some pretty high expectations you're placing on us first-timers."

Audrey laughed. "I'm sure you'll do great." She had no doubts.

"Hold your daughter." Her mom extended the little squirming bundle.

Mrs. Mitchel stepped gingerly around the doctor who was finishing her work at the foot of the bed. She sat down on the vinyl-covered hospital chair. Pastor Mitchel stood beside her, his hand on her shoulder. Her mom placed Grace into Mrs. Mitchel's open arms.

Darcy took pictures as everyone else looked on, tears of joy streaming down the faces of all present, including the doctor and nurse.

All attention was on the family of three, united for the first time. Audrey knew beyond a shadow of a doubt that God had designed this family. She was grateful to have had a part in its formation.

Chapter Twenty-Seven

THE FRIENDLY CHATTER OF WOMEN, THE CLINKING OF fine China, and the scent of baby powder filled the Hayes' home. Mrs. Mitchel chose a gift bag from the pile at her feet and folded back the tissue paper. She pulled out a set of board books, and held it up for everyone to see. "Thank you. I love Sandra Boynton books." There was a collective voice of agreement.

Audrey played with her wrist watch as she tried to contain her excitement. Her gift to baby Grace was next on the pile. Audrey had already given Grace numerous outfits and toys over the past four weeks since her birth, but this gift was special. Mrs. Mitchel read the small card aloud. "To: Grace. From: Aunty Audrey."

The room quieted as the guests anticipated Audrey's gift. You could hear a pin drop as Mrs. Mitchel peeled back the paper on the box. Peering inside, tears instantly filled her eyes. She removed the scrapbook from the box. Audrey prayed that Mrs. Mitchel would like it. On the first page was a heartfelt letter to Grace where Audrey told her she loved her very much. She explained that she wasn't ready to be a mother because she was very young but that God had chosen special parents for her.

She told Grace of God's great love. Lastly, she closed with the Bible verse that had given her the courage to follow God's will. 2 Corinthians 12:9. The next few pages were filled with pictures of Audrey from birth to the present time. The rest of the book was blank. "You can fill the rest of the book with cards, letters, and photos I send her throughout the years."

"She'll love it." Mrs. Mitchel wiped away tears with a tissue. She stood up and came to Audrey, pulling her into a hug. "We love you, Audrey."

"I love you too." The Mitchels were like family to her now.

The scrapbook was passed around the circle for each guest to admire while Mrs. Mitchel opened the rest of the presents. Baby Grace was also passed around. It was Darcy's turn to hold her, and she did a fine job of smothering her with kisses and "I love yous." Audrey was admiring the two of them when Mrs. Mitchel announced that she had a gift for Audrey. She handed the last package from the pile to Audrey, a small square box. Audrey opened it to find a gold ring with a row of delicate roses etched into it. It was simple, yet elegant.

"Thank you." She held it to her heart. "It's gorgeous."

"You're welcome." Mrs. Mitchel held out her hand, revealing a matching ring. "I also have one for Grace—for when she's older."

Audrey was moved beyond words. She removed the ring from the box, placing it on her finger. She hugged Mrs. Mitchel. "I'll never take it off."

Mrs. Mitchel smiled. "I'll always wear mine too."

Audrey showed off her ring to her mom and sister. Becca joined the huddle to check it out as well. Audrey held out her hand to Grace who was lying in Darcy's arms. "Look at my pretty ring, Grace. I'll wear it every day so that a connection to you will be with me everywhere I go." Audrey caressed the baby's hand, and Grace responded by wrapping her tiny fingers around Audrey's pinky. A warm feeling ran through Audrey from head to toe. She loved Grace so much it hurt. But at the same time, she was incredibly happy because she knew she was giving Grace the best life possible.

Her mom excused herself to cut the cake she had prepared. It was cherry chip, Audrey's favorite. Victoria Hayes started a pot of coffee brewing and put the tea kettle on the stove. Audrey sat on the couch next to Darcy, Grace holding her finger as she drifted to sleep.

"Do you want to hold her? I think everyone else has had a turn."

Audrey nodded. She had been aching to cuddle Grace all afternoon but allowed the guests to hold her first. Carefully, she removed the sleeping baby from Darcy's arms. Audrey gazed down at her angelic face, admiring her long eyelashes, rosebud lips, and round cheeks. Her look had already changed since Audrey had held her in the hospital four short weeks ago. The separation from Grace had been heart wrenching after carrying her for nine months, but it had also given Audrey an opportunity to begin healing and start planning for her future.

Pondering her plans, Audrey stared out the window at the same view she had from her own home. The pond was filled with ducks swimming lazily about and squirrels skipping among the branches in the lush trees. She was enrolled in classes for fall at Bethel. She'd be living off-campus in an apartment with a couple of runners from the cross-country team, whom had shown her nothing but love and support upon hearing the reasons for Audrey dropping out of school last winter.

Likewise, her coach was welcoming her back to the team with open arms. Audrey's life was on its way back to normal. But there was one more piece of her life's puzzle that needed tending to before she could really move forward. She let her eyes drift from the gorgeous view of the waterfront to one that made her heart beat wildly no matter how hard she tried to restrain it. Trevor.

He was standing at the grill, spatula in hand, shooting the breeze with the husbands of the shower guests. She'd visit the guys out back later.

Audrey wasn't sure what their future held, but she was hoping that Trevor could still find a place in his heart for her, whether it be friendship or something more. It wasn't a question of whether or not she loved him. She always had, and she always would. But she had become a changed person through all that she had endured. Now she carried baggage that could take a lifetime to sort through. Trevor was still young at heart, and his life remained a clean slate. Would the two of them still be compatible? Or would their differences be too great? There was only one way to find out. She needed to talk to him.

She ate her cake quickly and then asked Mrs. Mitchel if she could take Grace outside to show her off to the guys. "There's someone who hasn't met her yet." Audrey was nearly bursting with anticipation.

"Take all the time you need." Mrs. Mitchel stroked Grace's blonde hair. "Tell the men there's cake in here. We have enough left over to feed an army."

"I'll let them know."

Audrey lightly draped a receiving blanket over Grace's face to block out the sun's rays before stepping onto the patio. The warmth of the summer sun was a welcome sensation after sitting in the air conditioning for the better part of the day. It was a very nice shower, playing games and eating hors d'oeuvres. But Audrey felt that she was more in her element outdoors.

Her dad spotted her right away as she padded barefoot across the grass. He was in the middle of taking a bite of a big juicy burger. He waved her over to the picnic table where he was seated with Pastor Mitchel, Jake's dad, and Trevor's dad. Audrey made her way over, all the while completely aware of Trevor's gaze following her. He and Lucas were seated on lawn chairs, in the shade of an oak tree, balancing plates filled with burgers, chips, and pickles on their laps. Audrey smiled in his direction. She would go to him next.

"Hi, Dad." She took a seat on the end of the picnic bench.

Her dad wiped ketchup from his chin with a napkin. "Hi, honey, how's the shower? It's not wrapping up already, is it?"

"Not yet. I just thought I'd come out for a while."

"Any good loot?" Pastor Mitchel rubbed his hands together.

"Definitely. Grace got so much clothes, she might need a bigger closet. And thank you for the ring, Pastor Mitchel." She held up her hand for all to see.

His eyes sparkled. "You're so welcome. And you really need to start calling me by my first name. We're family now."

"That might take some getting used to." Pastor Mitchel had told Audrey this before. He and Mrs. Mitchel had also said that they would love to have Grace call her parents Grandpa Tom and Grandma Lydia. In fact, they insisted. They were thrilled that Grace would have grandparents living close by.

Grace squirmed in Audrey's arms. Peeking under the blanket, Audrey saw that she was getting restless. "I better get Grace in the shade." She scooted off the bench. "Oh, and we saved some cake for you guys. I was supposed to let you know."

"I told your mom that the cake would be more than enough, but she tossed and turned all night worrying about it."

Audrey laughed. "Sounds like Mom."

Jake's dad stood from the table, gathering his empty plate and cup. "Your mom makes the best cake of any lady in the whole church. Don't tell my wife I said that."

"It's no secret. Everyone knows my mom could open her own bakery." Audrey was happy that Mr. Preston had attended the shower. There had been a remarkable positive change in his demeanor recently. He'd been showing up to more church events, and he agreed to help Audrey find her perpetrator. It seemed that he and Jake had grown closer too. "Mr. Preston, thank you for helping with my case. I mean, we don't have much of a case yet, but maybe with your help we can actually catch my attacker."

"I won't rest until we find the slime ball and put him behind bars."

Audrey's dad nodded to Mr. Preston, a gesture of gratitude.

It was time to talk to Trevor. As she made her way over to him, her heart beat so loudly, she thought it would wake up Grace. The past month of reflection and prayer had led her to believe that she was ready to rekindle her relationship with Trevor. She felt terrible for the harsh way she had treated him, giving him the cold shoulder. She needed to be sure he understood that she only did it because she cared about him so deeply. But she should have gone about it in a different way. In hind sight, she should've been up front and honest with him about what had happened at that party and then explained that she needed time apart from him. But she couldn't undo the past. She could only ask for his forgiveness.

"Hey guys. I have someone I'd like you to meet."

Lucas stood up. "Take my chair, Audrey. I'll be going in for cake after I get a look at the little munchkin."

"Thanks." Audrey took him up on his offer, knowing that Lucas was allowing her and Trevor time alone. "Trevor and Lucas, meet baby Grace. Grace, this is Trevor and Lucas, our knights in shining armor who swooped in and delivered us to the hospital just in time."

Trevor scooted his lawn chair closer to hers to get a better look at the baby. "She's so cute." Sweetness dripped from his words. "Can I hold her?" He already had his arms outstretched, waiting.

Audrey placed Grace in his arms, instructing him to be mindful of the baby's neck. Trevor glowed as he held her, and Audrey wished she had a camera. Instead, she took a picture in her mind, memorizing the expression on Trevor's face, the awe and admiration he emanated. A lump formed in her throat. Not because she was sad. It was just such a beautiful moment. Trevor loved Grace. It was evident in the way he held her so gently, the way he caressed her soft cheek with his finger, and the way he closed his eyes when he snuggled her against his chest. He really loved her.

A tear slid down Audrey's cheek because the beautiful picture in front of her demonstrated the depth of Trevor's love not only for Grace, but for her. He really was amazing. He had been so patient with Audrey, persisting in his quest for answers when she ignored him, and then giving her the space she demanded. Most men would have given up long ago. But Trevor's love was steadfast.

"You did good, Audrey. She's adorable." Trevor's eyes remained fixed on the sleeping infant as he spoke.

"She's a cutie," Lucas chimed in. "I'll leave you three alone now while I go get myself some cake."

"Enjoy!" Audrey called out as he moseyed back to the house.

Now that they were alone, there was so much Audrey wanted to say to Trevor, but she didn't know where to begin. She decided an apology was a good place to start. "Trev, I'm so sorry."

He looked at her, his eyes twinkling. "For smacking me in the elevator? Don't worry about it. It's nothing a little plastic surgery can't cure."

Audrey laughed. It was just like Trevor to break the ice like that. "That's not what I meant."

"Oh, you meant for making me pass out and hit my head on the cold cement floor? I'll recover from that eventually too. It's not a problem."

Audrey doubled over in laughter. "That was your own fault. You need to buck up a little."

Trevor feigned insult. "My fault? I was being a perfect gentleman. I even offered to carry you over the threshold, and what kind of thanks did I get?" He scoffed. "A smack in the face and a goose egg on the side of my head."

"Okay, I'm sorry about all that." She was barely able to contain her laughter. She became more serious then. "But I'm also sorry for everything else. For shutting you out." Ashamed, she looked down, feeling lower than the dirt beneath her feet. "I hope you'll forgive me."

Trevor gently lifted her chin with his fingertips until their eyes met. "I forgive you. I'm just happy to have you back in my life."

Their eyes held. "Me too."

Grace let out a soft whimper that quickly morphed into a loud cry. Audrey lifted the baby to her shoulder, gently patting her back. "Shh, it's okay, Grace."

Grace's cries continued to grow in intensity. The men at the picnic table heard, and Andrew came over. "Sounds like somebody's hungry. Do you want me to have Maggie fix her a bottle? I can bring it out to you."

"Actually, do you mind bringing Grace in? I really need to finish talking to Trevor."

Andrew scooped the crying baby into his arms. "No problem. She could probably use a diaper change too."

Audrey watched Andrew walk away with the baby in his arms. Although Grace was still fussing, she was settling down. There was no question in Audrey's mind that she had made the best decision for her daughter.

There was a flutter of movement in the periphery of her vision. She turned to see a robin, perched on the gate that led down to the pond. Audrey watched as the bird landed on the grass and pulled a fat juicy worm from the soil. The robin flew to a nest in the oak tree where tiny baby robins squeaked in hunger. Audrey smiled. It was as if God were reminding her once again how he would take care of her, just as he takes care of the tiniest bird. She silently praised God.

Trevor didn't seem to notice the robin or the surge of emotion coursing through Audrey. He was still watching Andrew trying to soothe his daughter. He chuckled. "That little one has a temper."

Audrey smiled at his comment. "It's called a strong will, and it means that she will be very successful in life. She won't let anything get in her way." She laughed. "That's what my mom always said about me."

Trevor reached over and touched Audrey's arm, sending a current of electricity surging through her body. "Like mother, like daughter." His hand rested on her forearm, and it was all she could do to stop herself from squealing like a crazed pre-teen fan at a boy band concert. She hoped that he hadn't noticed her dramatic reaction to his touch. He hadn't meant for it to be romantic. This was exactly the reason why she had avoided him during her pregnancy. There was no way she could've stopped herself from falling madly in love with him had they kept in touch.

But now there was no reason to keep him at arm's length. On the contrary, it was time for her to move on with her life.

She had planned to take things slowly with Trevor, to allow time to rebuild their friendship and see what path it would travel. But now, sitting next to him, feeling his touch, and hearing his comforting words that held no remorse, she knew that more time was the last thing Trevor needed. He had faithfully stood by, waiting for her to come back to him. He had made his feelings clear all along, and now he deserved to know her true feelings.

She leaned closer to him, feeling the weight of his hand on her arm grow stronger. She looked into his alluring blue eyes and said the only words that held the power to convey her feelings. "I love you."

"I love you too."

They kissed. It was gentle and soft, filled with forgiveness and hope. When Audrey drew back from him, holding his gaze, she felt stronger feelings for him than ever before. In spite of everything that she had been through, he had loved her unconditionally. She knew at that moment, beyond a shadow of a doubt, that he was the love of her life.

Trevor cleared his throat, preparing to say something important. "Before this moment slips away, there's just one thing I need to tell you."

Audrey's heart pounded in her chest. She didn't know whether to be nervous or excited.

He took hold of her hands and looked deep into her eyes, putting her at ease. "Audrey Chapman, I want to marry you someday."

Audrey's heart flooded with joy. She'd never been so happy to hear those words. She giggled. "You promise?"

"I promise."

Epilogue

"STUDENTS, PLEASE TAKE YOUR SEATS." THE PROFESSOR, A librarian-type with reading glasses perched on the end of her nose and a tight bun situated at the back of her head, addressed the class.

Audrey claimed the seat next to Destiny and powered on her iPad. Happiness sparked her day as the home screen came into view. Sweet little Grace's face smiled back at her from the picture on the screen. Grace was sitting in the shade of an apple tree, a drooly smile lighting up her chubby face. The memory of that moment was etched on Audrey's heart. Maggie and Andrew had propped Grace in the sitting position several times before getting a decent picture. Grace kept toppling over just as Audrey was about to snap the photo. Grace belly laughed every time she landed in the soft grass.

A notification popped up. "This morning, we will review…" The professor's voice morphed into faint background noise as Audrey read a message that scrolled along the top of her screen. It was from Mr. Preston.

I BELIEVE WE HAVE A BREAK IN YOUR CASE.

Audrey gasped, drawing the attention of those around her. Destiny peered over at Audrey's iPad, her brow knit in concern. Audrey needed to read the rest of the message in private.

She hugged the device to her chest. "Take notes for me."

Destiny nodded, seemingly happy to play a role in Audrey's drama.

Audrey gathered her belongings, and hurried out of the classroom. She ran to the nearest vacant lounge area and dropped her backpack onto a chair. Her mind was a tangled web of what ifs. What if they found her attacker? What if Grace looked like him? What if this wasn't her attacker after all? She sat down, said a brief prayer, and read the message in its entirety.

CALL ME AT YOUR EARLIEST CONVENIENCE. A SUSPECT IN SERIAL SEXUAL ASSAULTS HAS BEEN DETAINED. INCRIMINATING EVIDENCE MAY LINK HIM TO YOUR CASE. SEVERAL PIECES OF JEWELRY, ALONG WITH A STASH OF DATE RAPE DRUGS, WERE CONFISCATED FROM HIS GLOVE BOX. IT IS BELIEVED THAT HE SAVES JEWELRY FROM EACH OF HIS VICTIMS.

A sick feeling roiled in Audrey's stomach. What kind of sicko keeps mementos from his victims?

She stood and began to pace. She'd always assumed she'd be elated to have her attacker found and punished. Instead, feelings of disgust rushed at her. She didn't want to lay eyes on the pervert.

Didn't want to know his name. Didn't want to waste another minute of her life thinking about him.

But in order to put him behind bars, preventing him from attacking another woman, she felt a responsibility to participate in the investigation.

She dialed Mr. Preston's number.

"Hello, Audrey. I was expecting your—"

"Was there a diamond necklace?" Audrey's voice was shaky, barely a whisper. Her throat felt almost too tight to speak.

"Audrey? We must have a bad connection. Can you repeat that?"

Audrey cleared her throat. She took a deep, calming breath, releasing it slowly. Her hand was so sweaty that she almost lost grip on her phone. "I need to know…was there a diamond necklace in his glove box? A teardrop diamond on a gold chain."

Mr. Preston hesitated for what felt like an eternity. Audrey heard a shuffling of papers on the other end of the phone. Finally, he answered.

"Yes."